"MONTY PYTHON MEETS
ALFRED HITCHCOCK . . .
Hilarious . . . Well-written . . . Satisfying . . .
A high-spirited romp through
low-life caverns of the Big Apple"
Hartford Courant

"McBAIN HAS STOOD THE TEST OF TIME.
He remains one of the very best."
San Antonio Express News

"**DOWNTOWN** HAS IT ALL:
the thrills of a good McBain,
the tension of a good movie."
London Daily Mail

"A STUNNING SURPRISE . . .
A mad scamper through the big city's
worst nightmares"
Wichita Falls Times Record

"NO LIVING MYSTERY WRITER
CREATES MORE SUSPENSEFUL SCENES
OR BUILDS PLOTS BETTER
THAN McBAIN."
Greensboro News & Record

DOWNTOWN

ED McBAIN

DOWNTOWN

AVON BOOKS  NEW YORK

AVON BOOKS
A division of
The Hearst Corporation
1350 Avenue of the Americas
New York, New York 10019

Published in hardcover by William Morrow and Company, Inc.; for information address Permissions Department, William Morrow and Company, Inc., 1350 Avenue of the Americas, New York, New York 10019.

First Avon Books Printing: June 1993

This is for
JAN AND ROY DEAN

DOWNTOWN

1

Michael was telling the blonde he'd never been in this part of the city. In fact, he'd been to New York only twice before in his entire life. Hadn't strayed out of the midtown area either time.

"But here you are now," the blonde said, and smiled. "All the way downtown."

She was wearing a smart tailored suit, gray, a white silk blouse with a stock tie. Briefcase sitting on the empty stool to her right. He figured her for someone who worked on Wall Street. Late business meeting—it was now seven o'clock—she'd stopped off at the bar here before heading home. That's what he figured.

She was drinking Corona and lime.

He was drinking scotch with a splash.

The place looked like an old saloon, but it probably wasn't. Etched mirrors, polished mahogany and burnished brass, large green-shaded lamps over the bar, smaller versions on all the tables.

There was a warm, cozy feel to the place. Nice buzz of conversation, too. Through the big plate-glass window facing the street, he could see gently falling snowflakes. This was Christmas Eve, a Tuesday night. It would be a white Christmas.

"What brings you to New York this time?" the blonde asked.

"Same thing that brought me here the last two times," he said.

"And what's that?"

"My ad agency's here."

"You're in advertising, is that it?"

"No, I'm in oranges."

The blonde nodded.

"Golden Oranges?" Michael said, and looked at her expectantly.

"Uh-huh," she said.

"You've heard of them?"

"No," she said.

"That's my brand name. Golden Oranges."

"Sorry, I don't know them."

"But you know Sunkist, right?"

"Sure."

"Well, I'm just a small independent trying to get big. Which is why I've got a New York agency handling my advertising."

The blonde nodded again.

"So what do you do?" she asked. "*Grow* the oranges and everything?"

"Yep. Grow them and everything."

"Where?"

"In Florida."

"Ask a stupid question," she said, and smiled, and extended her hand. "I'm Helen Parrish," she said.

"Michael Barnes," he said, and took her hand. "Nice to meet you."

"So when do you go back to Florida?" she asked.

"Well, not till the fourth of January, actually. I'm flying up to Boston tonight. Spend the holidays with my mother."

"Your mother's up there in Boston, huh?"

"Yeah. Be good seeing her again."

"Business all finished here?"

"Finished it this afternoon."

He realized that her hand was still in his. To the casual passerby, they must have looked like a man and a woman holding hands. Good-looking blonde woman with flashing blue eyes, suntanned man wearing rimless eyeglasses. Dark brown hair. Brown eyes. Average height, he guessed. Well, five-ten, he guessed that was average these days. In the army, he'd felt short. The army had a way of making you feel short. Come to think of it, he felt short nowadays, too. Jenny had done that to him. Made him feel short all over again.

"Do you work down here in this area?" he asked.

"I do," she said.

Still holding his hand.

"I figured you were with one of the brokerage firms," he said.

"No, I'm a lawyer."

"Really? What kind of law?"

"Criminal."

"No kidding?"

"Everybody says that. No kidding, or wow, or gee, or how about that, or words to that effect."

"Because it's so unusual. A woman, I mean. Being a criminal lawyer."

"Actually, there are three in our office."

"That many."

"Yes."

"Criminal lawyers. Women."

"Yes. Trial lawyers, in fact."

"Then you're a trial lawyer."

"Yes."

"Do you like the work?"

"Oh, sure."

She retrieved her hand gently, drained her glass, looked at the clock over the bar, smiled, and said, "Well, I think I'll . . ."

"No, don't go yet," he said.

She looked at him.

"Have another drink," he said. "Then maybe we can go someplace for dinner together," he said. "I've got a rented car outside, we can go anyplace in the city you like. I don't have to start for the airport till nine-thirty or so. Unless you've got other plans."

"I don't have any *plans* as such, but . . ."

"Then what's the hurry?"

"Well, I'll have another drink, but . . ."

"Good," he said, and signaled to the bartender for another round. The bartender nodded.

"This doesn't mean we're having dinner together," she said. "I hardly know you."

"Ask me anything," he said.

"Well . . . are you married?"

"Divorced."

"How long?"

"Nine months. More or less."

"And on the loose in the big, bad city, huh?"

"Well, my plane leaves at eleven-oh-five. It's the last one out tonight. I was lucky to get anything at *all*. It's Christmas Eve, you know."

"Yes, I know," she said. She was looking at him steadily now. Penetrating blue eyes. "How long were you married?" she asked.

"Thirteen years."

"Unlucky number."

"Yes."

"Do you have any children?"

"No."

"How old are you?"

"Forty-one," he said. "How old are you?"

"Thirty-two," she said at once.

He liked that. No coy nonsense like Gee, a woman's not supposed to tell her age. Just straight out thirty-two.

"Are *you* married?" he asked.

"Corona and lime, Dewar's with a splash," the bartender said, and put the drinks down in front of them. "Shall I keep this tab running?"

"Please," Michael said.

He lifted his glass. She lifted hers.

"To a nice evening together," he said. "Till plane time."

She seemed to be looking through him, or at least past him, toward the other end of the bar, almost dreamily. She nodded at last, as if in response to a secret decision she had made, and smiled, and said, "That sounds safe enough," and clinked her glass against his and began sipping at her beer.

"But you didn't answer my question," he said.

"What was your question?" she said.

"Are *you* married?"

"Would it matter?"

"Yes."

She waggled the fingers on her left hand.

"See any wedding band?"

"That doesn't mean anything."

"I'm not married," she said.

"Divorced?" he said.

"Nope. Just single."

"Beautiful woman like you?"

"Ha."

"I mean it."

"Thank you."

"So what I'd like to do," he said, "you must know a lot of good restaurants . . ."

"Slow down," she said smiling. "You didn't ask me if I'm engaged, or involved with anyone, or . . ."

"Are you?"

"No, but . . ."

"Good. Do you like Italian food?"

"Uh-huh," she said, and put down her glass, and slid her handbag over in front of her, and reached into it for a package of cigarettes.

"Well, if you know a good Italian restaurant, I'd like to . . ."

"All right," she said suddenly and coldly and somewhat harshly, "you want to give it back to me?"

He looked at her.

Her eyes had turned hard, there was no longer a smile on her face.

"The ring," she said.

She was whispering now.

"Just give it back to me, okay?"

She held out her right hand. Nothing on any of the fingers.

"The ring," she said. "Please, I don't want any trouble."

"What ring?" he said.

"The ring that was right here on this finger before

we started holding hands. A star sapphire ring that was a gift from my father. I want it back, mister. Right now."

"But I don't have it," he said. He realized there was a foolish grin on his face. As if she were in the middle of a joke and he was smiling in anticipation of the punch line.

She looked at him. Eyes as blue and as hard as the star sapphire she claimed was missing from her hand. Eyes somewhat incredulous, too. She'd told him she was a lawyer, a *criminal* lawyer, no less; was he some kind of idiot to have stolen her ring? This was in her eyes.

"Listen," she said, her voice rising, "just give me the goddamn ring, and we'll forget . . ."

"I don't *have* your . . ."

"What's going on here?"

Michael turned on the stool.

Big, burly guy standing there at his right shoulder, between the two stools. Tweed overcoat. Shoulders looked damp. Crew-cut hair looked damp, too. As if he'd just come in from outside. Beard stubble on his face. Hard blue eyes. Tonight was a night for hard blue eyes. If you had brown eyes tonight, you were out of luck.

"Detective Daniel Cahill," he said, and opened a small leather case and flashed a blue-enameled gold shield. He snapped the case shut. "This man bothering you?" he asked Helen.

"It's all right, officer," she said.

"I'd like to know what's happening here," Cahill said.

"I don't want to make any trouble for him," she said.

"Why? What'd he do?"

It occurred to Michael that they were both talking about him as if he were no longer there. Somehow this sounded ominous.

"If he'll just give it back to me," Helen said.

"Give *what* back, miss?"

"Look, officer," Michael said.

"Shut up, please," Cahill said. "Give *what* back?"

"The ring."

"What ring?"

"Officer . . ."

"I asked you please to shut up," Cahill said, and suddenly looked around, as if aware for the first time that there were other people in the bar. "Let's step outside a minute, please," he said. "You, too, miss."

"Really, I don't want to make any trouble for him," Helen said.

"Please," Cahill said, and gestured slightly with his chin and his raised eyebrows, which seemed to indicate he had some concern for the owner of the place and did not want to make trouble for him, either. Which Michael considered a good sign. Helen got off her stool and put on her overcoat and picked up her briefcase, and Michael followed her and Cahill to where he'd hung his coat on the rack to the left of the entrance door. He was digging for the coat under the pile of other coats on top of it, when Cahill said, "You won't need it, this won't take a minute."

Together the three of them went outside, Helen first, then Michael, and then Cahill. It was still snowing. Bigger flakes now. Floating gently and lazily out of the sky. The temperature was in the low thirties, Michael guessed, perhaps the high twenties. He hoped this little conference out here in front of the bar really would be a short one.

"Okay, now what is it?" Cahill said.

Sounding very reasonable.

"He has my ring," Helen said.

Also sounding very reasonable.

"Officer," Michael said, "I never even *saw* this woman's . . ."

"Over here," Cahill said, and indicated the brick wall to the right of the bar's plate-glass front window. "Hands flat against the wall, lean on 'em," Cahill said.

"Hey, listen," Michael said.

"No, *you* listen," Cahill said. "The lady says you've got her ring . . . what kind of ring, lady?"

"A star sapphire."

"So you just put your hands on the wall here, and lean on them, and spread your legs, and if you ain't got her ring, you got nothin' to worry about."

"You've got no right to . . ."

"Then you want to go down the precinct? Okay, fine, we'll go down the precinct, we'll talk there. Let's go, my car's up the street."

"Why don't you just give me the ring, mister?" Helen said. "Save yourself a lot of trouble."

"I don't *have* your goddamn . . ."

"Okay, fine, let's go down the precinct," Cahill said.

"All right, all *right*," Michael said angrily, and leaned against the wall, his arms spread, his legs spread, his fingers spread, "let's get this over with, okay? I don't have the ring, you can search me from now to . . ."

"Fine, we'll just *see* what you got," Cahill said.

Michael's immediate impulse was to attack; the army had taught him that. But the army had also taught him never to start up with an M.P. Indignantly, angrily, he endured the frisk. Cahill ran his hands up and down Michael's legs, and then tossed up Michael's jacket and reached into the right hip pocket of his trousers, and took out his wallet. Behind him, Michael could hear him rummaging through the wallet.

"This you?" Cahill asked. "Michael Barnes?"

"Yes."

"This your driver's license?"

"Yes."

"You from Florida?"

"Yes."

"These your credit cards?"

"Yes, everything in the wallet is mine."

"Okay, fine," Cahill said, and put the wallet back into Michael's hip pocket and then began patting down the pockets of his jacket.

"If you don't mind," Michael said, "it's goddamn cold out here. I wish you'd . . ."

"Well, well, well," Cahill said, and his hands stopped. Michael felt a sudden chill that had nothing to do with the weather. Cahill was reaching into the right-hand pocket of Michael's jacket. "What have we here?" he said.

Michael held his breath.

"Off the wall," Cahill said, "*off* it! Turn around!"

Michael shoved himself off the wall. He turned. Cahill was holding a star sapphire ring between the thumb and forefinger of his right hand.

"This your ring, miss?" he asked Helen.

"Yes," she said.

"Officer," Michael said, "I don't know how that got in my pocket, but . . ."

"Let's go," Cahill said, "we all three of us got

some work to do down the precinct."

"Could I have my ring, please?" Helen said.

"This is evidence, miss," Cahill said.

"No, it isn't *evidence*, it's a gift from my father, and I'd like it back, please."

"Miss, when we get down the precinct..."

"I'm not *going* down the precinct..."

"Miss..."

"... or *up* the precinct or *around* the..."

"Miss, this individual here stole your ring..."

"Yes, but now we've got it back, so let me have it."

"Miss..."

"I told you I don't want to make any trouble for him."

"This individual is a *thief*, miss."

"I don't care what he is, just let me have the ring," Helen said.

Cahill looked at her.

"I do not wish to press charges, okay?" she said. "Do you understand that?"

"That's how criminals go free in this city," Cahill said. "Because people are afraid to..."

"Just give me the goddamn *ring*!" Helen said.

"Here's the goddamn ring," Cahill said sourly, and handed it to her.

"Thank you."

She put the ring on her finger.

"Good night," she said, and walked off.

"You're a very lucky thief," Cahill said, and walked off in the opposite direction.

"I'm not a goddamn *thief*!" Michael shouted to the empty air.

The words plumed out of his mouth, carried away on the wind, the vapor dissipating into the lazy swirl of snowflakes. His dark brown hair was covered with snow, the shoulders of his brown jacket were covered with snow, he had not been in a snowstorm for a good long time now—since before his mother sold the hardware business in Boston and loaned Michael the money for the groves in Florida—but now he was up to his ass in snow. Well, not quite. Not yet. Only up to the insteps of his shoes so far. He realized all at once that he was shivering. He shoved open the door to the bar.

Mahogany and brass, green-shaded lamps, the gentle *chink* of ice in glasses, the buzz of conversation, the friendly sound of laughter. Everything just as it had been before the blonde accused him of stealing her ring. Shaking his head, still amazed by what had happened, he went back to where he'd left his glass on the bar. He downed what was left of the scotch in two swallows and signaled to the bartender for another one.

The bartender scooped ice into a glass, began pouring from the bottle of Dewar's.

"What was *that* all about?" he asked.

"Don't ask," Michael said.

"Was that guy a cop?"

"Yeah."

"What was it? The girl hit on you?"

"What do you mean?"

"Was he Vice?"

"No, no, nothing like that."

"'Cause I thought maybe she was a hooker . . ."

"No, she was a lawyer."

"So what was it then?"

"She said I stole her . . . look, I don't want to discuss it," Michael said. "It's over and done with, I don't even want to *think* about it anymore."

Shaking his head again, he picked up the fresh drink and took a long swallow.

A man sitting three stools down the bar said, "I was watching the whole thing."

"With the hooker, you mean?" the bartender said, turning to him.

"She was a lawyer," Michael said.

"Hookers will often claim to be lawyers, bankers, university professors, what have you," the man down the bar said. He was tall and lanky, with a Lincolnesque face, a pronounced cleft in his chin, and a thick mane of white hair brushed back from a widow's peak. He was in his early to mid-fifties, Michael guessed, wearing a dark gray suit with a red-and-black silk rep tie. Brown eyes. Long-fingered hands. A deep, stentorian voice. "I've been chatted up by hookers who claimed to be investment counselors, architects, delegates to the U.N., and even children's book editors. They are all nonetheless hookers."

"It's hard to tell a hooker, this day and age," the bartender said, nodding in agreement.

"Until they name their price," the tall, thin man said, and then got off his stool and came up the bar to where Michael was sitting. Taking the stool the blonde had vacated, he said, "Arthur Crandall," and took from his vest pocket a business card made of very thin black plastic. The lettering on the card was in white, and it read:

> CRANDALL FILMS, LTD.
> Arthur Crandall, Director

In the lower left-hand corner of the card, there was a New York address and telephone number. In the lower right-hand corner, there was a Beverly Hills address and telephone number. The card looked and felt like a strip of movie film. Which Michael now realized was its intent.

"Michael Barnes," he said, and took a little leather card case from the right-hand pocket of his jacket, and slipped a card free, and handed it to Crandall. The card was illustrated with an orange tree that grew out of the right-hand corner, its branches and leaves spreading upward and leftward across the top of the card, its oranges overhanging green lettering that read:

> GOLDEN ORANGE GROVES
> 16554 Fruitville Road
> Sarasota, FL 34240

In the lower right-hand corner was Michael's name, followed by the word "President," and below that his telephone number.

"Pleased to meet you," Crandall said. "You grow oranges, I see."

"That's what I do," Michael said.

"I grow *ideas*, so to speak," Crandall said. "A writer comes to me with an idea, and I nurture it along until we have, *voilà, un film!*"

"Would I know any of your movies?" Michael asked.

"War and Solitude?" Crandall said, and looked at him expectantly.

"Uh-huh," Michael said.

"You've heard of it?"

"No."

"That was my most recent film. *War and Solitude.*"

"I'm sorry, but I don't know it," Michael said. "I think I've seen almost every movie ever made . . ."

"I see," Crandall said.

"Either in an actual theater or else on cable or on videocassette

"I see," Crandall said again.

" . . . but *War and Solitude* doesn't ring a . . ."

"But you know *Platoon*, right?"

"Oh, sure,"

"War and Solitude was about the U.S. intervention in Nicaragua in 1926."

"Uh-huh," Michael said.

"It played art houses mostly," Crandall said.

"That must be why I missed it," Michael said. "We don't have too many art houses in Sarasota."

"It was meant to be a parable of sorts," Crandall said. "The film. But, of course, *Platoon* picked up all the marbles."

"It was a pretty realistic movie, I thought," Michael said. *"Platoon.* I was only over there for a little while, but . . ."

"Vietnam?"

"Yes. But I thought . . ."

"In combat?"

"Yes. I thought he really caught the feel of it. What it was like being there."

"You should see *my* movie," Crandall said. "You want the feel of war . . ."

"I'll look for it. Maybe it'll come to Sarasota someday."

"I doubt it," Crandall said.

"Well, you never know."

"Well, I *do* know, as a manner of fact," Crandall said somewhat heatedly. "Since the film was made eleven years ago, and it didn't make a nickel then, it sure as hell isn't going to be re-released *now* after *Platoon* got the girl, the gold watch, and everything. Which, by the way, the reason I was so fascinated by the conversation between you and the girl was that it read like a movie script. A classic Hooker-John scene. Until she accused you of stealing her ring. That threw me. I found myself thinking if this hooker is trying to *land* this guy, why is she all at once accusing him of stealing her ring?"

"Yeah, well."

"Very puzzling," Crandall said.

"Anyway, she got the ring back, so I guess . . ."

"What do you mean?"

"It was in my pocket."

"It was?"

"Yeah."

"How did it get in your pocket?"

"I guess she put it there. At least, that's what I thought until she refused to press charges."

"Then why'd she put it in your pocket to begin with?"

"That's just it. Listen, who the hell cares? She got her ring back, the cop let me go . . ."

"Well, aren't you curious?"

"No."

"I guess that's why you grow oranges and I make movies," Crandall said.

"I hate to interrupt this discussion," the bartender said, "but do you want me to keep your tab running?"

"No, I better be on my way," Michael said. "What do I owe you?"

The bartender handed him the bill.

Michael glanced at it, took out his wallet, opened it, and reached into the bill compartment.

There was no money in the bill compartment.

There were no credit cards in the various little slots on either side of the wallet.

His driver's license was gone, too.

So was his card for the Sarasota Public Library.

"Shit," he said.

2

"**B**e that as it may," the bartender said, "who's going to pay for these drinks here?"

"*I'll* pay for the drinks," Crandall said, somewhat testily. "Is that all you can think of is who's going to pay for the drinks? This man has just had his money and his credit cards stolen and all you can think of . . ."

"All right, all right," the bartender said.

"Is it any wonder that this city has a reputation for insensitivity? Here's a man visiting from Florida, on Christmas *Eve*, no less . . ."

"All right, all right . . ."

"He has his credit cards and his money and his driver's license stolen, and all *you* can think of . . ."

"I said all *right* already!"

"We've got to report this to the police," Crandall said, taking out his own wallet, looking at the check, and then putting a twenty-dollar bill on the bar. "What precinct are we in?"

"The First," the bartender said.

"Where is that?"

"On Ericsson Place."

"Where?"

"Ericsson Place. You gotta go all the way over the West Side from here. It's just off Varick and Canal."

"Do you know how to get there?" Crandall asked Michael.

"No," Michael said. "This is the first time I've been down in this part of the city."

"Last time, too, I'll bet," the bartender said.

"I'll show you the way," Crandall said.

"Well, look, I have to catch an eleven-oh-five plane to Boston. What I thought . . ."

"That gives you over three hours," Crandall said.

"Well, I thought I'd leave the city by . . ."

"Even so. You don't want these people . . ."

"I thought I'd call from Boston, report it . . ."

"No, no, you can't do that," Crandall said. "You have to go to the police in person. That's the way it works. Otherwise nothing'll get done. Don't worry, I'll go with you. I have a photographic memory, I can give them a good description of that fake cop."

"Well, thanks but . . ."

"Where'd you park your car?"

"But you see, I thought it might be simpler . . ."

"Come on, this won't take a minute," Crandall said. "It's your duty as a citizen."

"He's right," the bartender said.

Michael looked at him.

"Really," the bartender said.

"Well, okay," Michael said, and nodded.

"So where's the car?" Crandall asked.

"Right around the corner."

"Probably be a parking ticket on it," the bartender said.

Crandall gave him a look.

"Sorry," he said, and went to the cash register.

"Do you remember what name he gave you?" Crandall asked.

"Yes. Detective Daniel Cahill."

"Good. Although the name was probably as phony as he was."

"Here's your change," the bartender said.

"Thank you," Crandall said. He looked at the check again, left a tip on the bar, and then said, "Let's go."

They walked out of the bar into a raging snowstorm.

What had earlier been a Charles Dickens sort of *Christmas Carol*-ish snowfall—with fat, gentle flakes swirling and dipping on the air, and little puffy white hats on the street lamps, and people hurrying by with long mufflers trailing, their footsteps hushed on sidewalks and streets covered with a thin dusting of white—had now turned into a blustery blizzard blowing wind and tiny sharp snowflakes into every crack and crevice, covering the entire city with a fine, glistening, slippery coat of white already an inch thick.

"This we definitely do not need," Crandall said. "Where'd you say the car was?"

"Around the corner," Michael said.

They walked together to the corner, their heads ducked against the needle-sharp flakes driven by the wind, turned right, and then walked to the middle of the street where the rented car was parked under a street lamp. Michael unlocked the car on the driver's side, got in, and started it.

"If you'll flick open the trunk," Crandall said, "I'll see if we've got a scraper."

Michael reached for the trunk-release lever, close to the floor, and pulled on it.

"That's got it," Crandall said.

"Anything in there?" Michael called.

"Just a valise."

"Yes, that's mine."

"Nothing we can use," Crandall said, and slammed the trunk shut and came around the car to where Michael was sitting behind the wheel, the door open.

"One of those nights, huh?" he said.

"At least the defroster's working," Michael said.

"Good thing I wore gloves," Crandall said, and went around to the back of the car again, and began scraping at the rear window with the flat of his hand. It took them about five minutes to clear the windshield, the side windows, and the rear window. The car was toasty warm by then. Michael took off his glasses, wiped the lenses clear of condensation, and put them on again.

"You don't plan to drive, do you?" Crandall asked.

"What do you mean?"

"Well . . . he stole your license, didn't he?"

Michael said nothing.

He sat with his hands on the steering wheel, staring forlornly through the windshield, nodding.

At last he sighed and said, "Do you know how to drive?"

"Well, sure."

"Do you have a license?"

"Sure, but . . ."

"Would you please drive?"

"If you want me to, sure."

"I'd appreciate it," Michael said.

"I'll come around," Crandall said.

Both men got out of the car and walked around the front of it, through the snow, changing places. Behind the wheel now, Crandall familiarized himself with the dashboard instrumentation...

"Is this the headlight switch?"

"No, the one above it."

... and the gear-shift lever...

"Automatic transmission, huh?"

"Yes."

... and the brake and accelerator pedals.

"Shall I give it a whirl?" he asked.

"I'm ready when you are."

"I'll take it real slow," Crandall said, "make sure we don't get into any accidents."

He eased the car out of its space and into the street. The digital dashboard clock read 8:01, still early for a big-city night. But this was Christmas Eve, and there was not much traffic in the streets. Besides, news of the impending storm had probably driven everyone home even earlier than usual.

"How does the road feel?" Michael asked.

"Not too bad."

Crandall drove knowledgeably through the narrow twisting streets of downtown Manhattan, a mysterious maze to Michael, inching the car along until finally they came to Canal Street, where Crandall waited out a red light and then made a left turn.

"They usually clear the main thoroughfares first," he said. "Here comes a snowplow now. We should have pretty clear sailing over to Varick.

Why don't you put on the radio, see if we can get a forecast?"

Michael fiddled with the radio dial.

"Ten-ten is all news, all the time," Crandall said.

He was still driving slowly, although the road ahead was clear of snow. Wet but clear.

" . . . Arab leaders maintaining that the proposed oil hikes were more than adequately . . ."

"Pain in the ass, the Arab leaders," Crandall said.

" . . . justified by recent . . ."

"What the hell is *that?*" Crandall said.

" . . . developments in the Persian Gulf. Should OPEC decide . . ."

"Turn that off," Crandall said.

Michael turned off the radio.

"Did you feel that?" Crandall said.

"No. Feel what?"

"Listen."

Michael listened.

"I think we've got a flat," Crandall said.

"You're kidding."

"I wish I were, my friend."

He glanced into the rearview mirror, rolled down the window on his side, and hand-signaled that he was pulling over to the curb. He double-parked alongside a laundry truck, looked into the rearview mirror again, and sighed deeply. "It's a horror movie, am I right?" he said, and shook his head. "You want to check that right rear tire?"

Michael opened the door on the passenger side and stepped out into *Nanook of the North*. He closed the door behind him and sidled back between the laundry truck and the car, his coat flapping around his knees, his hair dancing wildly on top of his head, snow beginning to cake on his eyeglasses. He stopped before the right rear tire, kicked at it perfunctorily, and was kneeling to study it more closely when the car pulled away.

He threw himself back against the laundry truck, thinking in that split second that Crandall had accidentally stepped on the accelerator, and then realizing in the next split second that Crandall hadn't made any damn mistake, the car was speeding away, swerving a little as it sought purchase on the wet roadway, and then shooting off as straight as an—

"Hey!" he shouted.

The car kept speeding away into the distance.

"You son of a bitch!" he shouted, and began running after the car.

He ran up the middle of Canal Street, waving his arms and shouting, his coat flapping, horns honking behind him, headlights coming at him from the other side of the road, blinding him. A fearful blast immediately at his back caused him to leap to his right just as the sound of air brakes filled the snow-laden air, and then another blast of the horn, and a voice shouting, "You dumb fuck!" and the rush of the trailer truck as it came by him like a locomotive on the way to Albuquerque, wherever that was, and then the truck was gone as certainly as was Crandall in the rented car.

Sucking in great gulps of air, trying to catch his breath, Michael leaned against a red Cadillac parked at the curb. The window on the driver's side slid down suddenly and electrically. He jumped away from the car, turned, saw a girl on the passenger side with her blouse wide open and her breasts bulging out of her brassiere, and alongside her, behind the wheel, a teenage Puerto Rican with a scraggly moustache and a lipstick-smeared face.

"You mine not leanin' on dee wagon?" the boy said.

A sign in Spanish on the wall behind the muster desk advised Michael of his rights. To the right of the sign was the same warning in English—which was considerate, Michael thought. The sergeant sitting behind the desk and before both signs was a very fat man wearing a long-sleeved blue sweater over his blue uniform shirt. He looked up and said, "Help you, sir?"

"I want to report a few crimes," Michael said.

"Let me hear 'em," the sergeant said.

"A fake detective stole all my money and my . . ."

"How do you know he was a *fake* detective?" the sergeant asked.

"Well, if he *robbed* me, I have to assume . . ."

"Oh, yeah, right," the sergeant said. "What did he get from you?" he asked, and picked up the phone receiver.

"My money, my credit cards, and my driver's license."

Into the phone, the sergeant said, "Tony, there's a man here had his money and his credit cards and his license stolen from him by a fake detective."

"My car, too," Michael said.

"His car, too," the sergeant said. "You want to talk to him?"

"By a different person," Michael said. "The car."

"Right, I'll send him up," the sergeant said, and hung up. "Sir," he said, "if you'll go right up those steps outside there to the second floor and follow the signs that say Detectives, you'll ask for Detective Anthony Orso, that means 'bear' in Italian, he'll take good care of you."

"Thank you," Michael said.

"Don't mention it," the sergeant said, and picked up a ringing telephone. "First Precinct, Mulready," he said.

Michael walked up the iron-runged steps to the second floor, followed the signs with the word DETECTIVES and a pointing arrow on them, and at last came to a blue door with a glass panel. Painted onto the panel was a large facsimile of a gold and blue-enameled shield like the one Cahill had flashed in the bar. Under that was a sign that read:

```
1st Precinct
Detectives
Room # 210
```

Michael guessed this was the detective squadroom. He opened the door and stepped into the room and the first thing he saw was a little man sitting on a blue upholstered chair behind one of the desks. He was badly in need of a shave and he looked like a street hoodlum.

"Detective Orso?" Michael asked.

"Tony the Bear, that's me," Orso said. "You the one Gallagher ripped off?"

Michael blinked.

"Come in, come in," Orso said, and got up, and ushered Michael in. The squadroom was small but freshly painted in a blue the same color as the door. Electric IBM typewriters sat on all the desktops.

There were five or six desks in the room, but the room did not look crowded. A WANTED FOR MURDER poster with twelve photographs was taped to the wall over a small cabinet with fingerprinting equipment on it. A height chart was on the wall alongside the cabinet. Sitting on another blue-upholstered chair beside Orso's desk was a little man who looked remarkably like Orso's twin brother, except that his right hand was handcuffed to one of the chair rungs.

"We ain't got a detention cage," Orso explained.

"Some dump," the other man said.

"You shut up!" Orso said, pointing a finger at him.

"I know my rights," the man said.

"They all know their rights," Orso said sourly, and held out a chair for Michael. "Please, sir," he said.

From where Michael sat he could see both Orso and his look-alike in the other chair. The resemblance was uncanny. Michael wondered if Orso realized the man looked like him. And vice versa.

"So," Orso said. "Tell me what happened."

Michael told him what had happened. Orso listened. So did his twin brother.

"That's Gallagher, all right," Orso said.

"No, his name was Cahill," Michael said. "Detective Daniel Cahill."

"Are you sure? Was he working with a redhead calls herself Nikki Cooper, or sometimes Mickey Hooper, or sometimes Dorothy Callahan?"

"That don't rhyme," the other man said.

"Who asked you?" Orso said.

"Dorothy Callahan don't rhyme with the other two, that's all."

"I *know* it don't rhyme," Orso said. "Who says it has to rhyme?"

"She picks two names that rhyme, you figure the third one's gonna rhyme, too. But it don't."

"Do all *your* names rhyme?" Orso said.

"I got three names, too, and they all rhyme," the other man said, somewhat offended. "Charlie Bonano, Louie Romano, and Nicky Napolitano."

"What name were you using tonight when you stuck up the liquor store?" Orso asked.

"Charlie Bonano, and I didn't stick up no liquor store."

"No? Then who was it holding the gun on the proprietor?" Orso asked. "Musta been one of them two *other* guys, huh? Romano or Napolitano."

"Which ain't the point," Bonano said. "The point is a person chooses names that rhyme, then the names should rhyme. You don't go throwing in a Dorothy Calabrese."

"Callahan."

"Whatever."

"Shakespeare we got here in the squadroom," Orso said. "Worryin' about his iambic parameter."

"The point is . . ."

"The point is shut up. The point is we got this phony cop calls himself Gallagher runnin' all over the precinct workin' with a female redhead and rippin' off honest citizens like this gentlemen here. Also, if you want to know somethin', Bonano, it's wops like you give Italians a bad name."

"*Three* bad names," Bonano said.

"And you're ugly besides," Orso said.

"So are you," Bonano said.

"Maybe so, but I ain't going to jail," Orso said, and turned back to Michael. "We'll have to fill out some papers, sir," he said, "but I can tell you right now we ain't got a chance in hell of getting back the cash, and we'll be lucky Gallagher don't clean out Tiffany's tomorrow with your credit cards. First thing you better do is advise all the companies that your cards were stolen—do you know the numbers on the cards?"

"Nobody knows the numbers on their cards," Bonano said.

"Who asked you?"

"You asked *him."*

"But nobody asked you, did they?"

"What's the point askin' the man an impossible question to answer? Excuse me, sir, but do you know the numbers on your credit cards?"

"No," Michael said.

"There you are," Bonano said.

"It so *happens,"* Orso said, "I happen to *know* nobody knows the numbers on their credit cards. But it don't hurt to ask because one chance in a million, the person will know. It don't matter whether he knows or not, *anyway,* 'cause the credit card company has all this shit on a computer, and all you have to do, sir," he said, turning again to Michael, "is give them your name and address, and tell them your cards were stolen, and they'll make sure the word goes out. Otherwise, Gallagher's gonna buy himself a ticket on the Concorde to Paris and charge it to your Master-Card."

"Two tickets," Bonano said. "One for his girl-friend Dotty."

"You'll have to inform all your credit card companies," Orso said solemnly. "Now, sir," he said, and rolled some forms and some sheets of carbon into his typewriter. "Can you tell me your name, please?"

"Michael J. Barnes."

"What does the J stand for, sir?"

"Just J. Just the letter J."

"Yes, sir, and your address, sir? In case we catch Gallagher in the next hour or so."

"Ha!" Bonano said.

Orso gave him a look. Bonano shrugged.

"I *was* staying at the Hilton," Michael said. "But I've already checked out. In fact, my valise was in the . . ."

"On Fifty-fourth and Sixth?"

"Yes."

"I stayed at the Hilton once," Bonano said.

"What is it with you, huh?" Orso said. "Don't you know how to keep your mouth shut?"

"It's a very nice hotel, sir," Bonano said, as though complimenting its owner.

Orso rolled his eyes. "Your home address, please," he said.

"16554 Fruitville Road," Michael said. "Sarasota, Florida."

"Ah-ha," Orso said. "Something told me you were from Florida."

"Like maybe his suntan," Bonano said. "Are you near Hollywood Park? I go to Hollywood Park for the races."

"That's on the east coast," Michael said.

"So," Orso said, "from what the desk sergeant told me on the phone, Gallagher stole not only your money, your credit cards, and your driver's license, but also your car. What kind of . . . ?"

"No, it wasn't Cahill who stole the car," Michael said.

"Gallagher, you mean."

"Neither one."

"Then who was it?"

"Arthur Crandall."

"Who?" Bonano said.

"Arthur Crandall," Michael said. "He's a movie director. Here's his card."

"He stole your car and gave you his *card?*" Orso said, astonished.

"That is *some* classy thief," Bonano said.

Orso looked at the card.

"This looks like a piece of film," he said.

"It's his business card," Michael said.

"I can't get over it. A guy steals your car and hands you his card."

"He gave me the card first," Michael said.

"And *then* stole your car?" Bonano said.

"One thing I know for sure," Orso said, "a guy planning to steal your car hands you a business card with a name and two addresses on it, the name and the addresses are phony."

"For sure," Bonano said.

"So what we got here," Orso said, "is two unrelated cases. We got a phony cop and his copy editor girlfriend . . . did she tell you she was a copy editor?"

"No, a lawyer."

"Not a copy editor?"

"A criminal lawyer."

"Hmm," Orso said, and shook his head. "Well, what we got here nonetheless is this phony pair who stole your money and your credit cards and your driver's license . . ."

"My library card, too," Michael said.

"Do you read a lot?" Bonano asked.

"Yes," Michael said.

"I do, too. I developed the habit in the slammer."

"Sir, are you paying attention here?" Orso said.

"Yes, I'm sorry," Michael said.

"That's perfectly all right, sir. And we also got this phony movie director who stole your car . . ."

"It was a rented car," Michael said.

"Good thing," Bonano said.

"Which in no way diminishes the fact of Grand Theft, Auto," Orso said. "The point being we now got *two* cases here instead of one. Which now makes it *twice* as hard." He sighed heavily, and then said, "When did you plan on leaving the city, sir? In case we hear anything."

"I'm catching an eleven-oh-five plane out of Kennedy," Michael said, and looked at his watch.

"Do you have your plane ticket already?"

"Yes, I do."

"All paid for and everything?"

"Yes."

"That's very good, sir. How did you plan on getting to the airport, sir?"

"Well, I haven't given that any thought, actually."

"Since all your money was stolen, you see."

"Yes, that's true."

"In fact, sir, how did you plan on getting to Franklin Street?"

"Why would I want to go to Franklin Street?" Michael asked.

"Because that's where you can catch the train to Kennedy."

"Oh."

"Are you familiar with our subway system, sir?"

"No."

"I will give you a subway map, sir, which will acquaint you with all the lines in the city."

"How's he gonna ride the subway if he ain't got no money?" Bonano asked.

"Well, I have some change," Michael said, and reached in his right hand pocket. "What's the fare, something like a quarter?"

"A quarter!" Orso said.

"A quarter!" Bonano said.

Both men burst out laughing.

"The fare hasn't been a quarter since the *Dutch* were here!" Orso said, laughing.

"The *Indians!*" Bonano said, laughing.

"Well, I've got . . ." Michael quickly counted the coins on his palm. "Sixty cents," he said.

"Sixty cents!" Orso said, and burst into new gales of laughter.

"Sixty cents!" Bonano said. "I'm gonna wet my pants!"

"Sir," Orso said, "the fare has been a dollar-fifteen since Hector was a pup, sir. That is the subway fare in the city of New York. For *now,* anyway."

"How much does it cost in Sarasota?" Bonano asked.

"We don't have a subway," Michael said, and looked at the coins on his palm again. "Mr. Orso," he said, "do you think I can . . . ?"

"No, don't, sir," Orso said.

Michael looked at him.

"Please, sir."

Michael kept looking at him.

"Please don't ask me for a loan, sir. Please. I know that all you need is fifty-five cents to make up the difference between the subway fare and what you've got. But, sir, perhaps you don't know how many victims we get in here all the time, day and night, this city never sleeps, sir, victims who have had every penny taken from them and who need bus fare or subway fare to get them back home again. Sir, I can tell you that if I gave every one of those victims fifty-five cents, or even a quarter, or a dime, sir, even a thin dime, why, sir, I'd be giving away my entire salary to these people and I'd have nothing left to put clothes on my children's backs or food in their bellies. So, please, sir. As much as I'd like to . . ."

"You're breaking my heart," Bonano said, reaching into his pocket with his free hand. "Here's ten bucks," he said to Michael, and with some difficulty extracted two five-dollar bills from his wallet. "This'll get you to Kennedy."

"That is probably tainted money, sir," Orso said. "But do as you see fit."

Michael looked at the bills.

"Money from the proceeds of prostitution or drugs," Orso said. "But let your conscience be your guide."

Michael took the money.

"Thank you," he said to Bonano. "I'll pay you back."

"You can send your check to Sing Sing," Orso said.

"My luck, I'll get Attica," Bonano said.

"Write it out to any one of his names," Orso said.

"And, sir, I hope there are no hard feelings. It's just that if I lend money to . . ."

"Where are the violins?" Bonano asked.

"Actually," Michael said, "I wasn't about to ask for a loan."

"You weren't?" Orso said.

"You wasted a whole speech," Bonano said.

"I only wanted to use your toilet."

"Oh. Well, it's just down the hall."

"Thank you."

"But they have very nice toilets at the airport," Bonano said.

"You don't want my subway map?" Orso said, sounding hurt.

"I *do,*" Michael said. "Yes, thank you for reminding me."

"Here's what you do," Orso said, opening the map. "You go outside, you make an immediate right the minute you come down the steps, and the first street you hit is Varick. Okay, you make another right on Varick, and you walk past Moore, which there's a place called Walker's on the corner, and the next cross street you come to is Franklin. But you don't want to go all the way to Franklin . . ."

"I don't?"

"No, because just before you get to Franklin, what you'll see is a subway kiosk, that's the one right here," he said, and put his finger on the map. "Okay, you go downstairs, and you buy a token for a buck-fifteen and you go to the downtown platform, make sure it's the *downtown* platform, and you get on the A-train. You get off at Howard Beach—that's in Queens—and take a shuttle bus to the airport. There'll be directions when you get off the train," Orso said, and nodded in conclusion, and folded the map, and handed it to Michael.

"Thank you," Michael said.

"I hope you understand about the money and all. It's just that with all the victims in this city . . ."

"Bring on the Philharmonic," Bonano said.

"Will you let me know if you hear anything?"

"They *never* hear anything," Bonano said. "You'll get old and gray waiting for them to catch that phony cop and his girl. Or the phony movie guy, either."

"We caught *you,* didn't we?"

"Only 'cause my pants fell down when I pulled the gun," Bonano said.

"You're even uglier with your pants down," Orso said, and both men burst out laughing.

They were still laughing when Michael left the squadroom.

He went down the hall to use the toilet, and then came down the iron-runged steps, waving the subway map in farewell to a uniformed cop going up, and then opened one of the blue wooden doors leading to the street, and stepped outside into *Fang, Son of Claw.* The wind almost blew him off the front steps of the station house. It was snowing even more heavily now, the flakes swirling dizzily around the green globes on the station-house wall, the lights casting an eerie glow onto the thick carpet of snow on the steps and the sidewalk below. He pulled up the collar of his coat, walked to the corner, turned right on Varick, walked past Moore, and was just approaching the lighted subway kiosk ahead when a huge man wearing blue jeans, a leather jacket, black gloves, and a ski mask stepped out of a doorway and stuck a gun in his face.

3

One good thing Michael had learned in Vietnam was that a bad situation could only get worse. Either you reacted immediately or you never got a chance to react at all. Only three words came from the man's mouth, cutting through the wind and the slashing snow, but those words meant trouble. "Hands up, man!" and Michael moved at once, inside the gun hand, knee coming up into the man's groin, head rising swiftly to butt the ski-masked chin as the man doubled over in pain. There was the click of teeth hitting teeth. The man lurched, his hands flailing the air as he twisted partly away from Michael, who reached out for the collar of the leather jacket, caught it, twisted his hand into it, and yanked back on it.

He might have been in the jungle again, this could have been Vietnam again. But there was snow underfoot and not the damp rot of vegetation, and the man was wearing black leather instead of black pajamas. Nor was this a slight and slender Oriental who you sometimes felt you could break in half with your bare hands, this was a giant who measured perhaps six-feet two-inches tall and weighed two hundred pounds, and he wasn't about to be yanked over on his back by someone who was shorter by four inches and lighter by thirty pounds. Michael hadn't done this kind of work for a long time now. You got fat living in Florida. Eating oranges and watching the sun go down. You forgot there were such things as people wanting to hurt you. You forget there were such things as sometimes getting killed.

In the old days, there'd have been a knife in his hands, and he'd have gone for the throat. But that was then, and this was now, and Michael was working very hard and breathing very hard as the man turned and swung the gun at the same time, slamming the butt into the side of Michael's head, knocking the subway map out of his hand and knocking Michael himself to the sidewalk. He immediately rolled away in the snow, because jungle fighting had taught him yet another thing: if one man is holding a gun and the other man is on the ground and the first man doesn't fire, then the gun is empty and the next thing that's coming is a kick.

Michael didn't know how the gun could be empty since not a single shot had been fired, but the kick came right on schedule, aimed straight for the spot on his head where the gun had already hit him. His head wasn't there anymore, though. His head was perhaps six inches from where the kick sliced the air, eight inches now because he was still rolling away from the kick, a foot away now, rolling, rolling, and then scrambling to his knees and bracing himself because the man was coming at him again, bellowing in what seemed to be genuine rage although Michael hadn't done a damn thing to him but kick him in the balls and butt him under the chin a little.

"Freeze!" a woman's voice shouted, but nobody froze anything. Michael kept coming up off his knees because being on your knees was a bad position when a gorilla was charging you, and the gorilla kept right on charging and bellowing but not firing the gun, which caused Michael to think yet another time that the gun was empty.

"I said freeze, *police*!" the woman shouted again, which wasn't at all what she'd said the first time, and which this time caused the gorilla to hesitate for just the slightest bit of an instant, but that was all the time Michael needed. He feinted at the masked man's head with a right jab, and then kicked sideways and hard at his ankles, hoping the snow underfoot would help the maneuver, which it did. The man's feet slid out from under him and he went crashing down in the opposite direction, the gun flying out of his hand. This time Michael was on him in a wink, straddling him, and chopping the flat of his hand across the bridge of where the nose should have been under the mask. The man screamed. Michael hoped he'd broken the nose. The woman screamed, too.

"Police, police, break it *up*, goddamn it!"

She was standing at the top of the steps leading down to the subway.

She didn't look like any cop Michael had ever seen in his life.

She was, in fact, a very fat woman in her late thirties, he guessed, wearing a short black monkey-fur jacket over a red garter belt, red panties, red seamed silk stockings, and red high-heeled boots.

At first, Michael thought she was a mirage.

Coming up out of the subway that way. Half-naked. In a snowstorm no less.

Flaming red hair to match the lingerie and boots. Blazing green eyes, five-feet four-inches tall and weighing at least a hundred and fifty pounds.

Michael picked up the gun and pointed it at the man in the snow.

"Up!" he said. "On your feet!"

"Drop the gun," the fat redhead said.

Michael had no intention of dropping the gun. Not while the man sitting in the snow was still breathing.

"You hurt me," the man said.

High, piping, frightened voice.

"No kidding?" Michael said, and reached down for the ski mask, pulling it off his head, wanting to see just how *much* he'd hurt him.

The man was Chinese.

Or Japanese.

Or, for all Michael knew, Vietnamese.

Everything seemed suddenly like a dream. He was back in the jungle again, where everyone had slanted eyes, and where day and night he dreamed of naked redheaded women materializing in the mist, though not as short or as fat as this one was. Back then the women who materialized were very slender, but they were all carrying hand grenades in their armpits. The bad guys were slender, too. And very small. This bad guy was very large.

"You son of a bitch," he said.

In perfect English.

"Nice talk," the fat redhead said. "You," she said to Michael. "I told you to drop the gun."

"Where's your badge?" Michael said.

"Here's my badge," she said, and took from her handbag a shield that looked very much like the one Cahill had flashed in the bar, gold with blue enameling. "Detective O'Brien," she said, "First Squad."

"Officer," the Oriental man said at once, "this person broke my nose."

"No, I don't think so," Michael said.

"Get up," Detective O'Brien said.

"I think he broke some of my *teeth,* too."

He was on his feet now, tongue searching his teeth for chips, hand rubbing his nose at the same time. Michael knew the nose wasn't broken. He'd have jumped out of his skin just touching it. The teeth were another matter. He'd butted the man pretty hard.

"What are you doing sticking up people?" he asked.

He had the idea that Chinese guys—if he was Chinese—didn't go around sticking up people. Japanese guys, neither. He wasn't so sure about Vietnamese.

"What are *you* doing trying to *kill* people?" the man said.

"I was defending myself," Michael said.

"From what? A fake gun?"

Michael looked at the gun in his hand. It had the weight and heft of a real gun, but it was nonetheless plastic. By now, the man had decided that nothing was broken. Teeth all okay, nose still intact. Which put Michael in a dangerous position in that the gun in his hand was plastic and the man standing before him was beginning to look bigger and bigger every minute. Michael had never seen such a large Oriental in his life. He wondered if perhaps the man was a fake Oriental, the way Cahill had been a fake detective and the way the plastic gun in his hand was a fake Colt .45 automatic.

The gun Detective O'Brien pulled out of her handbag looked very real.

"I'll shoot the first one of you fucks who moves," she said.

Which sounded like authentic cop talk, too.

"You," she said. "What's your name?"

"Charlie Wong."

"Chinese, huh?" she asked.

"No, Jewish," Wong said sarcastically, which Michael figured was the wrong way to sound when a fat lady in only her underwear and a monkey-fur jacket was standing in the shivering cold with a pistol in her hand.

"And you?" she said to Michael.

"Presbyterian," he said.

"Your *name,*" she said impatiently, and wagged the gun at him.

"A cop," Wong said, shaking his head, "I can't believe it. I thought you were a hooker."

"Why, thank you," Detective O'Brien said.

"That's the way the hookers dress down here," Wong explained to Michael. "Even in cold weather like this. All year round, in fact."

"If you two *gentlemen* don't mind," Detective O'Brien said, sounding as sarcastic as Wong had earlier sounded, "what we're gonna do now is march to the station house, 'cause quite frankly I don't appreciate disorderly conduct on my . . ."

Wong shoved out at Michael, who in turn lost his footing and crashed into Detective O'Brien, who fell over backward onto her almost-naked behind, her silk-stockinged legs flying into the air, her gun going off. Michael figured that what he had here was a fat lady who was a real cop with a real badge and a real gun, but who thought he was a two-bit brawler instead of a two-bit victim. He decided he did not want to spend the rest of the night explaining that Wong had tried to hold him up. Especially since Detective O'Brien was now sitting up in the snow at the top of the steps leading down to the subway, her elbows on her knees, the pistol in both hands, taking very careful aim at him.

He had learned another thing in Vietnam.

"Aiiii-eeeeeee!" he yelled.

When you heard this in the jungle, your blood ran cold.

It worked here in downtown Manhattan, too.

Detective O'Brien screamed back at him in terror. Her gun went off wildly, and so did Michael, in the same direction Wong had gone, running back toward Moore, and crossing the street, and seeing Wong up ahead going a hundred miles an hour.

Michael took a quick look at his watch.

8:45.

His plane would be leaving in two hours and twenty minutes.

He could not go down into the subway to catch his A-train to the airport because Detective O'Brien was behind him, sitting between him and his transportation. There was not a taxi anywhere in sight, and besides the ten dollars Bonano had loaned him was not enough for cab fare to Kennedy. He did not know this goddamn city where everyone seemed to be either a cop or a crook and all of them seemed to be crazy. He did not know where there might be *another* subway station where he could catch a train to the airport, because his map was behind him, too, there on the sidewalk between him and O'Brien. He knew only that when you were lost in the jungle, you followed a native guide.

Behind him, Detective O'Brien fired her gun. Into the air, he hoped.

He ran like hell after Wong.

They ran for what seemed like miles.

Wong was a good runner. Michael was out of shape and out of breath. His shoes were sodden and his socks were wet and his feet were cold and his eyeglasses kept caking with snow, which he repeatedly cleared as he followed Wong, both of them padding silently over fields of white, the curbs gone now, no difference now between sidewalk and street, just block after block of white after white after white in a part of the city that was totally alien to him. But at last he turned a corner behind Wong and saw him ducking into a doorway with Chinese lettering over it. Michael looked at his watch again. 8:57. Wong disappeared into the doorway. Michael followed him.

He wiped off his glasses and put them back on again.

He was inside a Chinese fortune-cookie factory.

A Chinese man in white pants, a white shirt, a long white apron, and a white chef's hat stood behind a stainless steel counter stuffing fortune cookies with little slips of paper.

"Which way did he go?" Michael asked.

"True ecstasy is a golden lute on a purple night," the fortune-cookie stuffer said.

There was a door at the far end of the room. Michael pointed to it.

"Did he go in there?" he asked.

"He who rages at fate rages at barking dogs," the man said, and stuffed another cookie.

"Thank you," Michael said, and went immediately toward the door.

Behind him, the fortune-cookie stuffer said, "Dancers have wings but pigs cannot fly."

Michael opened the door.

He was suddenly in a downtown Saigon gambling den.

In Saigon, there were only three things to do: get drunk, get laid, or get lucky. There were a great many gambling dens lining the teeming side streets of Saigon, and he had gambled in most of them and had never got lucky in any of them. Nor had he ever seen anyone playing Russian roulette in any of them. That was for the movies. He had told Arthur Crandall—or whatever his real name was—that *Platoon* was a pretty realistic movie, but the operative word in that observation was "movie." Because however realistic it might have been, it was still only and merely a movie, and everyone sitting in that theater knew that he was watching flickering images on a beaded screen and that the guns going off and the blood spurting were fake. In the jungle, the guns going off and the blood spurting were real.

You could never show in a movie the *feel* of a friend's hot blood spilling onto your hands when he took a hit from a frag grenade. Never. You could never explain in the most realistic of war films that you had shit your pants the first time a mortar shell exploded six feet from where you were lying on your belly in the jungle mud. In war movies, nobody ever shit his pants. You could never explain the terror and revulsion you'd felt the first time you saw a dead soldier lying on his back with his cock cut off and stuffed into his mouth. In war movies, guys compensated for their terror and revulsion by playing Russian roulette in Saigon gambling dens. In real life, what you did in Saigon gambling dens was you bet on the roll of the dice, the turn of the card, or—occasionally—the courage and skill of a rooster. Cockfights in Saigon were as common as severed cocks in the jungle, but you never saw a cockfight in the same building where people were shooting crap or playing poker.

Here and now, in this section of the fortune-cookie factory, there were no cockfights. There were stainless steel ovens, and there were two crap games on blankets against one of the walls, and two poker games at tables, and a mah-jongg game at yet another table. The mah-jongg table was occupied entirely by Chinese men who looked as if they had stepped full blown out of the Ming Dynasty. This was by far the noisiest table in the room, the Chinese men slamming down tiles and shouting what sounded like orders to behead someone, and the men standing around the table shouting either encouragement or disparagement, it was difficult to tell. There was some noise, but not as much, coming from the two crap games on the blankets, where—as had been the case in Saigon—there were Orientals playing with white guys, black guys, and Hispanics. A television set on a shelf high on the wall was turned up to its full volume, and

Andy Williams had just come on in a Christmas special that contributed mightily to the overall din. In contrast to the television jubilance, the poker players were virtually solemn. A pall of smoke hung over the entire room. Charlie Wong was nowhere in sight.

Michael looked at his watch. 9:05. He had to get out of here and find a way to get to Kennedy by subway. His plane would be leaving in exactly two hours, the last plane to Boston tonight. He wandered over to one of the crap games, thinking he'd ask one of the players how to get to a subway stop that would connect with the Kennedy train. A short Hispanic—who looked remarkably like the young man who'd asked him not to lean on his car— picked up the dice, blew on them, said, *"Mama necesita un par de zapatos nuevos!"* and promptly rolled snake eyes. *"Mierda!"* he shouted, and immediately walked away from the blanket. On the television screen, Andy Williams was singing "Jingle Bells."

Michael stepped into the space the little Hispanic had vacated.

Taxi fare would be nice, he thought.

There were five players in the game now: two blacks, two Chinese, and a white man. One of the black men was named Harry. Michael discerned this when the dice were handed to him and one of the Chinese men said, "Come on, Hally, ketchem up hot," sounding like the cook in an old movie about the Gold Rush. At the mah-jongg table, one of the Chinese men there shouted something that sounded fierce and warlike, but everyone at the table laughed. Here at the blanket, Harry laughed, too. Michael figured he was laughing not because he spoke or understood Chinese but because it was now his turn to roll the dice, and a man holding a pair of dice in his hand is—for the moment, at least—in control of his own destiny.

Harry did indeed look like a man with the world on a string. Tall and wiry and chocolate-colored, he possessed in addition to his good looks a dirty Eddie Murphy laugh, a mischievous Bill Cosby twinkle, and the calm, confident air of a man about to make a fortune. Michael would have bet all the oranges on every tree in his groves on the roll of the dice this man held in his hand. But he had only the ten dollars Charlie Bonano had loaned him.

"Bet a hundred," Harry said, and put five twenty-dollar bills on the blanket. The hundred was covered in thirty seconds flat; apparently most of these players had seen Harry roll before and the air of confidence he exuded impressed them not a bit. The only man at the blanket who seemed to have any faith in him at all was the Chinese man who'd earlier urged him to ketchem up hot. He now said, "Twenny say Hally light."

"Ten says he's wrong," the other black man at the blanket said.

"Me, too, hassa ten long," the other Chinese man said, sounding like a stoker on an American gunboat during the Boxer Rebellion.

"Ten more says he's right," Michael said, and tossed onto the blanket all the money he had in the world.

The white guy—a burly man wearing a blue sweater and a blue watch cap, and looking like a seaman off a cargo ship—said, "Ten says he's wrong," and tossed his money onto the blanket.

On the television screen, Andy Williams and what appeared to be the entire Mormon Tabernacle Choir began bellowing "God Rest Ye Merry, Gentlemen."

"Come on, sugah," Harry whispered, and shook the dice gently, and let them roll easily off the pink palm of his hand and onto the blanket. The dice rolled and rolled and rolled, and hit the wall, and bounced off the wall, and one of them flew to the right and came up with a six-spot, and the other one flew to the left and came up with a five-spot, for a total of eleven, which was a winner.

Michael now had twenty dollars.

Was twenty enough for a taxi to Kennedy?

He looked at his watch.

9:15.

His heart almost stopped.

The girl walking toward the blanket was tall.

Five-nine, he supposed.

Much taller than the girls who'd worked the Saigon bars.

But every bit as beautiful. So achingly beautiful, those Vietnamese girls. Girls, yes, some of them were barely in their teens. That long glossy black hair and the slanted loam-colored eyes, the complexion as pale as a dipper of cream, a faint tint to it, not yellow, you could not call any Oriental on earth yellow, any more than you could call anyone black, or red for that matter, or even white, it was pointless to try to identify people by color because the colors simply didn't match. Here and now she came gliding sleekly out of the din and the smoke, a sinuous glide unique to Orientals, a green silk dress slit high on her right thigh, a red rose in her black hair, green satin high heeled pumps, the colors of

Christmas, fa-la-la-la-la, Andy Williams sang, and Michael wondered how many Saigon hookers he had fallen in love with. And later killed their sisters in the jungle.

"Hello, Harry," she said, "are you winning?"

"Jus' rolled me a 'leven," Harry said.

Michael smiled at her. She did not smile back. An hour and fifty minutes to plane time.

"Let the twenty ride," he said, and realized he was showing off for her, big spender betting all his money without batting an eyelash.

Harry picked up the dice, winked at him, and said, "Man knows a winner. Bet the two hunnerd."

"I'll take it all," the other black man said.

"You facin' disaster, Slam," Harry told him and laughed his dirty Eddie Murphy laugh.

"I'm facin' a man got lucky one time," Slam said.

"Oh, my my my," Harry said to the dice, "you hear this man runnin' his mouth?"

"Who wanna fiffy more?" the first Chinese man asked.

"I'll take thirty of that," the seaman with the watch cap said.

"I hassa twenny," the second Chinese man said.

Harry brought the dice up close to his mouth.

"Sugah," he whispered, "we don't wanna disappoint our friends here, now do we?"

He was talking to the dice as if he were talking to a woman. How could they possibly fail a man who speaks so gently and persuasively? Michael thought, and realized he was smiling. The girl thought he was smiling at her. Maybe he was. But she still did not smile back. Oh well, he thought.

"You know jus' what we need," Harry told the dice, "so I'm jus' goan let you do yo' own thing," and he shook the dice gently, and opened his hand again, and the dice rolled off his palm and strutted across the blanket, and kissed the wall, and skidded off the wall to land with a five-spot and a six-spot showing for a total of eleven again, which was another winner.

Michael now had forty dollars, certainly enough to get him to Kennedy by cab.

"How's that, James?" Harry asked.

"Good," the first Chinese man said, beaming.

"*No* good," the second Chinese man said sourly.

"Bet the four hundred," Harry said.

Michael looked at the girl one last time. She seemed not to know he existed. He pocketed his forty bucks and started moving away from the blanket.

"Don't go, man," Harry said softly.

Michael looked at him.

"You my luck, man."

In Vietnam—ah, Jesus, in Nam—too many young men had said those words to too many other young men. Over there, you needed something to believe in other than yourself, you needed a charm, a rabbit's foot, a buddy to stand beside you, to be your luck when it looked as though your luck might run out at any moment.

Michael looked at his watch.

9:30.

If he could get out of the city in the next half hour or so, he'd be okay. The roads to Kennedy would surely be clear of snow by now, it would be a quick half-hour run by taxi, walk directly to the gate, no luggage—thanks to Crandall—and off he'd go.

"You with me or not?" Harry asked.

There was something almost desperate in his eyes. "I've got forty says you're good," Michael said, and tossed the money onto the blanket and smiled at the girl. This time, she smiled back.

"What's your name?" she asked.

"Michael," he said.

"How do you do?" she said.

"We shootin' dice here?" Slam asked, "or we chattin' up Miss Shanghai?"

"Miss Mott Street, you mean," the seaman with the watch cap said.

"Miss China Doll," the second Chinese man said.

"Are you really all those things?" Michael asked.

"No, I'm Connie," she said.

"Willya please *roll* 'em?" Slam said.

Grinning from ear to ear, Harry picked up the dice.

He was good for the next pass, and three more passes after that, by which time Michael's initial ten bucks had grown to six hundred and forty dollars. He looked at his watch again—9:45—and decided to let all of it ride on Harry's phenomenal luck. He wondered if he was risking the money just so he could stay here by Connie's side. All at once, the plane to Boston didn't seem too very important. Missing a plane to Boston wasn't the end of the world. On the television screen, Andy Williams began singing "Silent Night."

Harry rolled a ten, a tough point to make.

Then Harry rolled a four . . .

And a nine . . .

And a six . . .

And an eight . . .

And Michael began wondering how many numbers he could roll before a seven came up and killed them both dead? Michael had never in his life won a nickel in a Saigon gambling house, but he'd kept rolling number after number out there in the jungle, never sevening out while everywhere around him brief good friends were dying.

"Tough point," he said.

"Very," Connie said, and smiled.

He smiled back.

Harry was whispering to the dice again.

This time I buy the farm, Michael thought.

"Sugah, we need a six and a four," Harry whispered.

It was almost ten o'clock.

On the television set, Andy Williams was saying good night to everyone, wishing everyone in America a Merry Christmas. Michael paid no attention to him. His eyes were on Connie and his six hundred and forty bucks were on the blanket.

"Two fives, baby," Harry whispered to the dice, and shook them gently in his fist, and opened his hand and said, "Ten the hard way, sugah," and the dice rolled out and away toward the wall.

On the television screen, the news came on. The headline story was a bombing in Dublin, but no one was listening to it.

One of the dice bounced off the wall.

A three.

The second die hit the wall.

Bounced off it.

A four.

Shit, Michael thought, there goes my taxi.

"In downtown Manhattan tonight," the male anchor said, "motion-picture director Arthur Crandall . . ."

Michael looked up at the screen.

" . . . was found shot to death in a rented auto-mobile. Police report finding a wallet in the car, possibly dropped by Crandall's murderer. It contained . . ."

Everyone around the blanket was looking up at the screen.

" . . . sixty-three dollars in cash, several credit cards, and a driver's license identifying . . ."

"Good night," Michael said, "thank you," and began walking toward the door across the room.

" . . . a man named Michael Barnes, who the Hertz company confirms rented the car at Kennedy last Fri . . ."

Michael closed the door behind him.

The same man was still behind the stainless steel table, stuffing fortune cookies.

"Have a nice holiday," Michael said.

"The down of white geese shall float upon your dreams," the man said.

The door opened again.

"Wait for me," Connie said.

4

It had stopped snowing.

She was wearing a short black coat over the green dress. The red rose was still in her hair. Black coat, black hair, green dress and shoes, red rose—all against a background of white on white. The silent night Andy Williams had promised. Still and white, except for the flatness of the black and the sheen of the green and the shriek of the red in her hair.

"You've got trouble, huh?" she said.

He debated lying.

"Yes," he said, "I've got trouble."

Their breaths pluming on the frosty air.

"Come on," she said, "I've got a limo around the corner."

He thought that was pretty fortunate, a rich Chinese girl with a chauffeured limo to take her hither and yon in the city. He didn't want to go anywhere in this city but out of it. Straight to Kennedy, where he would catch his plane to Boston and Mama, or else try to get a plane to Florida. Get out of this rotten apple as soon as possible, call his lawyer the minute he landed someplace. Dave, they are saying I murdered somebody in New York, Dave. What should I do?

Hushed footfalls on the fresh snow.

Everything looking so goddamn beautiful.

But they were saying he'd killed somebody.

The limousine was parked outside a Chinese restaurant on Elizabeth Street. Long and black and sleek, it looked like a Russian submarine that had surfaced somewhere on an Arctic glacier. There were Christmas decorations in both front windows of the restaurant, all red and green and tinselly. The building up the street seemed decorated for Christmas, too, with green globes flanking the—

"Hey," Michael said, "that's a . . ."

"I know," Connie said, "the Fifth Precinct. Don't worry about it. Just get in the back of the car the minute I unlock it."

She hurried ahead of him on the sidewalk, struggling through the thick snow in her high-heeled pumps while up the street a Salvation Army band played "Adeste Fideles," and a man with a microphone pleaded with passersby to be generous. It was a little past ten-fifteen by Michael's watch, but the streets here in Chinatown were still crowded with Christmas Eve shoppers. He watched Connie as she stepped off the curb, walked around to the driver's side of the car, and inserted a key in the lock. She opened the door, nodded to him, and immediately got into the car. He came up the street swiftly, stopped at the back door on the curb side, opened it. He got in at once, closed the door behind him, and said, "Where's the chauffeur?"

"I'm the chauffeur," she said.

"This is your car?"

"No, it's a China Doll car." She turned on the seat, looking back at him. "China Doll Executive Limousine Service," she explained. "I'm one of the drivers." To emphasize the point, she settled a little peaked chauffeur's hat on her head. The rose seemed suddenly incongruous. She handed him a card. Everyone in this city had a card. The card read:

CHINA DOLL
EXECUTIVE LIMOUSINE SERVICE
Charles Wong, President

"Charlie Wong!" he said.

"You know him?"

"He tried to hold me up!"

"Charlie? No. He's a respectable businessman. He has twelve limos."

"I don't care if he has a *hundred* limos. He stuck a gun in my face."

"Charlie?"

"Well, a plastic gun. Yes, *Charlie*! A big Chinese guy with . . ."

"No, you must be thinking of another Charlie Wong. Wong is a very common Chinese name. Sixty-two percent of all the people in China are named Wong."

"Is that true?"

"I think so. My name isn't that common. Kee. That's my family name. Connie is my given name."

"That's a very nice name," he said. "Connie Kee."

"Yes, it's illiterate."

"Alliterative."

"Yes. Although actually, it's Kee Connie. The same as it's really Wong Charlie. In China, they put the family name first."

"Then what should I call you?"

"Connie Kee. Because this isn't China, you know. This is America, you know."

"Right now I'd rather be in China," he said. "Would you like to drive me to Kennedy?"

"If you're going to China, you'll need a visa," she said.

"In that case, I'll go to Boston."

"I've never been to Boston, so I don't know. But when my uncle Benny went to Hong Kong—this wasn't even mainland China—I know he needed a visa. Anyway, you don't want to go to Kennedy," she said, shaking her head.

"How about La Guardia?"

"No good, either. They'll be watching all the bus stations, railroad terminals, and airports."

"Then how would you like to drive me to Sarasota?" he asked.

"I'd love to," she said, "but I have a twelve-thirty pickup. Why'd you kill that movie director?"

"I didn't kill any goddamn movie director," he said.

"The police think you did."

"The police are wrong."

"Right or wrong, everyone in this city knows what you look like."

"How can they know what I . . . ?"

"Because they showed your picture on television."

"My *picture*? Where'd . . . ?"

"Right on the screen, just as you were running out."

"Where'd they get . . . ?"

"On your driver's license. Nice big close-up of your face."

"Oh shit."

"Actually, it wasn't *that* bad a picture."

"Then they *will* be watching the airports."

"Is what I said."

"Because if they have my license . . ."

"Oh, they have it, all right."

"Then they know I'm from Florida . . ."

"Oh, they know, all right."

"And they have to be figuring I'll be heading down there."

"Is what anyone would figure."

"So I *can't* head down there."

"Not if you killed this guy Randall."

"Crandall," Michael said.

"I'm sure they said Randall."

"It was Arthur *Crandall,*" Michael said.

"Well. I won't argue with you. I guess you know who you killed."

"I *didn't* kill him. And it was *Crandall,* damn it, I have his card right here."

He fished into his jacket pocket.

"See?" he said, and showed her the card that looked like a strip of film. "Arthur Crandall, there's his name in black and white."

"There's his address, too," Connie said.

The entrance to the building on Bowery was a door with a plate-glass upper portion upon which the words CRANDALL FILMS, LTD. were lettered in big black block letters. Michael wondered what kind of film company would have its New York office here in this bedraggled part of the city; he guessed that *War and Solitude* had been a flop of even vaster dimensions than Crandall had described. He tried the doorknob. The door was locked. A dim light inside showed a steeply angled flight of steps leading upstairs. To the right of the door was a store selling plumbing appliances. To the left was a hotel that called itself the Bowery Palace. Michael stepped back and away from the door. He looked up at the second-story windows, where the name of Crandall's company was positioned in yet larger block letters. Not a light was showing up there. Apparently, the police hadn't got here yet. Either that, or they'd already come and gone.

A traffic signal was on the corner, and several enterprising Christmas Eve businessmen had set up shop there with buckets and chamois cloths, pouncing on the windshield of any car unfortunate enough to get caught by a red light. There was even less traffic in the streets now; the storm had frightened off all but a few hearty adventurers, and the rest were already home for Christmas. The windshield-washers on the corner kept looking up the avenue for signs of fresh customers. Meanwhile, they kept passing around a pint bottle of something that looked very dark and very poisonous. When one of them spotted the black limo, he started for it at once, bucket in his left hand, chamois cloth in his right. Connie waved him off. He kept coming.

"My windshield's clean," she said.

"I'm Freddie," he said. "Clean your windshield?"

"I just told you it's clean."

"Clean your windshield for a dollar?"

"A dollar!" Connie said. "That's outrageous!"

"So make it half a buck," Freddie said, and shrugged.

"Now you're talking," Connie said, and Freddie dipped the chamois into the bucket and slapped the cloth onto the windshield. A greasy film of ice immediately formed on the glass.

"Terrific," Connie said sourly.

"I want to find the backyard," Michael whispered.

"Why?" Connie asked.

"See if there's a fire escape."

"I'll come with you," she said.

"Are you a movie star?" Freddie asked Michael.

"No."

" 'Cause you look familiar," he said. "You wouldn't happen to have a scraper, would you?" he asked Connie.

"In the trunk," Connie said, and went around to the back of the car.

"Haven't I seen you on television?" Freddie asked.

"No," Michael said.

"In a series about Florida?"

"No."

"You sure look familiar."

"I have a very common face," Michael said.

"Ah, thank you," Freddie said, and accepted the scraper from Connie. "This should do the trick."

She was no longer wearing the green satin, high-heeled pumps she'd had on a few minutes ago. Black galoshes were on her feet now, the tops unbuckled. She looked like pictures Michael had seen of flappers in the Twenties, except that she was Chinese. She saw him looking down at the galoshes.

"I changed my shoes," she said.

He looked up into her face. So goddamn beautiful.

"I bought these in a thrift shop," she said, "to keep in the trunk. For inclement weather." On her lips, the word "inclement" sounded Chinese. She shrugged, and turned to where Freddie was already scraping the windshield. "You want to watch the car for me?" she asked.

"No, ma'am, I don't wash entire cars," he said, "I only do windshields."

"You keep an eye on the car for me, I'll give you that dollar you wanted."

"Make it two dollars."

"Two dollars, okay," she said, and locked the car and then turned back to Michael and said, "Let's go."

Michael looked at the Bowery Palace Hotel. He nodded, and then started toward its entrance door. Connie followed immediately behind him.

"Ask for room five-oh-five," Freddie called after them. "It has a mattress."

The hotel lobby was done in what one might have called Beirut Nouveau. Plaster was crumbling from the walls, electrical outlets hung suspended by dangling wires, the bloated ceiling bulged with what was certainly a water leak, wooden posts and beams seemed on the imminent edge of collapse, wallpaper was peeling, framed prints of pastoral scenes hung askew, and ancient upholstered furniture exposed its springs and stuffing. Altogether, the place looked as if it had recently been attacked by terrorists with pipe bombs. The clerk behind the scarred and tottering desk looked like a graying, wrinkled Oliver North who had just made his last covert deal with the Iranians.

"Good evening, Merry Christmas," Michael said to the clerk, and walked directly past the desk, and then past a hissing, clanging radiator that seemed about to explode and then past two men in long overcoats who were flipping playing cards at a brass spittoon against one of the flaking walls. It took Michael a moment to realize the spittoon wasn't empty. Behind him, he heard Connie clanking along in her unbuckled galoshes. "Merry Christmas," she said to the clerk, and he replied, "Merry Christmas," sounding somewhat bewildered, and then—as Michael approached a door under a red-and-white EXIT sign—"Excuse me,

sir, may I ask what you think you're . . . ?"

"Building inspector," Michael said gruffly, and would have flashed his driver's license or something if he'd still had it in his possession.

"Merry Christmas," the clerk said at once, "I'm sure you'll find everything in order."

"We'll see about that," Michael said, and opened the exit door, and stepped out into the backyard. Telephone poles grew from the snow-covered ground, their sagging wires wearing narrow threads of white. Fences capped with snow spread raggedly north, south, east, and west. Where tenements rose to the starry night, there were clotheslines stiff with frozen clothes. Not a breeze stirred now. Moonlight tinted the backyard world a soft silvery white.

"It's beautiful," Connie said beside him.

"Yes," he said.

He sighed then, and looked up at the back of the hotel, getting his geographical bearings, and then turned his scrutiny to the building on its left. A fire escape zigzagged up the snow-dusted, redbrick wall.

"You'd better wait for me here," he said.

"I'll go with you," Connie said.

He looked at her.

"There's no reward, you know," he said, and was sorry the instant the words left his mouth.

"Is that what you think?" she asked.

"I don't know what I . . ."

"I mean, is *that* what you think?"

"All I know is that a very beautiful girl . . ."

"Yes, I know."

" . . . has latched onto a stranger . . ."

"Yes."

" . . . who she thinks *killed* someone, which by the way I *didn't*. Not tonight, anyway."

"Then when?" she said at once.

"A long time ago. I've been living a very quiet life since I . . ."

"Are you married?" she asked.

"Divorced."

"Then what's wrong with my latching onto you?"

"I find it peculiar, that's all."

"You have a very low opinion of yourself, don't you?"

"No, I happen to have a very healthy ego, in fact."

"What happened? Did they break your spirit in jail?"

"Jail? Why would I . . . ?"

"For killing somebody."

"It was my *job* to kill those people."

"More than one?" she asked, astonished.

"Yes, but . . ."

"How many?"

"Eleven or twelve."

"Which? I mean, a person gives you a contract, you ought to know whether it's for eleven people or . . ."

"A contract? What con . . . ?"

"For eleven, twelve, fourteen, however many people you killed."

"It certainly wasn't fourteen."

"Then how many?"

"The figure was disputed . . ."

"Who disputed it? The defense attorney?"

"No, the RTO."

"The what?"

"The company radioman. He claimed *he* was the one who got the . . ."

"Listen, do you have a tattoo?" she asked.

"No, I . . ."

"Because forty-three percent of all convicts have tattoos, you know."

"I'm not a convict."

"Well, an *ex*-con."

"I've never been in jail in my life."

"You beat the rap, huh?"

"What rap? I was in the . . ."

"Listen, if a jury found you innocent, that's good enough for me."

"Connie, I never . . ."

"Do you have any children?"

"No."

"Do you think our lips would freeze together if you kissed me?"

He looked at her again.

"I know you didn't kill anyone," she said.

He kept looking at her.

"I knew it long ago," she said. "Because you

stayed for Harry. A man who killed somebody doesn't hang around like that. Not to bring another person luck. That's a kind and gentle person who does something like that. That's not a murderer. Anyway, I like your cute little face," she said, and raised her arms and then draped them on his shoulders, and stepped in closer to him. "So let's try it," she said.

And kissed him.

He had not kissed anyone this way since the divorce, which was exactly nine months and six days ago, the eighteenth of March, in fact, a very blustery Monday in Sarasota, Florida, he knew because he'd taken the boat out into the Gulf the moment the papers were signed, sailing off into a four-foot chop and drinking himself into oblivion the way he very often had in Vietnam, a wonder he'd got back to shore alive. Hadn't kissed anyone this way since the last time he'd kissed Jenny— well, no, that wasn't true.

The whole reason for the divorce, in fact, was that Jenny *hadn't* been kissing this way anymore, or at least not kissing *him* this way. It turned out that she'd been kissing the man who was the branch manager at the bank where she worked as a teller, kissed him a lot, in fact, fucked him a lot, too, in fact. Told Michael she was madly in love with the man—whose name was James Owington, the fat bastard—married him a month after the divorce became final, easy come, easy go, right?

No, Michael thought, they didn't break my spirit in any jail.

The V.C. did a pretty good job of breaking it in Vietnam, and Jenny finished the job later.

Kissing Connie Kee like this, he felt like weeping.

Not the bitter tears he'd wept in Vietnam when his closest friend, Andrew, died in his arms, or the kind of angry tears he'd wept that day on the boat with the waters of the Gulf threatening the gunwales. He did not know whether there were any kind of tears that could express what he was feeling here and now with this beautiful girl in his arms. Were there really tears of happiness? He had read a lot about them, but he had never shed such tears in his life. He knew only that kissing Connie Kee like this, he wished their lips *would* freeze together out here in the cold and the dark. He wanted to go on kissing Connie Kee forever. Or even Kee Connie.

He remembered, however, that the police in this winter wonderland of a city thought he had killed Arthur Crandall. He supposed he could go visit his old friend Tony the Bear Orso at the First Precinct, explain to him that the man who'd stolen the car was now the man who'd turned up dead in it— remember we were talking about all this, Tony, old pal, remember I showed you his card? Arthur Crandall, remember? You said it looked like a piece of film, remember? His card. Well, that's the man who's turned up dead. In the car he stole from me. So you see, Tony, I can't be the one who killed him. He stole my car, you see. And the other ones—the phony cop and his phony lawyer girlfriend—stole my credit cards and my license, so maybe it's the other ones who killed Crandall, but it wasn't me, it couldn't have been me. In fact, I was probably sitting right there chatting with you while Crandall was getting himself killed. That's a definite possibility and something you may wish to investigate. Meanwhile, I'll be running on back to Sarasota, Tony, give me a call when you break the case, I'll send you a crate of oranges.

So, yes, maybe he should drop in on the First, it wasn't everyone in this city who had Police Department connections. On the other hand, if he could not convince Tony the Bear that he had nothing whatever to do with the murder of Arthur Crandall he might find himself sharing a cell with Charlie Bonano—why were so many people in this city named Charlie? Except for *Charlie's News,* which was a store selling books, and magazines, and cards, and newspapers, Michael did not know a single Charlie in Sarasota. Did not know any other Charlies in the entire state of *Florida,* for that matter. But here in New York, three of them in the same night, and two of them named Charlie *Wong.* Remarkable. The very same night. Two Charlie Wongs. He wondered if Charlie was as common a name as Wong, and he thought of asking Connie— once they were finished with all this kissing—what the statistics on the frequency of Charlies in any given location might be. She showed no indication of wanting to stop the kissing, however, until a light snapped on overhead and someone shouted, "Hey! What the hell are you doing down there?"

They broke apart at once and looked immediately heavenward because this sounded like a demand from a vengeful God instead of a person shouting from the fourth-floor window of the tenement to the right of the hotel—which, they now discovered, was where the shout had come from: a light was showing in the fourth-floor window, silhouetting the person doing all the yelling.

"I'm gonna call the police!" the person—man or woman, it was difficult to tell—shouted.

"No, don't do that!" Michael yelled, and he

yanked Connie out of the glare of the moonshine and ran over the snow and into the shadows created by the rear of Crandall's building. They both listened. They could sense but not see the person up there straining to catch a glimpse of them in the dark.

"I know you're still there!" the voice shouted.

They said nothing.

A window slammed shut.

They waited.

Silence.

The light upstairs went out. The backyard was dark and still again. She grinned at him. He grinned back.

And then he leaped up like Superman for the fire-escape ladder, caught the bottom rung on the first try, and yanked it down.

There was a small Christmas tree on one of the filing cabinets, decorated with Christmas ornaments and lights that Michael now turned on to add a bit more illumination than was flowing in from the street lamp outside. The lights had a blinker on them. In fits and starts—on again, off again, yellow, green, red, and blue—Michael and Connie took in the rest of the office.

From the looks of the place, there'd been one hell of a party here. Someone had decorated the single large room with red and green streamers strung from wall to wall, crisscrossing the office like the rows and rows of protective barbed wire around the base camp at Cu Chi. Dangling from the streamers were cardboard cutouts of Santa Claus and Rudolph the Red-Nosed Reindeer and Frosty the Snowman, all of whom—together with the Easter Bunny and the Great Pumpkin and St. Valentine's Day, especially St. Valentine's Day— Michael had learned to distrust in Vietnam during the Tet Offensive in February of 1968, when Jenny (then) Aldershot forgot to send him a card asking him to be her valentine. And when, too, what with all that hardware flying around, he'd begun to doubt he'd ever get back home again to Jenny or anyone else, ever get back to shore again. He should have known then and there that one day she'd start up with a fat bastard bank branch manager, oh well, live and learn.

In addition to the streamers and the dangling reminders of Christmases past, there was a huge wreath hanging in the front window, which Michael hadn't noticed when he was looking up at the window from the street outside. There were also a great many ashtrays with dead cigarette butts in them, and a great many plastic glasses with the residue of booze in them, and a folding table covered with a red paper cloth upon which rested the tired remnants of a baked ham, a round of cheese, a crock of chopped liver, a tureen of orange caviar dip, a basket of crumbling crackers, several depleted bottles of gin, scotch, vodka, and bourbon, and a partridge in a pear tree. Or at least what appeared to be a partridge in a pear tree, but which was actually the tattered remains of a roast turkey on a wooden platter with a carving knife and fork alongside it. There were red paper napkins and green paper plates and white plastic knives and forks in evidence on every flat surface in the room. What at first appeared to be another red napkin lying on top of a large desk otherwise covered with plates and such—blink ON, blink OFF, went the Christmas tree lights—actually turned out to be a pair of red silk panties someone had inadvertently left behind. It must have been one hell of a party.

"Did you ever do it on a desktop?" Connie whispered.

"Never," Michael whispered back.

He wondered if she was propositioning him.

He also wondered if she was wearing red silk panties under her green silk dress.

"What are we looking for?" she whispered.

"I don't know," he said.

He did not, in truth, know what the hell they were looking for. He did not like this entire business of having been accused of murdering someone, did not like the sort of hospitality New York City extended to a visitor from the South, did not in fact like anything that had happened to him tonight with the exception of Connie Kee. He knew for certain—or, rather, *felt* for certain—that if he went to the police, he would find himself in deeper shit than was already up to his knees. He resented this. He was a goddamn taxpayer, and the police should have been working *for* him instead of *against* him. Why should he have to be doing *their* goddamn job? Well, a taxpayer in Sarasota, anyway.

He supposed he would have to learn how to do their job.

He hadn't wanted to learn how to avoid the punji sticks planted on a jungle trail, either, but he had learned. Had learned because if you stepped on one of those sharpened bamboo stakes it went clear through the sole of your boot and since Charlie had dipped the stakes in his own excrement—

Charlie.

Even in Vietnam, it had been Charlie.

For the Vietcong.

The V.C.

Victor Charlie.

And then just Charlie for short.

Good old Charlie.

Who had taught him to dance the light fandango along those jungle paths, live and learn. Or rather, learn and live. The way he had to learn now. Here in this city of New York, downtown here in this rotten city, his problem was a dead man. Arthur Crandall. And this was the dead man's office, as good a place to start learning as any Michael could think of.

"Cahill and Parrish," he whispered to Connie.

"Who?"

"We're looking for anything that might tie them to Crandall."

"Who are they?" Connie asked, sitting on the edge of the desk and crossing her long legs.

He explained who they were.

She listened intently.

She was so goddamn beautiful.

He kept wondering if she was wearing red silk panties.

Or any panties at all.

They began searching. The first thing they found in this office in holiday disarray, the first thing they found in this two-bit Sodom and Gomorrah show-biz office was a framed newspaper article on the wall alongside the blinking Christmas tree.

The article was written in French.

"Do you speak French?" he whispered.

"Chinese," she whispered back. "And English, of course. Cantonese dialect. The Chinese. Do *you* speak French?"

"A little. The Vietnamese spoke French. And my mother, too, every now and then."

The article was from a newspaper called the *Nice Matin*. In translation, the headline read:

DIRECTOR SHOWS WAR FILM

The article told about the showing of the film *War and Solitude* at the International Film Festival in Cannes. The article also summarized the critical reaction to it. Apparently, the reaction had been excellent. Everyone had thought, in fact, that *War and Solitude* would walk away with all the honors. Michael suddenly wondered if Oliver Stone, the director of *Platoon*, had killed Crandall and left him in Michael's car. The article had appeared in May, eleven years ago. Someone, probably Crandall himself, had inked in the newspaper's date in the margin on the right-hand side of the article. The caption under the accompanying photograph read: *Arthur Crandall before the showing of his film* War and Solitude *yesterday afternoon*.

The man in the photograph was not Arthur Crandall.

Or at least not the Arthur Crandall who'd been so helpful to Michael before stealing his car.

This Arthur Crandall—the one in the photograph—had a little round pig face with a pug nose and plump little cheeks. He was short and stout and he looked more like Oliver Hardy than Abraham Lincoln.

"This is not Arthur Crandall," Michael said. "I mean, this *says* he's Arthur Crandall, but he's not the man I met earlier tonight."

"Who later got himself killed."

"This isn't that man."

"Then who is he?"

"I don't know who he is."

"Let's see what's in his desk."

Together they went through the desk drawers. The red silk panties sat like a fallen poinsettia leaf not a foot from where they worked. He noticed that Connie smelled of oolong tea and soap, and he wondered if she knew she smelled so exotically seductive.

"I think we should take that picture with us," she said. "In case we need it later. Whoever he is. Because sailors who measure the tide sail with the wisdom of seers, you know."

He looked at her.

"Have you ever stuffed fortune cookies?" he said.

"No. Why do you ask?"

"Just wondered. You smell of oolong tea and soap, did you know that?"

"Did you know that the word 'oolong' is from *wu' lung,* which means black dragon in Mandarin Chinese?"

"No, I didn't know that," Michael said.

"Yes," she said. "Because oolong tea is so dark."

"I see."

"Yes."

He was getting dizzy on the scent of her.

"Here's his appointment calendar," Connie said, taking it from the top drawer of Crandall's desk.

"Do you think it's safe to turn on this lamp?" Michael asked, and snapped on the gooseneck desk lamp. Connie sat in the swivel chair behind the desk, and he dragged over another chair and sat beside her. Their knees touched. The calendar was of the Day-At-A-Glance type. She flipped it open to the page for Tuesday, December 24, and then automatically looked at her watch.

"*Still* the twenty-fourth," she said.

"Ten minutes to midnight," he said.

"Ten minutes to Christmas," she said.

There were several handwritten reminders on the page:

Call Mama

"Dutiful son," Michael said.

Send roses to Albetha

"Who's Albetha?" he asked.

"Who knows?" Connie said.

Mama @ Benny's
8:00 PM

"Mama again," Michael said. "But who's Benny?"

"Who knows?" Connie said, and flipped the calendar back to the page for Monday, December 23.

There were three entries for that date:

Bank at 2:30

"Deposit?" Connie asked. "Withdrawal?"

Charlie @ 3:30

"Another Charlie," Michael said.

"Huh?" Connie said.

"There are a lot of Charlies in this city."

"Yes," Connie said. "Now that you mention it."

"But not too many Albethas, I'll bet."

Christmas party
4:00–7:00 PM

"Let's find out why he went to the bank," Connie said.

"How?"

"His checkbook. If we can find it."

They began searching through the desk drawers again. In the bottom drawer, Michael found two large, ledger-type checkbooks, one with a blue cover, the other with a black one. The blue checkbook had yellow checks in it. Each check was headed with the names ALBETHA AND ARTHUR CRANDALL and an address on West Tenth Street.

"There's Albetha," Connie said.

"His wife."

"The roses."

"Nice."

"Yes."

"I wonder if she knows he's dead."

The black checkbook had pink checks in it. Each check was headed with the name CRANDALL PRODUCTIONS, LTD. and the address here on Bowery. Michael flipped through the business checkbook and found the stubs for the last several checks written, all dated December 23. There was a check to Sylvia Horowitz for a $200 Christmas bonus . . .

"His secretary?" Connie asked.

"Could be."

And a check to Celebrity Catering for $1,217.21 . . .

"The party, must be," Michael said.

"Some party," Connie said.

And a check to Mission Liquors for $314.78.

"More party," Connie said.

"Some party," Michael said.

No checks beyond the twenty-third. They leafed backward through the stubs. The last payroll checks had been made out on December 20, the ones before that on December 6. The firm paid its employees—apparently only Crandall and the woman named Sylvia Horowitz—on a biweekly basis.

"Let's try the personal checkbook," Connie said.

In the personal book, they found only one stub for a check written on Monday, December 23.

It was made out to cash.

For $9,000.

They both fell silent.

Outside, there was only the keening of the wind. Snow broke off from the telephone wires, fell soundlessly to the backyards below.

"It's almost Christmas, you know," Connie whispered.

Michael looked at his watch.

"Two minutes to Christmas," Connie whispered.

His digital watch blinked away time, tossed time into the past.

"I want to give you a present," she whispered.

It was one minute and twenty-two seconds to Christmas.

"Because you really do have a very nice face," she whispered. "And also, I like kissing you." She cupped his face in her hands. "You don't have anything communicable, do you?" she asked.

"No, I . . ."

"I don't mean like a common cold," she said. "I mean like anything dread."

"Nothing dread at all," he said.

"Good," she said.

He told himself that when this was all over and done with, if ever it was over and done with, he would remember this last minute before Christmas more than anything that could possibly happen afterward. Because in that slow-motion moment, Connie kissed him and murmured, "Merry Christmas, Michael," and moved in so close to him that he could feel her heart beating, or at least his own, and then he heard bells going off and he thought he'd died and gone to heaven until he realized it was only the telephone.

5

The telephone kept ringing into the otherwise blinking stillness of the room.

Michael picked up the receiver.

"Crandall Productions, Limited," he said.

"Arthur?" a woman's voice said.

"Who's this?" he said.

"Is that you, Arthur?" the woman asked.

"Yes," he said.

"You sound funny," she said.

"Who's this?" he said again.

"This is Albetha," the woman said.

"Uh-huh," he said.

"Arthur?"

"Uh-huh."

"Arthur, your children are waiting for Santa Claus, what are you doing at the office? It's Christmas morning already, do you know that? It's already five minutes past Christmas, do you know that? Now when do you plan on coming home, Arthur?"

Michael gathered she did not know he was dead.

"Did you get the roses?" he asked.

"Yes, I got the roses," she said. "Thank you very much for the roses, Arthur, but I'm *still* getting a divorce."

"Now, now, Albetha," he said.

"Arthur, the only reason I want you to come home here tonight is because it's Christmas and the children expect you to be here, that's the only reason. Tomorrow I'll explain to them how their daddy is a no-good philanderer, but this is Christmas right now, and you'd better come home here and get in your Santa Claus suit and be Santa eating the cookies and drinking the milk for your goddamn children, do you hear me?"

"I hear you," he said.

"Or is *she* there with you?" Albetha asked.

"Is who here?" he said.

"Jessica," she said.

"I don't know who that is," he said.

"Your blonde bimbo with her red panties," she said.

"Oh, her," Michael said.

"Come on home to your children, you *louse!*" Albetha said, and hung up.

"Albetha?" he said. He jiggled the rest bar. "Albetha?"

"His wife, huh?" Connie said.

"Maybe I ought to call her back," Michael said.

"No, I think we'd better get out of here," Connie said. "Because I think I heard a police siren."

Michael listened.

"I don't hear anything," he said.

"Not now," she said. "While we were kissing. I thought it was a siren, but maybe it was just a cat."

They both listened.

Nothing.

"It was probably just a cat," she said.

"Let's see if he's got an address book," Michael said, and went to the desk and began rummaging through the drawers again. "I want to call her back."

"Although it sounded very much like a siren," Connie said.

"Here we go. Do you think his home number might be in it?"

"I don't know anyone who lists his own number in his address book. Did you just see a light in the backyard?"

"No."

"I thought I saw a light," Connie said, and went to the window. "Yep," she said, "there's a light moving around down there. You know what? I think that *was* a siren I heard. Because those are two cops with a flashlight down there."

Michael went to the window.

"Shit," he said.

"Yes," she said. "Heading for the fire escape."

"Let's get the hell out of here," he said.

"Don't forget Crandall's picture . . ."

"I've got it."

" . . . and his address book," she said, "the tall one's starting up the ladder."

He pulled her away from the window and together they hurried to the front door. He turned the thumb knob on the lock, opened the door, and then followed her down the steep flight of steps to the street-level door. Through the thick plate-glass panel on the door, they could see a police car parked at the curb in front of the limousine, its dome lights flashing. Freddie was sitting on the limo's fender, looking innocent. The lock on the street-level door was a deadbolt. No way to unlock it on either side without a key. Michael backed off, raised his leg—

"Don't cut yourself!" Connie warned.

—and kicked out flat-footed at the glass panel.

A shower of splinters and shards exploded onto the sidewalk. Freddie, startled, jumped off the fender of the car. From the office upstairs, one of the cops yelled, "Downstairs, Sam!"

Michael was busy kicking out loose shards.

Cold air rushed through the open panel.

He helped Connie climb through, her long legs flashing, green panties winking at him for only an instant as she jumped clear. He climbed through after her and began running toward the limo. Connie slapped a five-dollar bill into Freddie's hand, ran around the limo's nose, and began unlocking the door on the driver's side. Behind him, Michael heard one of the cops yell, "You! Hey, *you!* Hold it right there!" The electric lock on his side of the car clicked open. He yanked open the door, climbed in, and slammed the door shut just as Connie stepped on the starter. There were gunshots now. He pulled his head instinctively into his shoulders, but the cops were only shooting at the deadbolt on the door to Crandall Productions, Ltd. The engine caught just as they kicked open the door and came running out of the building.

"Police!" one of them yelled. "Stop!"

Connie rammed her foot down on the accelerator. The car's tires began spinning on ice, its rear end skidding toward the curb, and then the tires began smoking, and suddenly they grabbed bare asphalt, and the car lurched away squealing from the curb and into the night.

Behind them, Freddie said to the cops, "Clean your windshield, officers?"

The house on West Tenth Street was a three-story brownstone just off Fifth Avenue. The address on the checks in Crandall's personal checkbook. Presumably the house he shared with Albetha and the kiddies.

"Every light in the house is burning," Connie said. "The lady's waiting up for you."

"For Crandall."

"Too bad he's dead," Connie said, and looked at her watch. "My twelve-thirty pickup is in the Village," she said. "Here's a China Doll card, call me when you're done here. If I'm free, I'll come get you. Otherwise, here's my home address. And here's twenty dollars."

"I don't want to take any money from you," he said.

"Then how are you going to get anyplace? If I can't come pick you up? Take it."

"Really, Connie . . ."

"It's a loan," she said.

He nodded, accepted the card and the money, and put both in his wallet. He now owed Charlie Bonano ten bucks and Connie Kee twenty. He was running up a big debt in this city.

"You sure you want to go see this lady?" Connie

asked. "Might be cops in there, for all you know."

"I don't see any police cars, do you?"

"Detectives drive unmarked sedans."

Michael shrugged.

"Pretty brave all of a sudden," Connie said.

Michael was thinking that sometimes you could sense things. You could smell the enemy. Sniff the trail and you knew whether it was clear ahead or loaded. He did not think he would find any policemen in Crandall's house. If he was wrong—

He shrugged again.

"I'll see you later," he said.

"Yes," she said, and waited till he walked to the front stoop of the building and up the steps before she eased the limo away from the curb. He watched the tail lights disappearing up the street, the red staining the snow. There was a sudden hush on the night. He looked up at the sky, expecting to see a star in the east. Disappointed, he looked at his watch instead. Twenty minutes past twelve. He rang the doorbell.

The woman who answered the door was perhaps thirty-four years old. She was almost as tall as Michael, her eyes brown, her mouth full, her hair done in the style Bo Derek had popularized in the movie *10*, more beautiful and natural on this woman in that her skin was the color of bittersweet chocolate.

"Yes?" she said.

"Is Mrs. Crandall home?" he asked.

"I'm Mrs. Crandall," she said.

"Oh," he said, and tried to hide his surprise. The newspaper photograph had shown Arthur Crandall as a white man.

"Yes?" she said.

"Well . . . we spoke on the phone a little while ago," he said. "You told me . . ."

"No, we didn't," she said, and started to close the door.

"Mrs. Crandall," he said quickly, "you called your husband's office . . ."

She looked at him.

"I answered the phone . . ."

Kept looking at him.

"You told me your kids were waiting for Santa . . ."

"What were you doing in my husband's . . ."

"Long story," he said.

Behind her, a small, excited voice said, "Mommy, come quick! Daddy's on television!"

"Who are you?" she asked Michael.

"My name is Michael Barnes," he said.

"Mommy, hurry *up*!"

Another voice. Two of them in the hallway now. And then a third voice from someplace else in the house.

"Annie? Are you *getting* her?"

Albetha Crandall looked him up and down. Sniffing the trail. Trying to catch the whiff of danger. She decided he was safe. "Come in," she said.

Two little girls in granny nightgowns were already running down the hall ahead of her. She let Michael into the house, closed and locked the door behind him, and then said, "You're not an ax murderer, are you?" and smiled in such marvelous contradiction that he was forced to give the only possible answer.

"Yes, I am," he said.

Albetha laughed.

"Mommmmmmmy! For Chriiiiiist's sake, come *on*!"

He followed her down the hall. It occurred to him that the police were showing pictures of the dead man on television. Arthur Crandall. His daughters were watching photographs of their dead father. And soon Albetha would be seeing those same photos. And they would undoubtedly be followed in logical sequence by the driver's license picture of the man alleged to have killed him, Michael Barnes the notorious ax murderer.

An eight-year-old girl in a granny nightgown sat on a couch facing the television set. The other two little girls—one of them six, the other four, Michael guessed—had just come into the room and were standing transfixed in the doorway, watching the screen. This was a newsbreak special. The words trailed incessantly across the bottom of the screen. NEWSBREAK SPECIAL NEWSBREAK SPECIAL NEWSBREAK SPECIAL. A very blond television newscaster was talking to the man whose picture had been hanging on the wall in Crandall's office. He was short and stout and almost bald, and he was wearing a three-piece suit with a Phi Beta Kappa key hanging on a gold chain across the vest.

He looked very much alive.

"I am very much alive," he said to the blond man. "As you can plainly see."

"Yes, I see that," the blond man said.

"What does he mean?" the eight-year-old on the couch said.

"Of *course* he's alive," the six-year-old said.

"Boy oh boy," the four-year-old said.

They all looked like different sizes of the little girl who played Bill Cosby's youngest daughter.

Albetha was watching the screen, an enormously puzzled look on her face.

"So what do you make of all this, Mr. Crandall?" the blond man asked.

"Well, if it weren't for the fact that there *is* a dead man . . ."

"Indeed there is," the blond man said, putting on a television newscaster's solemnly grieving face.

"Yes. But if it weren't for that, I'd think this was some kind of hoax."

"Ah, yes. But there *is* a real corpse, Mr. Crandall. And the police found your identification on him."

"Yes."

"Yes."

"Extraordinary."

"Really. So what do you make of it?"

"I can only believe that this Michael J. Barnes person is responsible."

Albetha gave Michael a sharp look.

"Yes, the man whose car . . ."

"Yes, the body . . ."

"Found in the . . ."

"Yes."

"For those of you who missed our newscast earlier tonight, I should mention that the body of a man carrying Mr. Crandall's identification . . ."

"Yes."

" . . . was found in an automobile rented by a visitor to New York . . ."

"Is this a series?" the four-year-old asked.

"No, Glory, it's a newsbreak special," Albetha said.

" . . . a man named Michael Barnes, whose wallet was also found . . ."

"Yes," Crandall said.

"In the automobile."

"Yes."

"So it would appear at least *possible* that the man the police are now actively seeking . . ."

"Are you *sure* this isn't a series?" Glory asked suspiciously.

"Positive," Albetha said, and gave Michael another sharp look.

" . . . *is*, in fact, the man responsible for the murder. But *why*—and this is the big question, isn't it, Mr. Crandall—why would he have put *your* identification in the dead man's pocket?"

"I have no idea," Crandall said.

"Nor does anyone else at this moment," the blond man said hurriedly, obviously having received an off-camera signal to wrap. "Believe me when I say, however, that we're happy one of our most talented screen directors is still with us. Mr. Crandall . . ."

His face taking on a sincere and solemnly heartfelt look, his voice lowering . . .

"Thank you so much . . . *literally* . . . for being here with us tonight."

"After the false reports of my death," Crandall said, smiling, "I'm happy I was *able* to be here."

"He's so full of shit," Albetha muttered.

"What?" the eight-year-old said.

"I said it'll be a while before Daddy gets home, so I want you all to go to bed now. If I hear Santa coming to drink his milk and eat the cookies you left by the tree, I'll come wake you. But you mustn't frighten him off or he won't leave any presents. All right now?"

"Who's this?" the four-year-old said, looking at Michael.

"One of Daddy's friends," Albetha said. "I'm sure."

Michael smiled.

"What's your name?" the six-year-old asked.

"Michael," he said.

"Come on, kids, bed," Albetha said, and shooed them off down the hallway.

Michael watched them go.

He debated running.

He decided not to.

When Albetha came back some five minutes later, she said, "You still here? I thought you'd be in Alaska by now."

"No," he said.

"A ploy, right? Murderer sticks around, lady thinks, Gee, he can't be the murderer."

"No, not a ploy."

"You going to slay my children in their beds?"

"No, ma'am."

"You better not. And don't call me ma'am. I'm at least five years younger than you are. What size suit do you wear?"

"Thirty-eight long."

"Arthur's a forty-six regular. Come along with me."

"Where are we going?"

"Put you in a Santa suit."

He followed her up the stairs.

"Why do they think you killed somebody?" she asked.

"I don't know."

"But you didn't, huh?"

"I didn't. It wasn't even my wallet. All they stole

from me were my credit cards and my driver's license. And my library card."

They were in the master bedroom now. Four-poster bed covered with a gauzy canopy. Imitation Tiffany lamp in one corner. Plush velvet easy chair. Old mahogany dresser.

"What are you doing here?" Albetha asked.

"I thought you might be able to help me."

"How?"

"This was before I knew your husband was still alive."

"Yeah, well, that's a pity," she said. "Him still being alive."

"You're divorcing him, right?" Michael said.

"Right."

"Because of Jessica."

"Right."

"Jessica who?"

"Here, put this on," she said, and handed him a Santa Claus suit on a hanger. "I'll get some pillows."

"Jessica who?" he asked again.

Albetha went to the closet. He began taking off his trousers.

"Wales," she said. "Why do you want to know?"

"What does she look like?"

"She looks like a bimbo," Albetha said. Her back was to Michael. She was reaching up for a pair of pillows on the closet shelf. The trousers were much too large for him. He suspected they'd be too large even with pillows in them.

"What color hair does she have?"

"The same color hair *all* bimbos have," Albetha said. "Blonde. Even *black* bimbos have blonde hair."

"Is she black then?"

"No," Albetha said. "Here. Stuff these in your pants."

He accepted the pillows.

"She's white?"

"Yes. Even as the driven snow."

"I need something to fasten these pillows with," he said.

"I'll get one of Arthur's straps."

She went to the closet again.

"Are her eyes blue?" he asked.

"No. Brown."

Which eliminated the woman in the bar. Whose star sapphire ring he hadn't stolen. And who'd called herself Helen Parrish.

"How does your husband happen to know her?" he asked.

"Intimately," Albetha said, and came back with a very large brown belt.

He took the belt, wrapped it around the pillows, and buckled it. He fastened the trousers at the waist. They felt good and snug now.

"How do you know she wears red panties?" he asked.

"Don't ask me about her goddamn panties. God-damn blonde bimbo with her red panties. God knows what I may have caught from her panties."

"What do you mean?"

"I had her panties on once."

"How'd that happen?"

"They were in my dresser drawer. Can you imagine that? He hides his bimbo's panties in my dresser drawer, mixed in with all my own panties. So I go to put on a pair of red panties, I put on *her* panties instead. I got out of them the second I realized I'd made a mistake. But who knows what I may have caught from them?"

"Well, you only had them on for a second."

"Even so. That's why they won't let you return panties, you know. Department stores. I wanted to call her and ask who she'd been intimate with lately. Besides my husband. You can get trichinosis from just eating the gravy," she said.

"You can?"

"Sure. From the pork. So don't tell me about only a second. Who *knows* what was in her panties?"

"Well, there's no sense worrying about it now," Michael said.

"Sure, *you* don't have to worry, you're not the one who was in her panties. Do you think I can get them analyzed? Put them in a paper bag and take them to a lab and get them analyzed?"

"For what?"

"For whatever she may have. I really *would* like to call her, I mean it. Hey, Jessie, how are you? Listen, do you remember those red silk panties Arthur left in my dresser drawer? They're walking across the room all by themselves, who've you been with lately, Jess?"

"I'm sure she wouldn't tell a perfect stranger who . . ."

"I'm not such a perfect stranger, I had her panties on. Also, she's no stranger to my husband, believe me."

"Does she work for him or something?"

"She's an actress," Albetha said. "She's in his new movie."

"I didn't know there *was* a new movie."

"How would you know there was any movie

at *all?*" Albetha asked, and looked at him suspiciously.

"A person who said he was your husband told me all about *War and Solitude*."

"When was this?"

"Earlier tonight. In a bar. Before he stole my car," Michael said, and put on the Santa Claus jacket.

"Was this person five-feet eight-inches tall, chunky, going bald, with brown eyes, a pot belly, and a Phi Beta Kappa key on his vest? From Wisconsin U?"

"No, he was . . ."

"Then he wasn't Arthur."

"I know he wasn't. *Now* I know. But he was very credible at the time. Told me all about your husband's work, gave me his business card . . ."

"Arthur's business card?"

"Yes."

"Well, anyone could have that. Arthur hands them out all over the place."

"Does the name Helen Parrish mean anything to you?"

"No."

"She's not an actress or . . . ?"

"No."

"Or anyone with whom your husband may have worked?"

"My husband has worked with a lot of women over the years, but I don't remember anyone named Helen Parrish. He was in television before he made *Solly's War,* and in television . . ."

"I'm sorry, what was that?"

"We called it *Solly's War.* Because the man who put up the money was named Solomon Gruber, and he was always yelling about budget, and about frittering away time, that was his favorite expression, 'Arthur, you're frittering away time.' Arthur hated him."

"What does *he* look like?"

"Gruber? An Orthodox rabbi."

"He wouldn't be a big, burly guy with a crew cut and a beard stubble, and hard blue eyes, would he?"

"No, he's tall and thin and hairy."

"Solomon Gruber."

"Yes."

"Who put up the money for *War and Solitude*."

"Yes. And lost it all. Or most of it."

"How much, would you say?"

"Did the film cost? Cheap by today's standards. Cheap even by the standards twelve years ago, when it was shot."

"How much?"

"Twelve million."

"That's cheap?"

"Here's the beard," Albetha said.

He put on the beard.

"And the hat," she said.

He put on the hat.

She studied him.

"The kids think *Arthur* is Santa Claus, but you'll have to do," she said. "Come on downstairs and drink your milk and eat your cookies. If you keep your back to them . . ."

"Tell me about your husband's new picture."

"Strictly commercial," she said. "Solly *hopes*. He financed this one, too."

"What's it called?"

"*Winter's Chill*. It's a suspense film. What the British call a thriller."

"I don't think I've seen it."

"It doesn't open till the second."

"Here in New York?"

"*Everywhere*. As we say in the trade, it is opening *wide*—which does not have sexual connotations, by the way. The expression refers to opening on thousands of screens simultaneously, as opposed to two or three dozen. The ads should break in Friday's papers. Arthur's giving it six days' lead time. He's hoping to make a killing, you see. Which may be the way to do it, who knows?"

Albetha shrugged.

"His last film was a class act. This is crap. But maybe the public wants crap. I find it ironic. In television, Arthur was doing crap. He left television to do a really fantastic film that didn't make a nickel. Now he's back to doing crap again."

He looked at her for a moment. She seemed to be searching his eyes for answers, but he had none for her.

"How do I find your husband's mother?" he asked.

"You don't," she said.

"He was supposed to call her yesterday. Maybe if I can learn what they talked about . . ."

"He didn't call her yesterday."

"It was on his calendar. Call Mama."

"His mother's been dead for ten years."

"Oh."

"May she rest in peace, the old bitch. And he didn't call *my* mama either 'cause they don't get along."

"Do you have Jessica Wales's address?"

"Yes. Why do you want it?"

"I want to talk to her."

"How do you know I won't call the police the minute you leave here?"

"I don't think you will."

"Why not? You're wanted for murder."

"Yes, but I'm Santa Claus," he said, and smiled behind the beard.

Albetha smiled with him.

"Have you ever been Santa before?" she asked.

"No. But I was Joseph a long time ago. In elementary school in Boston."

"When the world was still holy and silent," Albetha said.

He looked at her.

Tears were suddenly brimming in her eyes.

"Come," she said softly. "Be Santa for my little girls."

6

It was bitterly cold when he left the Crandall apartment. He had changed out of the Santa Claus suit and back into the clothes he'd been wearing to Bos—oh my God, he still hadn't called his mother!

She was probably suspecting the worst by now. His plane had crashed over Hartford, Connecticut. He was lying in a heap of wreckage, her Christmas gift smoldering beside him. If he knew his mother at all, and he thought he did, she'd be more concerned about her smoldering gift than his smoldering body. When he'd got back from the war, she'd seemed enormously surprised to see him. As if she'd already chalked him off. Later, when he began having the nightmares, an analyst told him this had probably been his mother's defense mechanism. Telling herself he was already dead, so that she'd be prepared for it when she found out he really *was* dead.

"But I was *alive*," Michael told the shrink. "I came home alive."

"Yes, but she didn't know you would."

"But there I was. Hi, Mom, it's *me*!"

"She must have been surprised."

"That's just what I've been telling you."

"You're lucky she didn't have a heart attack."

"She gave away all my clothes while I was gone. My civilian clothes."

"Yes, her defense mechanism."

"My blue jacket," Michael said.

"What?"

"My best blue jacket."

"Poor woman," the analyst said.

Well, maybe so. Poor woman had grieved for years after his father died. Poor woman had sold the hardware store and loaned Michael the money to buy the groves in Florida. A *loan,* she'd said, stressing the word. Paid her back every nickel, plus interest. He'd asked her to come live down there in Florida with him, she'd said, No, she wanted to keep living right there in Boston, even if the neighborhood *was* going to the dogs. She meant it was turning black. Michael's best friend in Vietnam had been black. Andrew. Died in his arms. Blood bubbling up onto his lips. Michael had held him close. First and only time he'd ever cried in Vietnam. He wondered later if Andrew's mother had given away *his* clothes while he was gone. He wondered if Andrew's mother had told herself he was dead in preparation for the Defense Department telegram that would confirm her worst fears. Michael wished he could forgive his mother for looking so surprised to see him alive. Surprised and perhaps a trifle disappointed. He wished he could forgive the poor woman for giving away his blue jacket.

He turned up the collar on his coat.

He had twenty dollars in his pocket, the money Connie had given him.

"A loan," she'd said.

Albetha Crandall had given him Jessica Wales's address, but he did not know this city's public transportation system and there did not seem to be any taxicabs on the street. It didn't seem to him that one-thirty was very late for Christmas morning; there were probably taxis on the street even in *Sarasota* at this hour. He began walking. He knew that the address Albetha had given him was downtown because she'd mentioned that it was. After he'd come only a block, he knew he was headed in the right direction because the streets were still numbered up here and the one following West Tenth was West Ninth. He told himself that after tonight he would never again go downtown in this city, maybe in any city, he would forever after stay *uptown,* where it was safe and well-lighted and patrolled by conscientious policemen. Meanwhile, he had to get to Jessica Wales's apartment because there were things he had to find out. Like, for example, why Crandall was now saying that Michael was the person responsible for the murder of the person who *wasn't* Crandall.

On television just a little while ago, Crandall had told the blond newscaster, "I can only believe that this Michael J. Barnes person is responsible."

Exactly what he'd said.

Go check it.

Rerun the tape, Blondie.

Michael J. Barnes.

His dear mother in Boston had given him the middle name Jellicle, after the Jellicle Cats in T. S. Eliot's *Old Possum's Book of Practical Cats,* which she'd read long before Andrew Lloyd Webber was even a glimmer in an Englishman's eye. Michael Jellicle Barnes, a name his schoolmates had found enormously amusing, reciting over and over again as they beat him up, "Yellow Belly Jellicle, Yellow Belly Jellicle," he could have killed his mother. He had tried unsuccessfully to hide the name from the girls he met in high school and later in college, all of whom naturally found out mysteriously and at once and who dubbed him "Jellybean Barnes," which was better, but not much, than getting beat up, he supposed. In the army, he had become "Jelly-ass Barnes" because of the slight accident he'd had the first time the squad went into battle, a name everyone had called him— except Andrew.

Dear, dead Andrew.

Easy come, easy go, right?

The moment Michael got out of the army, he'd become plain old Michael J. Barnes, and that was the name he'd used when he'd applied for his driver's license and his library card in Florida. And later on, his credit cards. Michael J. Barnes. No middle name, just the initial. And that's what he'd been ever since, Michael J. Barnes, no Jellicle, just plain old Michael J. Barnes.

This Michael J. Barnes person.

Was what Crandall had said.

This Michael J. Barnes person is responsible.

For murder.

He was suddenly lost.

Lost in thoughts as tangled as the Vietnam underbrush. Lost in time, because the Jellicle was out of his past and the present was an unknown man he had not killed. Lost in space as well, because the streets had run out of numbers and now there were only names and he did not know where in hell he was. Why was he all at once on Bleecker and then Houston and then King and Charlton and . . . where the hell was he? He looked at the slip of paper upon which Albetha had scribbled the address for him.

He looked up at the street sign on the corner.

He was on Vandam and Avenue of the Americas.

So where was St. Luke's Place?

Downtown, Albetha had told him. Between Hudson and Seventh. But where was Hudson? Or, for that matter, Seventh? He studied the empty avenue ahead as he would have studied a suspect trail, and then he looked to his right and looked to his left and decided it was six of one, half a dozen of the other, and began heading east, never once realizing that St. Luke's Place was to the north and west.

He walked for what seemed like miles.

Not a numbered street anywhere in this downtown maze. Sullivan and West Broadway and Wooster and Greene and Mercer and now Broadway itself though it did not seem like the Great White Way down here in lower Manhattan except for the snow in the streets. Kept walking east, although he did not have a compass and did not in fact *know* he was heading east. No sun up there in the sky. Just a cold, dead moon and stars that told him nothing. He turned corners, seemed at times to be doubling back on his own tracks, coming to the same street sign again and again, thoroughly lost now. He studied the sign on the corner. Mulberry and Grand. He looked up Mulberry. It was festively hung with welcoming arches of Christmas lights. Blinking. Beckoning. Surely there was a telephone somewhere on this beautifully decorated street.

He began walking.

Italian restaurants, all of them already closed for Christmas. Hand-lettered signs in some of the windows, advising that they would not be open again till the fourth of January. which, come to think of it, was when Michael had planned to head back to Sarasota. If he'd ever made it to Boston. He decided that if be found an open restaurant or an open *anything*, he would first call his mother to let her know he wasn't dead even though she didn't have any of his clothes she could give away prematurely, and then he would call China Doll Limo to see if Connie Kee was yet free to take him to St. Luke's Place, wherever the hell *that* was.

The awning over the restaurant read:

RISTORANTE BLUE MADONNA

The sign in the door read:

CLOSED

But there were lights blazing inside, and the sound of music—the Supremes singing "Stop in the Name of Love." The early Sixties came back in a rush. Boston before he was drafted. Sixteen-year-old Jenny Aldershot sitting on a wall over-looking the Charles River, her blonde hair blowing in the wind. He tried the door. It was unlocked. He opened it a crack. The music was louder now. He opened the door fully and stepped inside, and then he almost ran right out into the street again because the place was full of cops!

Beautiful young women wearing garter belts, panties, seamed silk stockings, and high heels— which was just what Detective O'Brien had been wearing earlier tonight. Dancing with men in business suits. As he started for the door again, someone clapped a hand on his shoulder. He turned to see a short roly-poly man who looked a lot like both Tony the Bear Orso and Charlie Bonano.

"Help ya?" the man said.

"I'm looking for a telephone," Michael said.

"This is a private party," the man said.

"I'm sorry," Michael said. "I thought this was a restaurant."

"It *is* a restaurant, but it's also a private party. Dinn you see the sign in the door? The sign says 'Closed.'"

"I'm sorry, I didn't see it."

"It says 'Closed' whether you seen it or not."

"All I want to do is make a phone call, it won't take a . . ."

"Are you a cop?" the man asked.

"No," Michael said.

The man looked at him.

"What are you then?"

"An orange-grower."

"My grandfather grew grapes," the man said. "I'm Frankie Zeppelin." He extended his hand to Michael. "What's your name?"

"Donald Trump," Michael said.

"Nice to meet you, Mr. Trump," Frankie said,

and shook hands with him. "Come on, I'll get you a drink. What do you drink, Mr. Trump?"

"You can call me Don," Michael said.

"Well, that's very nice of you, Don. And you can call me Mr. Zepparino. What do you drink, Don?"

"If you have a little scotch . . ."

"We have a little everything," Frankie said, and grinned as if he'd made a terrific joke. Putting his arm around Michael's shoulders, he led him toward the bar. "You look familiar," he said. "Do I know you?"

"I don't think so."

"Are you from the neighborhood?"

"I'm from Minnesota," Michael said at once, just in case Frankie had seen the earlier news broadcast.

"A lot of the girls here come from Minnesota," Frankie said. "These very dumb blonde girls with blue eyes, they must drink a lot of milk out there in Minnesota."

"Yes, it's called the Land of the Lakes," Michael said.

"I thought it musta been," Frankie said. "Kid," he said to the bartender, "pour Donny here some scotch."

The bartender picked up a bottle of Dewar's Black Label, and poured generously into a tall glass.

"Anything with that?" he asked.

"Just a little soda," Michael said.

"Hello?" a voice said over the loudspeaker system. "Hello? Can you hear me? Hello? One, two, three, testing, can you hear me? Hello, hello, hello, hell . . ."

"We can *hear* you already!" Frankie shouted.

Michael looked over to where a man wearing brown shoes and what looked like his blue confirmation suit was standing behind a microphone set up near a big copper espresso machine.

"Ladies and gentlemen," he said, "I want to wish you first, one and all, a very merry . . . is this thing on?"

"It's *on* already!" Frankie yelled.

"Hello?" the man at the microphone said. "Can you hear me?" He began tapping the microphone. "Hello? If you can hear me, please raise your hands please. Hello? Can you hear me?" Frankie threw up both his hands. All around the hall, people were putting their hands up. "Looks like a police raid in here," the man at the microphone said, which not too many people found funny, including Michael.

A redheaded woman wearing a black negligee over a black teddy and black garters and black silk stockings and black high-heeled patent leather shoes came over to the bar, said, "Hello, Frankie," and extended her glass to the bartender. "Just vodka," she said.

"I think I can safely say, at this our annual Christmas party here," the man at the microphone said, "that this year was a better year than any year preceding it. And I think I can say without fear of contradiction that next year is going to be an even better one!"

There were cries of "Tell us about it, Al!" and "Attaway, Al!" and "Let's hear the figures, Al!"

"Hi," the redhead said. "I'm Hannah."

"How do you do?" Michael said.

"You look familiar," she said. "Have I ever seen you on television?"

"No," he said at once.

"Aren't you the one who used to do the Carvel commercials?"

"Yes," he said, "come to think of it."

"No kidding? I *love* your Cookie Puss cakes."

"As an example," Al said, "in hotel encounters in the midtown area of Manhattan alone, revenues were up seven percent from last year for a total of . . ."

"Who's this?" a voice at Michael's elbow said.

He turned. He was looking at a very large man wearing a brown tweed suit, a yellow button-down shirt, a green knit tie, and an angry scowl.

"Jimmy, this is the man used to do the Carvel ice cream commercials," Hannah said.

"No kidding?" Jimmy said, immediately disarmed. He took Michael's hand, began pumping it vigorously. "I love your Black Bear cakes," he said. "I'm Jimmy Fingers."

"How do you do, Mr. Fingers?" Michael said.

"It's Finnegan, actually. But that's okay, everybody knows me as Jimmy Fingers."

"Especially the cops," Hannah said.

"Yeah, *them*," Jimmy said.

"Mobile encounters," Al said into the microphone, "by which I'm referring only to passenger automobiles and not vans or pickup trucks—and, mind you, I'm not even including figures for the Holland Tunnel or the George Washington Bridge—were up a full fifteen percent over last year."

"That's very good," Jimmy said appreciatively.

"Good? That's sensational," Frankie said.

"But it can give you backaches," Hannah said.

"Does anyone know where I can find a telephone?" Michael asked.

"Why you need a telephone?" Frankie said.

"I want to call a friend of mine. She may be able to take me to St. Luke's Place."

"Why you wanna go to St. Luke's? What's the matter with here?"

"Here is very nice, but . . ."

" . . . know I speak for all of us," Al said at the microphone, "when I extend our sincere appreciation and gratitude to our fine mayor, David Dinkins, and our excellent police commissioner, Lee Brown, and also the good Lord above us, thank you one and all!"

"Hear, hear," Jimmy Fingers said.

"And now, ladies and gentlemen, I am going to ask you to please enjoy the food and the beverage and the music and to stay as long as you like, although some of us may have made previous arrangements. To one and to all, to those of us in management, and to you—the rank and file in the front lines—I wish you a merry Christmas and a new year even more financially and spiritually rewarding than this one has been. Enjoy!" he shouted, and extended both arms in the V gesture Richard Nixon had made famous.

"You wanna go to St. Luke's, I'll take you to St. Luke's," Frankie said. "It's Christmas, I feel like Santa Claus. Anyway, it's on my way home."

"Well, thank you, that's very kind of you," Michael said.

"I got the car right outside," Frankie said.

At the microphone, four women began singing, "Deck the whores with boughs of holly, fa-la-la-

la-la, la-la-la-la. Look-in' for a good-time Charlie, fa-la-la . . ."

The moment they were seated in Frankie's red Buick Regal, he turned to Michael and said, "So they want you for murder, huh?"

Michael's hand shot out for the door handle.

"Relax, relax, maybe I can help you."

"I think you have the wrong party," Michael said.

"I seen you on television, I ain't got the wrong party. Relax."

"It's the kind of face I have, I'm often mistaken for . . ."

"Relax, willya please? I'm only tryin'a help here."

"Well, thanks, but how can you possibly . . . ?"

"I can hide you out for a coupla days," Frankie said.

"But I didn't kill anybody," Michael said.

"Well, of *course* you didn't, nobody *ever* killed anybody. But this is *me* you're talkin' to."

"Well . . ."

"So you want to go under or not?" Frankie asked. "You surface again sometime next week, the cops'll forget you even existed."

"Excuse me," Michael said, "but I don't think that's the way to go."

"Then what *is* the way to go?" Frankie said, sounding a bit irritated. "I mean, no offense meant, but you're the fuckin' guy *murdered* somebody, not me."

"I think I've got to find out who got killed."

"Who got killed is this guy Crandall."

"No, it wasn't Crandall."

108

"On television, they said he was the dead guy. And they said *you* killed him. Which, by the way, your name ain't Donald Trump."

"That's right, it isn't."

"I mean, nobody in this whole fuckin' *world* could be named Donald *Trump*. I mean, if you had to pick a phony name . . ."

"It's Michael Barnes," Michael said.

"Which also sounds phony. I'm tryin'a help you here, and you keep layin' this bullshit on me. Is it that you don't trust me? I mean, I spent all my life in this fuckin' downtown community, tryin'a build a reputation for honesty and trust, so if there's one thing you can do, it's trust me."

"I do trust you," Michael said.

"Good," Frankie said, and pulled a gun from a holster under his jacket and stuck it in Michael's face. "You know what this is?" he asked Michael.

Michael knew what it was. It was a Colt .45 automatic. He had handled many guns exactly like it while he was in the army.

"Yes," he said, "I know what it is."

"Good," Frankie said. "You know how to use it?"

"Yes."

"Good. 'Cause I want you to use it."

Michael looked at him.

"There is a person I would like you to kill," Frankie said.

Michael kept looking at him.

"Because I understand you're very good at that," Frankie said.

Everyone in this city is crazy, Michael thought.

"You already killed this movie guy," Frankie said, "so it . . ."

"No, I *didn't* kill this movie . . ."

"Hey," Frankie said, *"listen, okay?"* and put the gun to his ear as if it were a finger. "This is *me,* okay?" he said, and winked. "Never mind what you tell nobody else, this is me. Now. If you already killed one guy and the cops are lookin' for you . . ."

Michael sighed.

" . . . then it won't make no difference you kill another guy, 'cause the cops'll *still* be looking for you, am I right?"

"No, you're wrong," Michael said. "Because killing *two* people is a lot more serious than killing *one* person."

"Well, you certainly should know," Frankie said.

"And besides, I *didn't* . . . look, do me a favor, okay? It was nice meeting you, really, and I enjoyed being there at your union meeting . . ."

"We're not a union," Frankie said. "We're a social and athletic club."

"Whatever, it was very nice. I'm glad business was so good, I'm very happy for you. And I appreciate your offer to drive me to St. Luke's Place . . ."

"So then take the gun and help me out," Frankie said. "I mean, that's the fuckin' *least* you can do."

"You make it sound as if I *owe* you something," Michael said.

"I'm not turnin' you in, am I?"

"Goddamn it, I didn't *kill* anybody!"

"If you can't do the time, don't do the crime," Frankie said.

"Mr. Zepparino," Michael said, "I'm going to get out of this car now."

"Please take the gun," Frankie said, "or I'll blow your fuckin' brains out."

"All right, give me the gun," Michael said.

"Now you're talkin' sense," Frankie said, and handed him the gun.

"Thank you," Michael said, and pointed the gun at him. "And now I'm going to bid you a fond . . ."

"That won't do no good," Frankie said.

Michael looked at him.

"The gun ain't loaded," he said.

"What?"

"The clip's here in my pocket."

"What? What?"

"Also, if a person asks you nice to kill somebody for him, why don't you just *do* it?"

"Because I . . ."

"Instead of threatening that person with an empty pistol?"

Michael was thinking first Charlie Wong with his fake gun, and now Frankie Zeppelin with an empty one. He was thinking he had to get out of this city. He was thinking that he had to get out of here before he himself went crazy.

"The person I want you to kill is Isadore Onions," Frankie said.

"I'm not about to kill Mr. Onions or anyone else," Michael said wearily.

"There's a deli on Greenwich Avenue," Frankie said, "which is where he hangs out all the time. He should be there now, this is still very early in the day for Isadore, even if it's Christmas. What I'm going to do, I'm going to drive to that deli, it's called the Mazeltov All-Nite Deli. When we get there, Donny, I'll give you . . ."

"Michael," Michael said.

"Michael, sure," Frankie said, and rolled his eyes. "What I'll do when we *get* there, *Michael,* I'll give you the clip to put in the gun, and then I want you to go in and blow him away. Does my calling you Michael make you feel better, *Michael?*"

"I am not going to kill anyone," Michael said.

"I admire a man who sticks to his guns," Frankie said, "but you don't understand. Isadore Onions *needs* killing."

"But not by me," Michael said.

"Then by who?" Frankie said. "Me? And then *I'll* get in trouble with the law, right? When you're *already* in trouble with the law. Does that make sense? Try to make sense, willya please?"

"Mr. Zepparino, have you ever . . . ?"

"Isadore Onions is a very fat man with a Hitler moustache," Frankie said. "He usually dresses very conservative except he wears red socks. If you aim for the moustache you will probably kill him."

"Probably. But . . ."

"Just don't let the socks distract you."

"Look, Mr. Zepparino . . ."

"You can call me Frankie. Now that we're doing business together. Did I mention that there is five bills in this for you? If you do a good job? Five big ones, Donny."

"Mr. Zepparino, have you ever heard of a Mexican standoff?"

"No. What is a Mexican standoff?"

"A Mexican standoff is where *I* have the empty gun and *you* have the clip to put in it, and neither one of us can force the other one to do a goddamn thing. That is a Mexican standoff."

"Have you ever heard of a Russian hard-on?" Frankie asked. "A Russian hard-on is where *you* have the empty gun and *I* have the clip to put in it, but I also have *this,*" he said, and pulled another gun from inside his coat. "This is a .38 caliber Detective Special, and it is loaded. Which means that you are going to get out of this car outside the Mazeltov All-Nite Deli on Greenwich Avenue, and you are going to go inside and shoot Isadore Onions in the moustache or I will have to shoot you instead and throw you out on the sidewalk. On a very cold night."

The car was suddenly very still.

"Which they will prolly give me a medal for shooting a cold-blooded murderer," Frankie said.

"Where's Greenwich Avenue?" Michael asked.

7

In Vietnam, one of the first things Sergeant Mendelsohnn told him was, "When the going gets tough, the tough get going." This did not mean going home. Or going back. It meant going forward. Advancing. Blowing apart the whole fucking jungle as you moved *toward* the enemy. Leaves flying, mounds of earth exploding, whole trees coming down as you trashed the countryside, rat-tat-tat, pow, zowie, boom, bang, Rambo for sure, only you didn't have glistening muscles you bought in a Hollywood gym.

You were a lean, somewhat scruffy-looking eighteen-year-old kid from Boston, and you wore eyeglasses, and you just wished your glasses wouldn't get shattered in all that noise and confusion while you were bringing down the countryside hoping you'd get some of the bad guys. But you never refused to advance. And you never pulled back unless you were ordered to.

This had nothing to do with patriotism. It had to do with the fact that Mendelsohnn or somebody even higher up would shoot you in the back if you either refused to advance or turned tail and ran back to safety when the shit began flying.

As Michael got out of that red Buick on Greenwich Avenue, he knew that Frankie Zeppelin was sitting there behind him with a .38 Detective Special trained on his back, and he knew that if he did not advance into the Mazeltov All-Nite Deli as ordered, he would be shot in the back. *Plus ça change, plus c'est la même chose,* as his mother had been fond of saying back in Boston each time winter howled in off the Common. His mother's ancestry was French. His father's was English. An odd match, considering that the English and the French had been traditional enemies even before Agincourt. Sometimes their house resembled a battlefield. Well, not really. Nothing but a battlefield even remotely resembled a battlefield. This empty, windblown, bitterly cold street was not a battlefield, either, even though Michael had one pistol in the pocket of his coat and another pistol trained on his back, and there was a man sitting inside whom he was expected to kill.

Like fun.

This was not a battlefield, and Frankie Zeppelin was not a sergeant.

Michael opened the door to the deli.

For a little past two o'clock on Christmas morning, the place was thronged. Men in suits or sports jackets or tuxedos; women in slacks or dresses or evening gowns. Radiators clanging and steaming. Wooden tables, no tablecloths on them, paper-napkin holders, salt and pepper shakers. Waiters in black jackets and unmatching black trousers, white shirts, no ties, running frantically back and forth, to and from a counter behind which a steam table added yet more warmth to the place. The sudden aroma of food reminded Michael that he hadn't had anything to eat since lunch with Jonah today— yesterday actually, although his mind-clock always considered it the same day until the sun came up in the morning, no matter *what* time it really was.

Jonah Hillerman of the Hillerman-Ruggiero Advertising Agency. Who had proposed a scenario for the upcoming Golden Oranges television campaign. Beautiful suntanned blonde girl doing the commercial, okay? Wearing nothing but a bikini. Sun shining. Eating an orange in the first scene, juice spilling onto her chin. "Eat 'em," she whispers, and wipes away the juice with the back of her hand. In the next scene, she's squeezing an orange. Frothy, foaming juice bubbles up over the rim of the glass. "Squeeze 'em," she whispers. "Mmmm, good," she whispers. "Mmmm, sweet. Mmmm, Golden. Mmmm, *Oranges*!"

"Subliminal sex," Jonah said. "The viewer thinks we're asking him to eat the blonde's pussy and squeeze her tits. We're telling him the blonde is good, she's sweet, she's golden. Eat her, squeeze her! What do you think?"

"What about women?" Michael asked. "They're the ones who go shopping for the oranges."

"That's a sexist attitude," Jonah said.

Michael was almost faint with hunger. He went to the counter and ordered two hot dogs with sauerkraut and mustard, a side of French fries, a Coca-Cola, and a slice of chocolate cake. Isadore Onions—wearing a dark suit, red socks, a Hitler moustache, and the worst hairpiece Michael had ever seen in his life—was sitting at a table with a blonde wearing a very tight fluffy white sweater and a narrow black leather mini-skirt. Michael figured she could make a fortune doing orange juice commercials. Or even working for Frankie Zeppelin.

"Two dogs," the man behind the counter said. "Fries, a Coke, and a slice a chocolate. Pay the cashier."

Michael picked up his tray and went to the cash register.

The cashier tallied the bill.

"Seven-forty," she said.

Michael reached into his pocket for his wallet.

His wallet was gone.

Not again, he thought.

He patted down all his other pockets. No wallet. He wondered if Frankie Zeppelin had stolen his wallet. The cashier was looking at him.

"Seven-forty," she said.

"Just a second," Michael said.

He left the tray at the cash register, walked over to Isadore Onions's table, pulled out a chair, sat, and said, "Mr. Onions?"

"Mr. Ornstein," the man said. "No relation."

"To who, honey?" the blonde asked.

"Nick Ornstein, the gangster who was Fanny Brice's husband."

"That was Nick *Arn*stein," the blonde said.

"Exactly," Ornstein said. "So who are *you*?" he asked Michael.

"Mr. Ornstein," Michael said, "there's a contract out on you."

"Thank you for telling me," Ornstein said, "but what else is new?"

"What else is new is that I'm the one who's supposed to shoot you," Michael said.

"Don't make me laugh," Ornstein said.

"But you won't have to worry about that if you give me seven dollars and forty cents to pay for my food over there."

"Who is this person?" Ornstein asked the blonde.

"Michael Barnes, sir."

"You look familiar," the blonde said.

"You've probably seen me on television," Michael said. "I'm already wanted for a murder I committed earlier tonight. So another one won't matter at all to me. I work cheap, Mr. Ornstein. All I want is seven dollars and forty cents to forget the whole matter."

"Get lost," Ornstein said.

"Mr. Ornstein, I'm a desperate man."

"Who isn't?"

"I'm starving to death . . ."

"So starve."

"If I don't get something to eat soon, I'll fall down on the floor here."

"So fall."

"I think it was nice of him to tell you," the blonde said, and shrugged.

"Sure, very nice," Ornstein said. "He comes in, he sits down, he tells me he's supposed to shoot me, this is a nice thing to say to a person? And then ask him for a loan besides? This is nice by you?"

"He only asked for seven dollars," the blonde said.

"And forty cents, don't forget," Ornstein said. "On my block, seven dollars and forty cents don't grow on trees."

"Come on, Izzie, it's Christmas."

"Too bad I'm Jewish."

"If this man falls down on the floor . . ."

"Let him, who cares?"

"If there's a commotion, there'll be cops in here."

"I hope not," Michael said.

"Me, too," Ornstein said. "Here," he said, immediately taking out his wallet and reaching into it and handing Michael a ten-dollar bill. "Get lost."

"Thank you, Mr. Ornstein," Michael said, "thank you very much, sir," and got up at once and went to the counter to pay for his order and to pick up his tray. He looked around the room. The only vacant chair was at Ornstein's table. He went to it, said, "Hello, again," sat, and began eating.

"I thought I told you to get lost," Ornstein said.

"No, it's better he came back," the blonde said.

"Why?"

"Because now he can tell us who put out the contract on you."

"Yeah, who?" Ornstein asked Michael.

Michael was busy eating.

"I never seen such a fresser in my life," Ornstein said.

"He's cute when he eats," the blonde said, and smiled at him.

Michael had the distinct impression that she had just put her hand on his knee.

"Who sent you to kill me?" Ornstein asked.

In the army, they had told Michael that if he was ever captured by the enemy, he should tell them nothing but his name, rank, and serial number. He was not to tell them where the Fifth Division was, or the Twelfth, or the Ninth, he was not even to tell them where the nearest latrine was.

"Frankie Zeppelin," he said.

"Of course," Ornstein said, and nodded to the blonde.

"Of course," she said, and her hand moved up onto Michael's thigh.

"Excuse me," he said, "but I don't believe we've met."

"Irene," she said, and smiled.

"You know why he wants me killed?" Ornstein asked Michael.

"No, why?"

"Because of *her*," Ornstein said.

"Really?" Michael said.

"He's insanely jealous," Ornstein said. "So am I."

"I think I'd better go," Michael said. "If you'll let me have your name and address, I'll . . ."

"Finish your meal," Irene said, and smiled again. Her hand was still on his thigh.

"What I was going to say . . ."

"Yes?" Irene said.

" . . . was I'll send Mr. Ornstein a check. When I get home."

"Frankie Zeppelin will kill anyone so much as *looks* at this girl," Ornstein said.

"That's true," Irene said, and smiled again at Michael.

Michael was very careful not to look at her.

"So you can imagine how he feels about us sleeping together," Ornstein said.

"I can imagine," Michael said.

"But who can blame him?"

"Not me," Irene said.

"Not me, neither," Ornstein said, and belched. His hairpiece almost fell off his head. He adjusted it with both hands, looked across the table at

Michael as if wondering if he'd noticed either the belch or the adventurous wig, and then said, "I myself would kill anyone got funny with her."

"Oh my," Irene said.

"I would," Ornstein said.

Michael kept eating. He wondered if Ornstein knew he had a terrible wig. He wondered if Ornstein knew that Irene's hand was on his thigh. He wondered if Frankie Zeppelin was still outside in the Buick, counting the money in Michael's wallet and waiting to shoot him. He was beginning to think he had a better chance of getting killed here in this city than he'd ever had in Vietnam.

"So, Michael," Ornstein said, "this is what I . . . it *is* Michael, isn't it?"

"Yes."

"Is what I thought it was, what a dumb name. Michael, I want you to go back to that goniff . . ."

"Which means thief," Irene said, and smiled.

" . . . and tell him if he ever sends anybody *else* around here to shoot me . . ."

"Oh my," Irene said.

" . . . I'll send him back in a box," Ornstein said. "You think you can remember that, Michael?"

"I think I can remember it," Michael said.

"So go tell him," Ornstein said.

Michael stood up, pulling his coat around him like a cloak.

"Thank you," he said.

"Don't mention it," Irene said.

"For the loan," he said.

"Of *course* for the loan," Ornstein said. "What else?"

He almost started for the front door, and then remembered that Frankie Zeppelin was sitting out there in the red Buick with a .38 caliber Detective Special in his fist. He turned abruptly, almost knocking over a woman carrying a tray of what appeared to be four bowls of soup, incurring her wrath and a question he assumed to be strictly New York: "Whattsamatter you're cockeyed?"

The men's room was at the rear of the deli, in a corridor that dead-ended at a door marked EMERGENCY EXIT. A sign warned that this was to be used only in an emergency, and advised that a bell would sound if anyone opened the door. Michael went into the men's room, washed his hands at one of the sinks, tried the window over the toilet bowl, discovered it was painted shut, and then went out into the corridor again.

The sign was still there on the door.

A push bar was set on the door about waist-high.

Michael read the sign yet another time.

Then he shoved out at the bar.

The door flew open.

Sergeant Mendelsohnn had told him that the war in Vietnam was merely a piss-ant war compared to the one in Korea, in which noble war he had been proud to serve because it had been a *true* test of manhood. In Nam, the way Charlie scared you shitless was he crept around the jungle in his black pajamas and you never *saw* him. It was a phantom army out there. That's what was so terrifying. You *imagined* Charlie to be something worse than he really was. But in Korea . . . ah, Korea. Mendelsohnn waxed entirely ecstatic about Korea. In Korea, the Chinese lit up the whole battlefield at night! Could you imagine that? You were advancing in the dark and *whappo,* all of a sudden these floodlights would light up the whole place, it was like having your ass hanging on the washline in broad daylight. And *also* in Korea—man, what a war that had been—there were Chinese cavalry charges! Could you imagine *that?* Cavalry charges! With bugles and gongs! Unlike the gooks in Nam, the ones in Korea made all the noise they possibly could. They terrified you with their noise. You were ready to die just from the noise alone.

Like now.

The minute Michael shoved open the door, the instant the door opened just the tiniest little crack, the bells went off. Not *a* bell, as had been promised on the warning sign, *A Bell Will Sound.* These were *bells.* Bells in the plural, bells in the multiple, bells that would have deafened the hunchback of Notre Dame, bells that would have sent the entire American Army in Korea fleeing in terror with or without bugles or horses or floodlights, bells that if Hitler had mounted them instead of whistles on his Stuka dive-bombers, there would now be his picture on American hundred-dollar bills.

Michael reeled back as if he'd been struck in the face with a hammer.

And then he remembered that when the going got tough the tough got going, and he pushed the door open wider and hurled himself out into the night, the cold air joining with the bells to assault his ears in fierce combination as he stepped onto and into the unshoveled snow behind the diner. The bells would not stop. Or perhaps they had stopped and he was now hearing only their echo. Perhaps—

And suddenly there were lights!

And horns!

The goddamn Chinese were coming!

This was Korea, and this was the test of his manhood!

Standing there trapped in the glaring lights, with the gongs still echoing in his ears and the horns blowing, Michael knew they would come riding out of the night on their Mongolian ponies and slash him to ribbons with their sabers. And then . . .

Oh Jesus . . .

The first Chinese soldier came out of the glare of the lights and moved toward him slowly as if in a dream, white snow underfoot, white covering the world, white and green and long black hair and . . .

"Michael!" she shouted.

"Connie!" he shouted back.

"This way! Quick!"

She grabbed his hand in hers, and together they crashed through the fans of brilliant illumination coming from the limo's headlights. Snow thick underfoot. Shoes sodden. Socks wet. They reached the car. She ran around to the driver's side. He opened the door on the passenger side. No bells went off. The bells were still ringing in his head, though. He got in.

"You okay?" she asked. "I've been searching all over for you."

"Yes," he said.

Her voice reverberated inside his head.

He pulled the door shut. The good solid sound of a luxury car's door settling snugly and securely into its frame. And then a small, expensive electric-lock click that miraculously cleared his ringing ears.

Behind them, he heard someone shouting.

He didn't know who and he didn't care why.

"Where to now?" Connie asked, and eased the limo into the night again.

St. Luke's Place was a tree-shaded street with a public park on one side of it, and a row of brownstones on the other. It was exactly one block long, a narrow oasis between the wider thoroughfares that flanked it. At three in the morning, the only house with lights showing was in the middle of the block. Michael looked up at the third-floor window, located the name Wales in the directory set in a panel beside the door, rang the bell, identified himself as the man who'd telephoned not five minutes ago, and was immediately buzzed in.

The woman who answered the door to the third-floor apartment was perhaps thirty-three years old, a Marilyn Monroe look-alike with a Carly Simon mouth. She had short blonde hair ("The same color hair *all* bimbos have") and wide brown eyes, and she was wearing high-heeled silver slippers and a long silver robe belted at the waist. Michael did not think either the robe or the slippers were *real* silver, but they certainly did look authentic. Like the gun in Detective O'Brien's hand had looked authentic. All those many years ago, it seemed. Was it still only Christmas morning? Had it been only three hours since he'd first learned from Albetha Crandall on the telephone that there was a bimbo with red silk panties in her husband's life? He wondered if Jessica Wales was wearing red silk panties now.

"Please come in," she said.

Little tiny breathless Marilyn Monroe voice.

Carly Simon smile.

She stepped back and away from the door, the robe parting over very long, very shapely Cher legs. It suddenly occurred to Michael that Jessica Wales was not wearing red silk panties or anything else under that robe. There was nothing and nobody but Jessica Wales under there. Here I am with a famous movie star who's wearing nothing under her robe, he thought.

A Christmas tree was in one corner of the large living room, festively decorated with ornaments that looked expensively German in origin, and minuscule white lights and angel's hair spun into tunnels that seemed to recede into a distant childhood where sugarplum fairies danced in everyone's head. Wrapped Christmas packages in different sizes and colors were spread under the tree and a pair of bulging red stockings with white cuffs were hanging over a fireplace in which cannel coal was burning. The record player, or the radio, Michael couldn't tell which, was playing what sounded like Old English carols. He stepped past Jessica, the scent of *Poison* wafting up from her, and heard the door clicking shut behind him. She turned the lock, put on the safety chain.

"So," she said, "how can I help you?"

"Well, as I told you on the phone . . ."

"Yes. But I don't know where he is."

"I thought he might be here."

"No. In fact, until you called, I still thought he was dead."

"No, he's alive."

"You're sure?"

"Yes. I saw him on television."

"I'm so happy to hear that," she said, "would you like a drink?"

"No, thank you. Miss Wales, it's urgent that I find Mr. Crandall."

"Yes, so you told me. Are you sure? A little cognac?"

"Well, just a little, thank you."

Jessica moved like molten silver to a built-in bar on the wall alongside a unit containing a television set, a VCR, a turntable, a tuner, a tape deck, and a compact disc player. Michael still didn't know whether he was listening to a recording or to the radio. He looked around as Jessica began pouring the cognac. The living room adjoined the dining room, an open swinging door between them. Beyond the dining room, he could see only a portion of a kitchen with sand-colored cabinets. On the other side of the room there was an open door with a small library beyond it, and a closed door leading to what Michael guessed was the bedroom. The place was luxuriously furnished. He wondered how long Jessica had been a famous movie star he'd never heard of.

On the radio—it was the radio, he now discovered—an announcer was telling the world or at least the tri-state area that this was WQXR and that an uninterrupted program of Christmas music would continue immediately after the three A.M. news. Michael moved closer to one of the speakers. Jessica handed him a snifter half full of cognac.

"Roll it around in your hands," she said. "Like this."

She was holding her own snifter in both hands, close to her abundant breasts, rolling it gently between her palms. Michael was suddenly reminded of the commercial Jonah Hillerman had pitched at lunch yesterday. Eat 'em. Squeeze 'em.

Mmmm, good. Mmmm, sweet.

"To bring out the bouquet," Jessica said.

On the radio, a newscaster was giving the latest on the continuing conflict in the Middle East.

Jessica kept rolling the snifter between the palms of her hands.

The newscaster said that a large American corporation had sold one of its divisions to the Japanese for a billion dollars.

"Mmmm, good," Jessica said, and brought the snifter to her nose.

The newscaster said that a United States senator had been indicted for violating the law against . . .

Jessica was sniffing the bouquet.

. . . said in a televised news conference that he would be exonerated once the true and complete story was . . .

"Mmmm, sweet," Jessica said.

The newscaster said that the dollar had fallen against most major currencies in U.S. trading.

"Taste it," Jessica said.

The newscaster said that a new cold front was moving in from the Canadian Rockies.

It seemed to Michael that he might have been listening to this very same newscast yesterday or two weeks ago or two months ago. Some American corporation was always selling off something to the Japanese, elected senators were always being indicted for breaking one law or another and then assuring the public that they would be proven innocent once the true facts were known, the American dollar was always weaker against most major currencies, there was always a cold front moving in from the Canadian Rockies, even in the summertime, and there was always and forever a continuing conflict in the Middle East. Even at Christmastime. Peace on earth, the man had said, but where was it? Meanwhile, Jessica was sipping her cognac.

The newscaster started giving the weather forecast for New York City and vicinity. Continued cold . . .

"Mmmm," Jessica said.

. . . temperatures in the single digits . . .

"This is sooo good," she said.

. . . possibility of more snow before morning.

"Terrific," Michael said.

"But you haven't tasted it yet," she said.

"I meant the weather."

The newscaster was now telling everyone to stay tuned for an uninterrupted program of Christmas music. No mention of the dead body found in the rented automobile. No mention of Michael Barnes, the wanted desperado. Another voice came on, saying there would now be uninterrupted music until the next news report at four A.M. Something medieval flooded from the speakers.

Michael took a sip of the cognac.

"Yes," he said, "delicious. Who's Mama?"

"Mama?"

"In Crandall's appointment calendar, it said 'Call Mama.' And he was also supposed to meet her at eight o'clock last night. So who's Mama?"

"Arthur's mama is dead."

"I know. So whose mama was he calling and meeting?"

"Maybe Albetha's."

"No, they don't get along."

"Well, certainly not *my* mama. She's on vacation in London, England."

"Then whose?"

"I have no idea. How'd you see Arthur's calen . . . ?"

"Do you know why he went to the bank on Monday?"

"I think he goes to the bank *every* day," Jessica said, and shrugged.

"He wouldn't have gone there to cash a check, would he?"

"How would I know?"

"For nine thousand dollars?"

"I really couldn't say."

"Which is exactly a thousand dollars less than has to be reported to the IRS."

"Really? Gee."

"Who else was at that Christmas party?"

"What Christmas party? How do you know about the Christmas party?"

"I was in Crandall's office earlier tonight. Do you know anyone who lost a pair of red silk panties?"

"Gee," she said, "no."

"Okay, who's Charlie?"

"Which Charlie? There are a lot of Charlies in this city, you know."

"Yes, I know. Which Charlie did *Crandall* know?"

"Well, there's Charlie Nichols, no relation to Jack Nichols the big movie star."

"You mean Jack Nicholson, don't you?"

"Exactly. Charlie Nichols used to be on *Mister Ed* years ago. Arthur used him in *Winter's Chill.* To do one of the voices."

"A horse's voice?"

"No, a ghost's voice. There are a lot of ghosts in the picture. Or at least I'm supposed to *think* they're ghosts. The character I play. She thinks they're ghosts. They're trying to drive her crazy, you see. The character I play."

"Like Ingrid Bergman in *Gaslight*?"

"No!" she said sharply. "Not at *all* like *Gaslight*. Don't even *breathe* the word *Gaslight*. This is a very scary picture."

"So was *Gaslight*."

"Will you please stop with *Gaslight*? This is a much better picture than *Gaslight*, you'll see when it opens."

"When will that be?"

"On the second. That's a Thursday. So we'll catch the *Weekend* section of the *Times*. When they review all the new movies. The Friday paper."

"What does Charlie Nichols look like?"

"What difference does it make? He's only a voice."

"Yes, but what does he look like?"

"I never met him. I just told you, he's a voice."

"Have you met any Charlies who are *more* than voices?"

"Everybody has met a Charlie who is more than a voice."

"I mean, who is also a Charlie that Crandall knows."

"I can't think of any other Charlies he knows."

"You said he knows a *lot* of Charlies."

"No, I said there are a lot of Charlies in this *city* is what I said."

"But Charlie Nichols is the only Charlie that Crandall knows."

"He's the only Charlie that I know Arthur knows. For all I know, Arthur may know a *hundred* Charlies, maybe even a *thousand* Charlies, there are probably *millions* of Charlies in this city. All I'm saying is that Charles R. Nichols is the only Charlie . . ."

"Okay, I've got it. Do you know where he lives?"

"No."

"But I do."

The voice came from behind him.

A man's voice.

He turned at once.

Arthur Crandall was standing in the doorway to the bedroom. Fat and short and bald and wearing the same three-piece suit he'd worn on television, a Phi Beta Kappa key hanging on a gold chain across the front of his vest.

"Merry Christmas, Mr. Barnes," he said.

"Who's the dead man?" Michael asked. "And why are you running around town telling people *I* killed him?"

"Which of course you didn't do," Crandall said, and looked at his watch.

"And why are you looking at your watch?" Michael asked.

"I was wondering when the police would get here," Crandall said. "I called them the moment you arrived. They should be . . ."

"Thank you for the warning," Michael said, and started for the door. "It was nice meeting you both, there certainly are some charming and delightful people here in downtown New . . ."

"No," Crandall said, and reached into his pocket.

His hand came out with a gun in it.

Everybody in this city has a gun, Michael thought.

And took a step toward him.

"No, please don't," Crandall said. "This is a gun, you know."

"So is this," Michael said.

8

You usually knew in that first split second whether the other guy was serious.

In Vietnam, lots of guys had to prove they were big macho killers, had to keep telling this to themselves over and over again because otherwise they'd go weak with terror whenever a leaf rattled out there in the jungle. So one way they tried to prove it was to lean on anybody they thought would back down. Come to think of it, this may have been the origin of all that Russian roulette stuff in *The Deer Hunter*. Because lots of times out there, weapons came into play during the showdown process.

Now if you were going to lean on somebody, it was usually better not to choose some guy who weighed three hundred pounds and was built like the Chesapeake and Ohio. Because this man would chew up both you *and* your rifle and then spit out railroad spikes. So you didn't go bumping on him, you didn't go waving your weapon around in his face unless you felt it would be patriotic to get killed by a fellow American instead of a gook.

What you tried to do, if you were looking to bolster your own courage and make yourself feel like a great big macho killer, was you tried to pick on somebody who wore eyeglasses and who looked sort of scrawny and whose middle name was Jellicle, was what you tried to do. Shove your rifle in *his* face, man. See if you could get *him* to back down. And usually you knew in that first split second whether you had him or not.

And vice versa, if you were the one who was looking into the barrel of the rifle—as had so often been the case with Michael—you knew immediately whether the guy threatening you would really paint the jungle with your blood if you didn't back off *toot sweet,* as they all used to say in their bastardized, learned-from-the-gooks French.

Michael had never backed off.

Even when he knew the other guy was dead serious.

The ones who were all bluff and bravado, you dismissed with a wave of the hand, boldly turned your back on them, went back into the hootch to smoke a joint.

But the red-eyed ones . . .

The ones who'd had too much of the jungle and were no longer capable of telling friend from foe . . .

The ones who had murder scribbled crookedly on their mouths . . .

These were the ones it was essential to stare down.

Because if you backed off from them now, if you let the barrel of that automatic rifle force you to turn away, why then one day they would shoot you as soon as look at you. No warning next time. Just *pow* when the jam was on, in the back, in the face, in the chest, it didn't matter, they knew you were nothing but dog shit and they could waste you whenever they wanted to, and wasting you would give them the magical power to kill all the gooks in the jungle. It was like eating your testicles or your heart or whatever Long Foot Howell had told him the Indians used to eat after they'd scalped you.

What you did, you said, "Fuck off, okay?"

And if he didn't choose to do that, you walked right up to him, and you slapped the muzzle of the rifle aside with the palm of your hand.

And if the muzzle refused to be slapped aside, if those little red pig eyes in the man's head were telling you that he was going to blow you away in the next count of three, why then what you had to do was kick him in the balls the way Michael had kicked Charlie Wong in the balls only several hours ago. And while the man was writhing on the ground in pain, you stepped on his face hard, which Michael guessed he'd have done to Charlie Wong if Detective O'Brien hadn't shown up in her sexy underwear, braving the cold and all. And once you'd stolen the man's face, why then you could turn your back on him the way you did with the other kind, just saunter away into the hooch for a little smoke. Maybe ask him to join you if you were feeling generous. And maybe he'd shoot you anyway one fine day, but chances were he wouldn't.

The situation here was identical to all those showdowns Michael had survived in Vietnam, where he'd sometimes thought he'd rather face a whole platoon of gooks rather than another red-eyed American trying to show he wasn't scared. Crandall wasn't doing such a good job of showing he wasn't scared. It was Michael's guess that the man had never held a gun in his hand before this very moment and that the sight of the larger weapon in Michael's hand was causing him to have some second thoughts about keeping him here until the police showed. Panic was in his eyes. He definitely did not want a gunfight here at the old O.K. Corral.

So Michael did what he would have done in Vietnam when facing a bluff. He dismissed Crandall with a wave of his free hand, turned his back on him, and started for the door.

Which should have worked.

But it didn't.

Because apparently Michael hadn't learned a lesson he should have learned many, many years ago, and the lesson was Watch Out For That Harmless Little Vietnamese Woman With Her Gentle Smile And Her Innocent Eyes Because She Is Deadlier Than A Crack Male Regiment.

It was Jessica Wales who hit him.

She hit him very hard on the back of his head with something that sent him staggering forward toward the front door, in which direction he'd been heading anyway. He knew better than to let go of the gun. He also knew enough to roll away, the way he'd rolled away into the snow when Charlie Wong was trying to kick his brains into New Jersey. This time the foot that came at him was wearing an ankle-strapped shoe with a stiletto heel that looked like silver or perhaps stainless steel as it came flashing toward—

The woman was trying to stomp him.

He had seen many black soldiers in Vietnam stomping other soldiers. They had learned this art while growing up in lovely ghettos here and there across the United States.

Where lovely Jessica had learned it was anyone's guess.

But she definitely was trying to stomp him.

Not kick him.

Stomp him.

Kicking and stomping were two different things, although often used in conjunction. When you kicked someone, you were trying to send his head sailing through the goal posts. When you stomped someone, you were trying to break open his head like a melon. Squash it flat into the pavement. The pressure point in the stomping process was the heel. In Vietnam, the heel had been flat and attached to a combat boot. Here in the living room of Jessica Wales's apartment, it was four inches long and tapered to a narrow point. If that heel connected with his head—

Michael kept rolling away.

There were here-again gone-again glimpses of long legs flashing, white thighs winking, the silver robe parting and flapping as Jessica tracked him across the floor, searching for an opportunity to step on him good. He rolled, rolled, rolled blindly into the wall, came to a frightening dead stop, and was scrambling to his feet when he saw Jessica bending her right leg and reaching down for the shoe. Tired of stepping and stomping, she had undoubtedly decided it would be better to wield the shoe like a hammer. And was now in the process of getting the shoe off her foot and into her hot little hand.

Fascinated, he watched her little balancing act.

Blonde Jessica standing on one foot, opposite leg bent backward at the knee, right hand sliding the heel of the shoe off the heel of her foot—

He would never have a better shot.

He lunged forward, ramming his shoulder hard against the leg she was standing on, knocking her off balance. The shoe flew off her foot and out of her hand. As she tumbled over backward, legs splayed, the robe opened disappointingly over a triangular patch of very black hair.

Michael leaped to his feet.

"I warned you!" Crandall shouted.

And fired.

At first, Michael thought he'd made a terrible and perhaps fatal mistake. For the first time in his life, he'd wrongly identified a genuine shooter as a bluffer. But then he saw that Crandall was looking at the smoking gun in his hand as if it had suddenly developed fangs and claws. This thing here in his hand had actually gone off! That's what his astonished face said. He had pulled the trigger and this thing had exploded in his hand and a bullet had come out of it and had in fact whistled across the room to shatter a mirror on the wall above where Jessica was already getting up off the floor in a tangle of legs and open robe and mons veneris and one silver shoe.

Michael wondered if he should walk over to Crandall, push the muzzle of the gun aside, tell him to fuck off, and then go back into the hooch for a smoke. He figured it just might work. While he was doing all this calculation, he forgot about Jessica for the second time that night, and remembered too late that once may be oversight but twice is stupidity.

The way he remembered was that Jessica hit him on the head again with the same object she'd used earlier, which he now realized was a metal tray of some sort, this time connecting more solidly and causing him to stagger forward almost into Crandall's arms. Crandall backed away as if being attacked. He certainly did not want this thing in his hand to go off again. Nor did he want to catch Michael in his arms, which he would have to do if Michael kept stumbling toward him. But Michael suddenly brought himself up short because even in his dizziness he had clearly and finally perceived that Jessica and not Crandall was the real danger.

Where? he thought.

And turned, hoping he would not get shot in the back, after all, because getting shot in the back would be a first for him. On Christmas Day, no less. Which would not be such a terrific surprise since he seemed to be experiencing a great many firsts here in festive New York City, the least of which was being attacked by a ferocious movie star who now looked not like Marilyn Monroe but that lady, whatever her name was, in *Fatal Attraction* with the frizzed hair and the long knife in her hand.

Jessica did not have a knife in her hand.

Jessica had a poker in it.

Which she had grabbed from a little stand alongside the fireplace, leaving a shovel and a brush still hanging from it. She came limping at Michael, one shoe on, one shoe off, her lips skinned back, her capped movie-star teeth glistening with spit, her eyes blazing. He figured she was angry because he'd knocked her on her ass.

But then Crandall put a very clear perspective on the entire situation.

"Careful!" he shouted. "He's a killer!"

And Michael realized in a dazzling epiphany that Crandall either really believed he had murdered someone, or else was putting on a damn good show of believing it. Convincing Jessica—who did not seem to need very much convincing—that Michael was an armed and dangerous murderer, and this was a simple matter of survival. Which explained the desperate look in Jessica's eyes and the headlong rush at him with the poker. But which did not explain why Crandall stood there with a weapon in his hand and his thumb up his ass.

Michael had never hit a woman in his life.

When he'd learned about Jenny and her branch manager, he'd wanted to hit her, but then he'd wondered what good that would do. He'd already lost her. James Owington had already taken her from him, so what was the sense of hitting her? Wouldn't that be more punishing to him than it would be to her? The eternal knowledge that he had hit a woman who was only five-feet six-inches tall and weighed a hundred and twenty pounds? Who wasn't even working for the Viet Cong?

Jessica wasn't working for the Viet Cong, either.

She was merely a sensible woman trying to save her own life. She had a good cheering section, too. As she came at Michael, the poker swinging back into position, Crandall whispered little words of encouragement like "*Hit* him, *kill* him!" From the look on her face, she needed no urging. Crandall had warned her that Michael was a killer; unless she took him out, he would kill again. The thing to do now was knock off his head. Before he knocked off hers.

Which Michael did.

He hit her very hard.

There was nothing satisfying about the collision of his fist with her jaw. He hit her virtually automatically, bringing his fist up from his knees as if he were throwing an uppercut at a sailor in a Saigon bar, repeating an emotionless action he had gone through at least a dozen times before, unsurprised when he heard the click of teeth against teeth, unsurprised when he saw her eyes roll back into her head. He watched as she collapsed. One moment she was standing, the poker back and poised to swing, and the next moment she folded to the floor as if someone had stolen her spine.

Michael walked to where Crandall was standing with the gun in his hand.

"Fuck off, okay?" he said, and took the gun from him and went to the door.

He now had two guns.

Like a Wild West cowboy.

One in each pocket of his coat.

He was happy that the two uniformed cops who came up the steps as he was going down did not stop and frisk him.

"Are you looking for the guy beating his wife?" he asked.

"No, we're looking for Wales," one of the cops said.

"That's near England, I think," Michael said, and continued on down.

Connie was waiting outside in the limo, the engine running.

"I think it's time we went home," she said.

She drove the limo to the garage China Doll used on Canal Street, and they began walking from there to her apartment on Pell. As promised, the temperature was already starting to drop. Michael guessed it was now somewhere in the low twenties or high teens. They walked very rapidly despite the packed snow underfoot and the occasional patches of ice on sidewalks that had been shoveled, their heads ducked against the wind, Connie's arm looped through his. Under the other arm, she carried the green satin high-heeled shoes she'd retrieved from the limo's trunk. The streets were deserted. This was four o'clock on Christmas morning, and everyone was home in bed waiting for Santa Claus. But Michael was brimming with ideas.

"What we have to do is find out where Charlie Nichols lives," he said.

"Okay, but not now," Connie said. "Aren't you cold?"

"Yes."

"I mean, aren't you *freezing*?"

"Yes, I am. But this is important."

"It's also important not to die in the street of frostbite."

"You can't die of frostbite."

"For your information, frostbite is freezing to death."

"No, it's not."

"Can you die of freezing to death?"

"Yes."

"All right then," she said.

"Connie, the point is we've got to talk to Nichols. Because if he's the Charlie in Crandall's calendar . . ."

"Please hurry."

"Then maybe he can tell us who Mama is, or why Crandall drew nine thousand dollars from the bank, *if* he did, or what he did with that money, or what his connection is with the two people who took all that stuff from my wallet and the one who stole my car."

The words came out of his mouth in small white bursts of vapor. He looked as if he were sending smoke signals. The clasps on Connie's galoshes clattered and rattled as she led him through yet another labyrinth, this goddamn downtown section of the city was impossible to understand. None of the streets down here were laid out in any sensible sort of grid pattern, they just crisscrossed and zigzagged and wound around each other and back again, and they didn't have any numbers, they only had names, and you couldn't get anywhere without a native guide, which he supposed Connie was. A very fast one, too. She walked at a breakneck pace, Michael puffing hard to keep up, both of them sending smoke signals with their mouths. He hoped there weren't any hostile Sioux on ponies in the immediate neighborhood. He would not have been surprised, though. Nothing that happened in this city could ever surprise him again.

They came at last to a Chinese restaurant named Shi Kai, just off the corner of Mott and Pell. The restaurant was closed, but a sign in the front window advised:

**OPEN FOR BREAKFAST
AS USUAL
CHRISTMAS DAY**

Connie took a key from her handbag, unlocked a door to the left of the restaurant, closed and locked it behind her, opened another door that led to a flight of stairs, and began climbing. There were Chinese cooking smells in the hallway. There were dim, naked light bulbs on each landing. She kept climbing. Behind her, he watched her legs. Her galoshes rattled away. He hoped they wouldn't wake up anyone in the building. On the third floor, she stopped outside a door marked 33, searched in the dim light for another key on her ring, inserted it into the latch, unlocked the door, threw it open, snapped on a light from a switch just inside it, and said what sounded like "Wahn yee" or "Wong ying," Michael couldn't tell which.

"That means, 'Welcome' in Chinese," she said, and smiled.

"Thank you," he said, and followed her into the apartment.

He supposed he'd expected something out of *The Last Emperor.* Sandalwood screens. Red silk cloth. Gold gilt trappings. Incense burning. A small jade Buddha on an ivory pedestal.

Instead, against a wall painted a pale lavender, there was a long low sofa done in a white nubby fabric and heaped with pillows the same color as the wall, and there was an easy chair and a footstool upholstered in black leather and there was a coffee table with a glass top, and a bar unit hanging on the right-angle wall, and several large framed abstract prints on the wall opposite the sofa.

Connie sat, took off her galoshes, and then padded in her stockinged feet to the bar unit.

"This has been *some* night," she said, and rolled her eyes, and lowered the drop-leaf front of the bar. "I had a man vomit all over the backseat, did you notice?"

"No, I didn't."

"I mean that the limo I picked you up in outside the deli wasn't the same one I'd dropped you off in when you went to see Crandall's wife?"

"No, I couldn't tell any difference."

"Charlie was very upset. Charlie Wong. *My* Charlie Wong. About the stink in the car."

"I can imagine."

"Do you know how to make martinis?" she asked.

"Yes, I do," he said.

"Why don't you mix us some very nice, very dry martinis while I go take my shower, and then you can take your shower, and then we can sip our martinis in bed, would you like to do that?"

"Yes," he said.

His voice caught a little.

Because he was thinking about what she'd just said.

Not about mixing the martinis or taking the showers.

But about sipping the martinis.

In bed.

That part.

"A twist, please," she said.

You came through the bedroom doorway and the first thing you saw was the bed facing the door, its headboard against the far wall, a window on each side of it, a night table under each window. It was neither a king nor a queen, just a normal double bed. With a paisley-patterned quilt on it. There was a dresser on the wall to the right of the bed, and bookcases on the wall to the left, and a door to the closet on that same wall, and on the entrance-door wall, which he didn't really see until they got into bed together, there was an easy chair with a lamp behind it to the left of the door, and a full-length mirror to the right of it.

They left the quilt on the bed because it was so damn cold.

Every few minutes, they poked out from under the quilt to take a quick sip of their drinks, and then they hurriedly put the glasses back on the night tables on either side of the bed. They did this until the glasses were empty. Then they pulled the quilt up over their shoulders and settled in close together.

"He turns the heat off at eleven o'clock every night," Connie said. "There's nobody cheaper in the world than a Chinaman."

Under the quilt, the whole world was cozy and warm and safe.

Under the quilt, with Connie in his arms, he felt the way he'd felt long long ago in Boston, when his father was still alive and there to take care of him, and when the house was full of the smells of his mother's good French cooking and when at night she wrapped him in a big white fluffy towel after his bath, and patted him dry, and then tucked him into bed and pulled the covers to his chin, and told him Good Night, Sleep Tight, Don't Let The Bedbugs Bite, and kissed him on the cheek. In the darkness, he would smile. And fall asleep almost instantly.

After Boston, he hadn't slept too well for a long time. That was because the Cong's main job was keeping the Americans awake all night, never mind killing them. If the Cong could keep the Americans awake, why then they'd have to go home eventually in order to get a good night's sleep. He was sure that had been the strategy. It worked, too. Even when you knew they couldn't possibly be out there, even when intelligence reports told you they were fifty miles away, a hundred miles away, *retreating* even, you still imagined them out there creeping up on you while you slept. So you never really slept. Never completely. You closed your eyes, yes, and occasionally you caught ten minutes here, ten minutes there, even a half hour's deep sleep sometimes until your own snoring startled you into frightened wakefulness, and you jumped up in a cold sweat, your rifle fanning the jungle even before your eyes were fully open.

When he'd got back home . . .

Boston.

Home.

Jenny told him he'd filled out a lot.

She had learned how to soul-kiss.

From *Cosmopolitan* magazine, she told him.

His mother had given away all his clothes.

And his father was sick and dying.

He'd come back to where it was safe—the Boston he remembered, the Boston he'd longed for all those months, the Boston that was the reality as opposed to the jungle nightmare—but his father was sick and dying and his mother, who was only forty-two, looked suddenly old, and the nightmare was here, too, here in Boston where it was supposed to be safe.

They buried his father on a cold November morning.

It was raining.

He remembered thinking he would never be safe again.

He told his mother one night that his dream was to marry Jenny and take her someplace where it was warm all year round. He almost said warm and *safe* all year round. His mother had looked at him with that sad, grieving expression she wore all the time now, and then she'd merely nodded. He wondered what she was thinking. Was she thinking it did not pay to dream because eventually all dreams die? His father's dream had been to own a chain of hardware stores all across New England. But cancer had cut him down when he was forty-four, and all he'd left behind him was the big old house and the one store. Good Night, Sleep Tight, Don't Let The Bedbugs Bite, and don't let the Cong creep up on you in your sleep, either. How can you dream if they won't let you sleep?

It took his mother two years to get over his father's being dead. At the end of that time, she told Michael she'd had a good offer for the store and was going to sell it. Said she could lend him the money for his dream. At prevailing interest rates. Told him to go find his Someplace Warm, take his Jenny there with him. He'd never known whether she was trying to get rid of him or trying to help him. He'd had the feeling that maybe . . .

Well, he'd discussed this with the shrink.

That somehow his mother blamed *him* for his father's death.

That because she'd prayed so hard for Michael to come home safe and sound, the gods had somehow taken payment for his survival. Had spared his life and taken his father's instead.

That she hated him for this.

The shrink wondered out loud if she'd given away Michael's clothes the day she'd learned his father had cancer.

Michael said he didn't know.

In Vietnam, Sergeant Mendelsohnn had told him to shoot first and think it over later. Michael took the money, asked Jenny to marry him, and moved down to Florida with her.

Where he'd felt safe for a while.

Until Jenny started up with James Owington at the bank.

And after that, you know, a man began to think there wasn't much sense to *anything* anymore. You go fight a dumb fucking war where nobody will let you sleep and everybody including the people on your own side are trying to kill you, and you get through it by the skin of your teeth and you come home to find your father dying and your mother blaming you for it and your girlfriend soul-kissing her way through Boston and its suburbs, you begin to think, Hey, *sheeee*-it, as Andrew would have put it. And when even the sweet Florida dream turns sour, when the enemy creeping up on your sleep now is a fat fucking branch manager who's getting in your wife's pants, hey, man, what was the sense of *anything*?

Part of his dream . . .

Well, he'd wanted to start a family down there.

Little girl, little boy. Two kids, that would've been nice.

Name the girl Lise, after his mother.

Well, maybe not.

But *shit,* Mom, it really wasn't my fault he died. Name the boy Andrew for sure.

But if you can't sleep you can't dream, and anyway all the dreams died forever—or so he'd thought—nine months and six days ago, *seven* days ago now, but who was counting? All the dreams had drowned in the Gulf of Mexico on that blustery March day, drowned together with his sorrows.

But tonight . . .

He could see snow beginning to fall again outside the window on his side of the bed. Fat fluffy flakes drifting down in the light of the lamppost.

He held Connie in his arms.

She felt so small and delicate.

He held her close and watched the snow coming down.

And almost instantly, he fell deeply asleep.

And for the first time in years, he dreamed again.

9

It was Christmas Day.

Cooking smells from the restaurant downstairs drifted up the stairwell and seeped under the door and wafted across the apartment into the bedroom where he lay with Connie Kee in his arms. It was still snowing. He guessed there had to be eight feet of snow out there by now. Maybe ten feet. It had to be Minnesota out there by now.

He had fallen asleep instantly, but now he was wide awake and a bit leery of waking up Connie, who might discover there was a stranger here in bed with her and go running out into the snow naked. The last time he'd been to bed with anyone was with a woman named Zara with a Z Kaufman in Miami, where he'd gone to an orange-growers' convention. That was in September, it was still hurricane season down there in Florida, there were in fact hurricane warnings posted for southeast Florida and the Keys. He had not been to bed with anyone since the divorce in March, but there he was with the palms rattling outside his motel window and the wind blowing at forty miles an hour and a fifty-year-old woman who grew oranges in Winter Haven teaching him a few tricks he hadn't learned in Saigon.

Zara with a Z Kaufman.

A very lovely person.

He had never seen her again after that night.

So here he was now with a Chinese girl dead asleep in his arms, afraid to wake her up because whereas last night there had been only two of them here in this bed, this morning there were three of them if you counted his hard-on, which Connie suddenly seized in her right hand, leading him to believe she hadn't been asleep after all.

They kissed.

It was like their kiss last night under the stars in that snowbound backyard where telephone poles grew from an endless field of white and snow-capped fences ran forever. Except better. Because although last night there had been the attendant if remote possibility that their lips might in fact freeze together—she always seemed to be worried about freezing, he now realized—the bed today was quite warm under the quilt, thank you, and there was in fact steam banging in the radiators, and no one was about to freeze, not today when Christmas was upon the world.

And whereas last night someone up there in a fourth-floor window had asked them what the hell they were doing and had threatened to call the police, which he or she had in fact later done, the bastard, there was now no one here in this radiator-clanging, steam-hissing room to hurl a challenge or to dial 911 to report a dire emergency. There was no dire emergency in this room. Unless the urgency of their mutual need could be considered an emergency of sorts, and a dire one at that. He could not recall ever wanting a woman as much as he wanted this one. Nor could he recall any woman ever wanting him as much as Connie seemed to want him.

They could not stop touching each other.

They could not stop kissing.

Her murmuring little sounds hummed under his lips.

His hands were wet with her.

When at last he entered her—

"Oh, Jesus," they whispered together.

It was Christmas Day.

There were four Charles Nicholses listed in the Manhattan telephone directory, but none of them had an *R* for a middle initial.

Which meant that none of them was the Charles R. Nichols who was no relation to Jack Nichols the big movie star.

Charles R. Nichols, who had been on *Mister Ed* years ago, and who had played a ghost's voice in Crandall's latest, as-yet-unreleased film, *Winter's Chill.*

Connie suggested that perhaps the Nichols they wanted was listed in the Bronx, Brooklyn, Queens, or Staten Island directories instead. In which case, she and Michael could run over to Penn Station and check out the phone books there.

"The police will be watching the railroad stations," Michael said.

"Then I'll go alone."

"The police know what you look like, they saw you driving me away from Crandall's office," he said. "Connie . . . maybe I . . ."

"No," she said.

"What I'm trying to say . . ."

"You're trying to say you love me."

"Well . . ."

"And you're worried about me. That's so nice, Michael. You say the sweetest things, really."

"Connie, the point . . ."

"But I'm not afraid," she said. "So you don't have to . . ."

"I *am,*" he said.

She looked at him.

"Afraid," he said.

She kept looking at him.

"The time to be afraid," he said, "is when you don't know what's happening. And when you feel helpless to stop whatever *is* happening."

"Then what we have to do is find *out* what's happening. And *stop* it from happening. Then you won't be afraid anymore and we can just make love all the time."

He took her in his arms. He hugged her close. He shook his head. He sighed. He hugged her again.

"What was that other man's name?" she asked.

"What man?"

"The one Crandall's wife told you about. The one who put up all the money for his war movie."

"Oh. Yes."

"She told you he looked like a rabbi . . ."

"Yes, tall and thin and hairy . . ."

"Magruder!" Connie said.

"No."

"Magruder, yes!"

"Connie, there are no rabbis named Magruder."

"Then whose name is Magruder?"

"I have no idea. But that's not *his* name."

"Then what *is* his name?"

"I don't remember. It had something to do with the movie."

"Yes, he put up the money for . . ."

"Yes, but not that. Something about *War and—Solly's* War! His first name is Solly! No, Solomon! *Solomon* something!"

"Magruder!"

"No!"

"I'm telling you it's Solomon Magruder!"

"And I'm telling you no!"

"Then what?"

"I don't know."

"Gruber!" she shouted.

"Yes!"

"Solomon Gruber!"

"Yes!"

"The phone book!" she said.

"Be there," he said. "Please be there."

There were no Solomon Grubers listed in the Manhattan directory. There were a lot of S. Grubers, but no way of knowing which of them, if any, might be a Solomon. There was, however, a listing for a Gruber Financial Group, and another listing for a Gruber International, and yet another for a Gruber Foundation, all of which sounded like companies that might have had twelve million dollars to invest in a flop movie eleven years ago. Michael tried each of the three numbers. No answer. This was Christmas Day. But in studying the S. Gruber listings a second time—

"Look!" Connie said.

"I see it."

"This S. Gruber has the same address . . ."

"Yes."

" . . . as the Gruber Financial Group."

"But a different phone number," Michael said. "Let's call him."

"Let's eat first," Connie said.

The S. Gruber whose address was identical to that of the Gruber Financial Group lived in Washington Mews, which was a gated little lane that ran eastward from number 10 Fifth Avenue to University Place. Connie explained that they were still in what she considered downtown Manhattan.

"As far as I'm concerned," she said, "it's all downtown till you get up to Forty-second Street. Then it starts to be *mid*town. This is the Sixth Precinct here. Driving a limo, I like to know where all the precincts are, in case I get some weirdo in the back. The precincts are funny in this city. For example, the First starts at Houston Street on the north and ends at Battery Park on the south. Which means if you get killed, for example, on Fulton Street, you have to run all the way uptown and crosstown to Ericsson Place to report it. Anyway, this is the Sixth, which is mostly silk stocking."

They were walking up what could have been a little cobblestoned lane in a Welsh village. Doors that only appeared to be freshly painted flanked the pathway, their brass knockers and knobs gleaming in the noonday light. The cobblestones had been shoveled clean of snow. There were wreaths in the windows, electrified candles in them. The twinkling multicolored glow of illuminated Christmas trees behind diaphanous lace curtains. Classical music wafting through a street-level window opened just a crack. Swelling violins. And now a clarinet. Or maybe a flute. Dying with a dying fall on a Christmas Day already half gone. Michael wished he could identify the composition. Or even its composer. There were so many things he wished. Down in Sarasota he read *The New York Times* all the time, and he listened to WUSF 89.7, which was the public radio station, but he never could tell one piece of classical music from another. To him, they all sounded like somebody practicing.

"A penny for your thoughts," Connie said.

"I was just vamping till ready," Michael said.

"I hope you're ready now," she said, "because here it is."

A black door.

A brass escutcheon on it.

Solomon Gruber, engraved in script lettering.

To the right of the door, set into the doorjamb, a heavy brass bell button.

Michael pressed his forefinger against it.

Inside, chimes began playing a tune you didn't have to be Harold Schonberg or even Newgate Callendar to recognize.

The tune was "Mary Had a Little Lamb."

They listened to it. It sounded nice on the frosty Christmas air.

When the chimes reached "fleece as white," the door opened.

The man standing there in the doorframe was not tall and thin and hairy, and he did not look like a rabbi, either. The man standing there was wearing a red turtleneck sweater with a black velvet smoking jacket over it. He had a very bushy handlebar moustache, which may have been why Albetha Crandall had thought he was hairy. Otherwise, he wore his hair in a crew cut that made him look like a German U-boat commander. Why she'd thought he was tall and thin was anyone's guess. Perhaps she'd meant in comparison to her husband, who was short and chubby. Solomon Gruber, if that's who this man turned out to be, was of medium height and build. Compact, one might say. Chunky. Like a bulldog.

"Yes?" he said.

He looked as if he expected them to start singing Christmas carols. He looked as if he would close the door in their faces if they did. Or run up to the roof to pour boiling oil on them.

"Mr. Gruber?" Michael asked.

"Yes?" he said again.

"My name is Michael Bond, I'm with *The New York Times*, I wanted to talk to you about *Winter's Chill*. This is Constance Keene, my assistant."

Gruber blinked.

"Come in," he said at once, and stepped aside to allow them entrance. *"Mary!"* he shouted. "Come quick, it's *The New York Times*! Come in, come in, please," he said.

Michael wondered if it was a crime to impersonate a person from *The New York Times*.

Gruber's townhouse was furnished the way Michael hoped one day to furnish the house in Sarasota, now that Jenny was out of it and living with her fucking branch manager. In recent months, he had browsed through enough home furnishing magazines to know that the extremely modern furniture here in Gruber's living room was either Herman Miller or Knoll, all leather and glass and chrome and wood. The house in Sarasota was at the end of a dirt road that ran alongside the groves. Behind the house was a man-made lake that had been dug by the former owner of the groves. Sliding glass doors opened onto the lake. Modern furniture would look good in that house. He knew Connie liked modern because of the way her apartment was furnished. Now he wondered if she'd like the Sarasota house.

The walls in the Gruber living room were done in rough white plaster, except for the fireplace wall, which was done in black marble, with a chrome surround for the hearth. A painting that looked like a genuine Matisse hung on one of the white walls. Another that looked like a real van Gogh hung on the wall adjacent to it. A Christmas tree was in the far corner of the room, near the windows facing the lane outside. A woman came in through a rosewood swinging door that led to the kitchen. She was wearing a long red gown that matched Gruber's red turtleneck sweater. She was taller than Gruber, and she had blonde hair—but she was not the woman who'd conned Michael in the bar last night. It occurred to Michael that there were a lot of blondes in the city of New York. Just as there seemed to be a lot of Charlies. Which was why he was here.

"Mr. Gruber," he said, "I . . ."

"Mary, this is Michael Bond," Gruber said, "and his assistant, Constance Keene."

"How do you do," Mary said.

Which was why the doorbell played "Mary Had a Little Lamb," Michael guessed.

"Can I get you something to drink, Mr. Bond?" Gruber said.

"Some hot toddy?" Mary said.

She was smiling like one of the women in *The Stepford Wives*. Michael wondered if she had wires and tapes inside her.

"Mary makes a great hot toddy," Gruber said.

He was smiling like a shark approaching a Sarasota beach at the height of the season. Probably because *The New York Times* was in his living room.

"I'd like to try a hot toddy," Connie said. "I've never had one."

"One hot toddy coming up," Mary said. "Mr. Bond, what will you have?"

"A diet Coke, if you've got one."

"Will a diet Pepsi do?"

"Yes, thank you."

"One hot toddy and one diet Pepsi coming up," she said, and went out into the kitchen.

"From what I understand," Michael said, "the Gruber Group put up all the financing for Arthur Crandall's new film."

"Boy oh boy oh boy, *The New York Times*," Gruber said, shaking his head. "On Christmas Day, no less. You guys have sources not to be believed."

"That's true, though, isn't it?"

"Yes, the Gruber *Financial* Group—it's Gruber *Financial* Group, not Gruber *Group*."

"Yes, sir, Gruber *Financial* Group."

"Maybe you ought to jot that down," Gruber said.

"Yes, sir, have you got a pencil and some paper?"

"I've got some," Connie said, and reached into her shoulder bag and took from it a bill pad with the lettering CHINA DOLL LIMOUSINE across its top. She handed this to Michael together with a ballpoint pen that had tobacco shreds clinging to its tip.

"Gruber Financial Group, yes, sir," Michael said, and wrote it onto the pad.

Mary came out of the kitchen. She was carrying a tray with a mug and a glass on it. The mug had a cinnamon stick poking up out of it like the periscope on a miniature submarine.

"Here you are," she said, and extended the tray.

Connie picked up the mug.

Michael picked up the glass.

Mary put down the tray and said, "We were in Japan last year, Miss Keene. It's a lovely country."

"Thank you, I've never been there," Connie said, and sipped at the toddy. "This is very good," she said. "Would you like to taste this, Michael?"

"No, thank you," Michael said. "Mr. Gruber, do you know a man named Charles Nichols?"

"Huh?" Gruber said.

"Charles R. Nichols."

"What part of Japan do your people come from?" Mary asked.

"I'm Chinese," Connie said.

"Oh, dear," Mary said.

Gruber shot her a look that said *Now* look what you've done, you've offended a Chink on the fucking *New York Times*! Mary started to shrink, as if he'd thrown water on a witch. Michael hoped she wouldn't melt right down into the carpet, leaving only her red gown behind. Gruber turned back to Michael.

"Are you doing a piece on *Charlie*?" he asked. There was a look on his face that said there was no understanding the ways of *The New York Times*. Charlie Nichols, who had been on *Mister Ed* years ago, and who now played the voice of a ghost in *Winter's Chill*? Of all the actors in the film, *this* was who *The New York Times* had singled out for a piece? Incredible.

"Do you know where we can reach him?" Michael asked.

"Is this for the Arts and Leisure section?" Gruber asked.

"Yes," Michael said.

"That's the approach you're taking, huh?"

"We thought we'd like to talk to him."

"I mean . . . look, I certainly don't want to tell *The New York Times* what approach it should take. Far be it from me. But what *is* the approach you're taking? I mean . . . why *Charlie,* of all people?"

"Because of his *Mister Ed* affiliations," Michael said.

"He wasn't the horse or anything," Mary said.

"That's right, thank you, Mary," Gruber said.

"I mean, he didn't do the *horse's* voice, you know. He was just a regular actor."

"He had a bit part, in fact," Gruber said.

"This is all very good stuff," Michael said, writing.

"It is?" Mary said, looking astonished.

"This begins to hit you after a while, doesn't it?" Connie said, and took another sip of the toddy.

"You're supposed to stir it," Mary said. "With the cinnamon stick."

"Oh," Connie said, and began stirring it.

"All he does is play one of the ghosts in *Chill,*" Gruber said.

"One of the voices," Mary said.

"There are ghost voices," Gruber said.

"Trying to make her crazy."

"The character."

"The woman Jessica plays."

"Jessica Wales," Gruber explained.

"They're trying to make her crazy," Mary said.

"Like in *Gaslight*," Michael said, nodding.

"Oh *no!*" Gruber said at once.

"No, no, no," Mary said. "Not at *all* like *Gaslight*."

"This is a highly suspenseful film about a woman on the cutting edge of terror and deceit," Gruber said, sounding like the headline of an ad for the movie.

"Is she mad or is she only too sane?" Mary said, sounding like another headline.

"This makes your fingers sticky, doesn't it?" Connie said.

"A true departure for Arthur," Gruber said. "I don't know if you saw *War and Solitude*, but . . ."

"No, I didn't."

"A beautiful film," Mary said, looking soulful.

"Wonderful, the man's a genius," Gruber said. "We lost a fortune, of course, but does this take away from the man's genius? Does *Jaws* take away from the genius of Steven Spielberg?"

"But *Jaws* didn't *lose* money, did it?" Michael said.

"Exactly," Gruber said. "This beautiful film went down the tubes . . ."

"Not *Jaws.*"

"No, *Solitude.* Because of Vincent Canby's lousy . . . excuse me, I bear no ill will toward the *Times*, believe me. I lost twelve million dollars plus another two million in advertising and promotion, but Canby is entitled to his opinion, would I deprive a man of his right to free speech? I notice, of course, that six years later he thinks *Platoon* is a masterpiece, but listen, bygones are bygones, we're talking about *Winter's Chill* now, am I right? Despite the fact, by the way, that in Cannes *Solitude* almost walked off with all the marbles and *Cahiers* called it the best war film ever made. This was six years *before* Mr. Canby decided to fall in love with *Platoon,* a genius before his time, Arthur Crandall, mark my words. And *Chill* is an even better film."

"There are murmurings, however," Michael said, and he saw panic flash suddenly in Gruber's eyes, "that whereas Crandall's last film was a class act"— quoting Albetha now—"this new one is crap, you'll pardon the . . ."

"Nonsense!" Gruber said.

"Why, he's being compared to *Hitchcock*!" Mary said.

"That's right, thank you, Mary," Gruber said.

"At the peak of his career! Hitchcock!"

"His *Psycho* days!"

"His *Birds* days!"

"Why, when people in the motion-picture community thought Arthur was *dead* last night . . ."

"Then you'd heard about that," Michael said, suddenly alarmed.

"Yes, of course, it was all over television."

"We were *so* relieved when he called," Mary said.

"To say he was alive."

"We couldn't believe it was him calling. He was supposed to be dead. But there he was on the *phone*! It was a miracle!"

"Believe me," Gruber said, "there was universal mourning in the motion-picture community when . . ."

"MGM, too," Mary said.

"When his murder . . ."

"United Artists, Columbia, Disney. Not only Universal," she said.

"When his murder was erroneously reported. Genuine and universal *grief* for this *genius* cut down in his prime, this new master of . . . excuse me, what did you say your name was?"

"Bond," Michael said. "Michael Bond. No relation."

"Because you look familiar."

"I'm sure I don't."

"Have I seen you in anything?" Mary asked.

"No, I'm just with *The New York Times."*

"Exactly my point," Gruber said. "Mr. Bond, I think you understand what I'm saying. I'm saying there is greed and malice everywhere in this world, but honesty and truth will prevail as surely as the cry of a newborn babe."

"Do you write fortune cookies?" Connie asked.

"Do you understand me, Mr. Bond? Whoever told you that Arthur Crandall's new film is . . . *what* did you say you'd heard?"

"I heard it was crap."

"Crap, I can't believe it," Gruber said.

"The man's a fucking *genius,"* Mary said.

"Crap," Gruber said again, shaking his head. "Who told you this?" Gruber asked.

"His wife, actually," Michael said.

"That bitch!" Mary said, and her husband gave her a look that said, This is *The New York Times* here, so watch your fucking language.

"What she said, actually," Michael said, "was that in television he'd been doing crap . . ."

"Absolutely," Gruber said.

" . . . and he left television to do a really fantastic film . . ."

"Truly fantastic!"

" . . . that didn't make a nickel . . ."

"Not a dime," Gruber said.

" . . . but now he was back doing crap again."

"False," Gruber said. "Do you know how much this new movie cost to make?"

"How much?" Michael asked.

"Three times what *Solitude* cost."

"Thirty-six million dollars," Connie said at once. "This is very good, this toddy. Why do they call it a toddy?"

"Thirty-six million, correct," Gruber said, "plus I have to figure at least another five, six million for prints and advertising, and it'll come to forty, forty-five million before all is said and done. Now tell me something, Mr. Bond, how can a forty-five-million-dollar picture be crap? Can you tell me that, please? You don't plan to *print* that, do you? His wife's remark?"

"I mean, she *is* a bitch," Mary said, shaking her head.

"What we planned to do," Michael said, "was leave the review to the daily reviewer . . ."

"Who?" Gruber said at once. "Canby? Or Maslin? Don't say Canby or I'll have a heart attack."

"I don't think it's been assigned yet."

"It hasn't been *assigned* yet? It's opening on the second, we had screenings all last week, it hasn't been *assigned* yet?"

"Not that I know of. But the Sunday section's approach would be . . ."

"I'll bet it's Canby," Gruber said to his wife.

"*That* prick," she said.

"We thought we'd talk to Charlie Nichols, take an oblique approach to . . ."

"Why don't you talk to Jessica Wales? She's the *star* of the fucking thing," Gruber said, "why don't you talk to her?"

"Well, we wanted a unique approach . . ."

"I thought you said oblique."

"*And* unique."

"We've got some great stills of Jessica, you could use those with the story."

"The scene where they're coming at her with the knife, oooooo," Mary said, and shuddered.

"The ghosts," Gruber said.

"What she *thinks* are ghosts."

"Don't give it away, for Christ's sake," Gruber said.

"They aren't *really* ghosts, don't worry," Mary said to Michael, as if trying to still the fears of a very small child.

"That's right, tell him," Gruber said, shaking his head. "Give away the whole fucking plot."

"Are you really a rabbi?" Connie asked him.

"What?" he said.

"Because I didn't know rabbis talked that way." Gruber blinked.

Mary rolled her eyes and said, "*Whatever* you do, don't mention *Gaslight.*"

"Very good, tell him not to mention *Gaslight,*" Gruber said. "That's like telling somebody not to stare at somebody's big nose. Did you see that picture?"

"No," Michael said.

"The Martin picture."

"Sheen?"

"Steve. Anyway, this isn't *Gaslight* we did, this is an entirely new and original approach to psychological suspense. Jessica Wales gives the performance of her career and Arthur Crandall has never been . . ."

"I wonder, Mr. Gruber, do you think you could let me have Charlie Nichols's address, please?"

"You're determined to do this interview with Charlie, huh?"

"That's my assignment, sir."

"Who thinks up these crazy assignments? Gussow?"

"I'll bet it's Canby," Mary said.

"Do we even *have* his address?" Gruber said. "I mean, he's a bit player. Why the hell do you want to interview *him*?"

"I just take orders," Michael said.

"Oh, sure, everybody just takes orders," Gruber said. "The Nazis just took orders, Canby just takes orders, *you* just take orders, where's the address book?" he asked Mary.

"I'll get it," she said, "don't get excited. He gets so excited," she said to Michael.

"Maybe I oughta just call Arthur, he's probably got the address right at his finger . . ."

"No, I don't think you should do that," Michael said.

"Why not? You said you want to talk to Charlie . . ."

"We'd like to surprise Mr. Crandall."

"Oh, he'll be surprised, all right, don't worry. An interview with Charlie Nichols? Oh, he'll wet his pants, believe me. When's this thing gonna be in the paper?"

"Next Sunday."

"You work that close, huh?"

"Yes."

"Here it is," Mary said, and handed the address book to her husband.

The chimes suddenly began playing "Mary Had a Little Lamb."

"I love this song," Mary said.

Gruber waited until the entire little song had played.

Then he said, "Who is it?"

And a man answered, "Police."

10

It was as if someone in the platoon had yelled "Charlie!"

His heart stopped.

He almost threw himself flat on the ground. But the ground was a thick white carpet, across which Gruber was now walking to the front door. Michael glanced quickly at Connie. Connie smiled back mysteriously. It occurred to him that Mary's little hot rum toddy had done a real number on her.

Gruber opened the door.

There were two men standing there.

They were both wearing blue jackets with yellow ribbed cuffs and waistbands.

"Mr. Gruber?" one of the men asked.

He was about Gruber's height and weight. He had curly red hair and blue eyes that matched his jacket.

"Yes?" Gruber said.

"Detective Harold Nelson, Seventh Precinct," he said, and immediately turned his back to Gruber.

Across the back of the blue jacket, in yellow script lettering, were the words SEVENTH PRECINCT BOWLING TEAM. He turned to face Gruber again. "I called a little while ago," he said. "This is my partner, Detective Marvin Leibowitz."

"How do you do?" Leibowitz said. He was taller than Nelson, with black hair and brown eyes. Together they looked like *Car 54, Where Are You?* In bowling jackets.

"Marvin is our captain," Nelson said.

"An honor to meet you," Gruber said.

"Not of the precinct," Nelson said. "The team."

"Still an honor," Gruber said. "Come in, please."

The way he was treating them, Michael figured Gruber had paid off a great many cops on the streets of New York while filming this or that wonderful motion picture. When he was still living in Boston, they had shot a movie titled *Fuzz* up there, which was about cops. Burt Reynolds had played the detective in it. Raquel Welch was in it, too, though they never got to kiss because Reynolds was already married to a woman who couldn't hear or speak. Michael went to see it later, it turned out to be a lousy movie. But while they were shooting this movie, there were so many *real* cops hanging around that Michael was sure the entire Boston P.D. was on the take. He suddenly wondered if *Winter's Chill,* the new Arthur Crandall masterpiece, had been shot right here in New York City.

"The reason we're here, sir," Nelson said, "as I mentioned on the telephone, is we're the detectives investigating this homicide which we caught in our precinct . . ."

"Yes, I realize that," Gruber said.

"Although you wouldn't know it from the jackets,

would you?" Leibowitz said.

"We're playing later tonight," Nelson explained.

"The Ninth," Leibowitz explained.

"Who's conducting?" Connie asked.

Both Nelson and Leibowitz looked at her. Michael wished they weren't looking at her that way. She still had the mysterious smile on her face, which made her look somehow insulting. To cops, anyone smiling that way was either mentally retarded or trying to be a wise guy. He could sense both cops bristling at the way she was smiling. It never occurred to either of them that she might have had too much toddy. They merely saw this Oriental smiling in a superior manner, and they figured her for somebody challenging authority. In Vietnam, sometimes you got an American soldier questioning a native who either lowered his eyes or looked away, and the soldier figured he had something to hide. Couldn't look you straight in the eye, then he had to be lying or something. Didn't realize this was a sign of respect, not looking a superior directly in the eye. It caused a lot of trouble in Vietnam. In Vietnam, a lot of innocent people had got themselves shot because they wouldn't look an American soldier in the eye when he was asking them questions. He wished Connie would stop smiling.

"Is there something comical, miss?" Nelson asked.

"Yes," she said.

"May I ask *what*?"

"No," she said, and kept smiling.

Nelson looked at her as if trying to freeze her solid with his icy blue stare. Leibowitz, standing behind him and to his left, was scowling now. Suddenly, they no longer looked like *Car 54*. Instead, they looked like two mean detectives who would kick Connie's ass around the block as soon as look at her.

"At *any* rate," Nelson said, dismissing her and turning to Gruber again, "we thought that since you are an associate, so to speak, of Mr. Crandall . . ."

"Yes, I am."

"Who at first we thought was the dead man, but who isn't . . ."

"Oh, thank God," Mary said, "such a genius."

Nelson looked at her.

"I don't believe I have met these other people, sir," he said to Gruber.

"My wife, Mary," Gruber said.

"How do you do?" Nelson said.

"Ma'am," Leibowitz said, and almost touched the bill of a cap he was no longer wearing, a holdover from his days as a uniformed cop.

"Mr. Bond and Miss Keene of *The New York Times*," Gruber said.

Michael said, "Nice to meet you."

Connie smiled mysteriously.

"What're you gonna do?" Nelson asked her. "Write about how *incompetent* the cops in this city are?"

"Because we ain't got the killer yet?" Leibowitz said.

"You look familiar," Nelson said to Michael.

"I don't think so," Michael said.

"You ever done a story up the Seventh Precinct?"

"No, sir, I'm sure I haven't."

"Me, neither," Connie said.

"I could swear I know you," Nelson said. "How

about the Two-Six uptown? You ever write about the Two-Six?"

"Never."

" 'Cause I used to work up the Two-Six."

"I've never been there."

"Up in Harlem? On a Hun' Twenny-sixth Street?"

"No, sir, I'm sorry."

"Five-twenny West a Hun' Twenny-sixth?"

"No."

"Boy, I could swear I seen you someplace."

"Me, too," Leibowitz said, staring at him.

"Mr. Gruber," Michael said, extending his hand for the book Gruber was clutching like a hymnal, "if you'll just let me have that address . . ."

"When *do* you expect to catch him?" Gruber asked.

"Barnes? Who knows? The man's from Florida, for all we know he's already back there by now."

"Well, as a matter of *fact,*" Michael said, bristling somewhat, "for all you know, he may not have killed that person at *all*. Whoever that person may be."

"Oh, so *that's* gonna be the *Times* approach, huh?" Nelson said, and nodded knowingly to his partner.

"Of course," Leibowitz said. "The police in this city don't know if Michael Barnes *really* done it . . ."

" . . . and we *also* don't know who got killed."

"Who *did* get killed?" Michael asked.

"We don't know," Nelson said.

"But that doesn't mean . . ."

"That doesn't mean *Barnes* didn't kill him," Nelson said.

"Well, I'm sure you'll work it out," Michael said. "Connie, let's go. Mr. Gruber, if you'll . . ."

"Okay, Michael," Connie said.

" . . . let me have . . ."

"Michael, did you say?" Leibowitz asked.

Michael thought Uh-oh.

Leibowitz was looking at him.

"Mr. *Who,* did you say?" Nelson asked.

Nelson was looking at him, too.

Both of them trying to remember if this was the man they'd seen on television.

The picture on the license.

Not a very good likeness, but—

"Bond," Michael said.

It wasn't going to wash.

"Mr. Bond," Nelson said, reaching under his jacket for the gun holstered to his belt, "I wonder if you'd . . ."

Michael did two things almost simultaneously.

Three things, actually.

In such rapid succession that he might just as well have been doing them all at the same time.

He grabbed Connie's hand; he yanked the address book out of Gruber's hand; and he hit Nelson with his shoulder.

"Oh my *God!*" Mary yelled.

"Stop or I'll shoot!" Nelson yelled.

"Don't!" Gruber yelled. "The paintings!"

The door seemed so very far away.

Moving through the jungle with Andrew in his arms, his life leaking away. The medical choppers so very far away. The jungle path a long, dark tunnel through overhanging leaves of green, vines of green, everything dripping green except Andrew, who kept spilling red. Behind Michael, someone called, "We no wanna hurt you, no run, Yank, we wanna help you," and he wondered why every fucking Cong soldier in this country sounded like a Jap in a World War II—

Nelson fired.

He didn't hit any pictures.

What he hit was Michael.

In the left arm.

He dropped the address book.

He said, "Oh shit."

Which sobered Connie at once. Or maybe the sudden sight of blood sobered her. She yanked open the door, picked up the book, grabbed the hand on Michael's good arm, and pulled him through the doorway after her. Behind them, Nelson—or perhaps Leibowitz—fired a shot that sent splinters flying out of the jamb.

Here we are again on the streets of Fabulous Downtown New York, Michael thought, with the fun just about to begin, folks, because my arm is bleeding very badly, and there are two cops chasing us with guns in their hands, and I can't shoot at either one of them because I'm as innocent as the day is long, which so far happens to be the longest day in my life.

He told himself he could not afford to pass out, even though his arm was killing him—where was the address book, had Connie picked up the address book? Charlie Nichols was in that book and Charlie just might know what the hell was going on here. If this were a War Movie, which with all this shooting it was beginning to resemble a lot, he'd have told the Chinese girl guiding him through enemy lines to go on without him, he was hurt too bad and he wasn't going to make it. Or if this were a Show Biz Movie, he'd have told his Chinese dancing partner to accept the job Ziegfeld had offered because he himself was only a second-rate hoofer who didn't want to stand in her way. But this wasn't a movie at all, this was real life, and so he clung to Connie's hand as if he were hanging outside a tenth-story window with nothing but her support between him and the pavement below. Behind him, he heard Nelson yelling like a fucking Cong Jap, "We don't wanna hurt you, Barnes," although he'd already hurt Michael pretty badly.

They had almost reached the sidewalk now.

"Police!" someone yelled. "Freeze!"

They both stopped dead in their tracks.

A green-and-white car was at the curb.

The lettering on it read SIXTH PRECINCT.

Two uniformed cops in what looked like padded blue parkas with fake-fur collars were running toward them.

"Freeze!" one of them shouted again.

"Police!" the other one shouted.

Still running toward them.

"Drop those guns!" one of them yelled.

What? Michael thought.

And then he realized that these nice police officers had heard gunfire, and had pulled their car to the curb and had seen a bleeding man and a nice Chinese woman running out of this nice little Welsh lane here, and chasing them were a menacing tall guy and an equally menacing short guy in bowling jackets, both of them screaming, and each of them with a gun in his hand.

Michael wondered if Nelson and Leibowitz would turn to flash the yellow SEVENTH PRECINCT BOWLING TEAM lettering on their jackets.

But Connie was rushing him away from the alley.

* * *

This was some city, this city.

Here was a man bleeding from a bullet wound in his left arm, the blood staining the sleeve of his overcoat—though admittedly the coat was a dark blue and the blood merely showed on it as a darker purplish stain—being rushed into a taxi by a gorgeous Chinese girl, and nobody on the street batted an eyelash. Michael found this amazing. In Sarasota, if you belched in public, you got a standing ovation.

The cab driver said, "What is that there? Is that blood there?"

"Yes, my husband just got shot," Connie said.

"Sure, ha-ha," the cabbie said.

Michael realized she had called him her husband.

He tried the name for size: Mrs. Michael Barnes.

Constance Barnes.

Connie Barnes.

"So what *really* happened?" the cabbie wanted to know.

"We were walking down the street minding our own business," Connie said, "when this man came along from the opposite direction with a tiger on a leash."

"Boy oh boy," the cabbie said, shaking his head, watching her in the rearview mirror.

"So my husband told him he thought that was against the law, having a tiger on a leash . . ."

Again.

She'd said it again.

" . . . and the man said, 'Sic him!'"

"To the tiger?"

"Yes."

"Sheeesh," the cabbie said. "What a city, huh?"

"You said it," Connie said.

"So what'd the tiger do? This musta been a trained tiger, huh?"

"Oh, yes. He jumped on my husband."

"An attack tiger, huh?"

"Oh, yes."

"Mauled him, I'll bet. Your husband."

"Exactly what happened."

"Sheeesh," the cabbie said again. "What was his name?"

"I don't know. He was a tall, dark man wearing . . ."

"No, I mean the tiger."

"Why do I have to know the tiger's name?"

"So you can report this to the police."

"I don't think I heard his name."

"Then how you gonna identify him? All tigers look alike, you know."

"I know, but . . ."

"So you have to know his name. If the police should ask you his name."

"Well, why would they do that? I mean, I don't think there are too many tigers on leashes in this city, do you?"

"Who knows? There could be."

"I mean, have *you* ever seen a tiger on a leash in this city?"

"I'm just now hearing about one, ain't I?" the cabbie said.

"His name was Stripe," Connie said.

Michael was thinking that everybody in this city was crazy.

"That's a good name for a tiger," the cabbie said. "So what's this address on Pell Street? A doctor?"

"No, it's where I live," Connie said.

" 'Cause don't you think you ought to see a doctor?"

"I want to look at it first."

"Are *you* perhaps a doctor, lady?"

"No, but . . ."

"Then what good is it gonna do, *you* looking at it?"

"Because if it looks bad, *then* I can call a doctor."

"On Christmas Day? This is Christmas Day, lady."

"I'll call a Chinese doctor."

"Do *they* work on Christmas Day?

"Yes, if they're Buddhists."

"Look, suit yourself, lady," the cabbie said. "You want a Buddhist doctor, go get a Buddhist doctor."

He was silent for the rest of the trip to her apartment. Michael guessed he was offended. When they got to Connie's building, he pocketed the fare and her generous tip, and then said, "Also, they got rabies, you know. Them attack tigers." Michael himself was beginning to believe he'd really been attacked by a tiger. As he got out of the cab, he looked up and down the street in both directions, to make sure there weren't any more of them around. He also looked up toward the roof to make sure one of them wasn't going to jump down into the street from up there. He got a little dizzy looking up. He swayed against Connie, suddenly feeling very weak. But he did not pass out until they were safe inside the apartment.

"Ah, ah, ah," the doctor said.

He looked like Fu Manchu.

A scarecrow of a man with a long, straggly beard

and little rimless eyeglasses. He wasn't wearing silken robes or anything, he was in fact wearing a dark suit and a white shirt and a tie with mustard stains on it, but there was something about his manner that seemed dynastic. He was bent over Michael, his stethoscope to Michael's heart. Michael's shirt was open. He had bled through the bandage Connie had put on his arm before calling the doctor. The sheet under him was stained with blood. The doctor moved the stethoscope. He listened to Michael's lungs.

"Very good," he said.

"Yes?" Connie said.

"Yes, the bullet did not go through his lungs."

"Perhaps because he was shot in the arm," Connie said respectfully.

"Ah, ah, ah," the doctor said.

His name was Ling.

He took the bandage off Michael's arm.

"Mmm, mmm, mmm," he said.

"Is it bad?" Connie asked.

"Someone shot him in the arm," Ling said.

"Is the bullet still in there?" Connie asked.

"No, no," Ling said, "it's a nice clean wound."

Good, Michael thought.

"Good," Connie said.

"You'll be able to play tennis in a week or so," Ling said, and chuckled. "Are you left-handed?"

"No."

"Then you'll be able to play tennis tomorrow," he said, and chuckled again.

Michael watched as Ling worked on his arm. He was wondering if he planned on reporting this to the police. He felt certain that reporting gunshot wounds was mandatory.

"How did this happen?" Ling asked.

He was sprinkling what Michael guessed was some kind of sulfa drug on the wound. In the field, you stripped a sulfapak and slapped it on the wound immediately. In the field, people were spitting blood on you while you worked. In the field, everyone got to be a doctor. You lost a lot of patients in the field.

"We were walking down the street minding our own business," Connie said, "when this man came along from the opposite direction with a gun in his hand."

"Ah, ah, ah," Ling said.

"So Michael said to the man . . ."

"Excuse me, but is this your husband?" Ling asked.

"Not yet," Michael said.

Connie looked at him.

Ling looked at them both.

"You must be cautious," Ling said. "There are many problems in East-West marriages."

"Like what?" Michael asked.

"Like food, for example," Ling said.

"But I like Chinese food," Michael said.

"Exactly," Ling said.

"I see," Michael said.

"So what did you say to this man?"

"Which man?"

"The one who shot you."

"Oh."

"What he said," Connie said, "is that he thought it was against the law to be walking down the street with a gun in your hand."

Not in Florida, Michael thought.

Florida was the Wild West these days.

Though not as much as New York seemed to be.

"So the man shot him," Connie said.

"Tch, tch, tch," Ling said.

"Are you going to report this?" Connie asked flatly.

Ling looked at her.

"Are we both Chinese?" he asked.

"I'm only walking wounded," Michael said. "And walking wounded are allowed to walk."

Dr. Ling had bandaged his arm neatly and tightly, and it was no longer bleeding and certainly in no danger of becoming infected unless Michael went rolling around in the dirt someplace. Moreover, it hardly hurt at all now, so what he wanted to do . . .

"No," Connie said. "What we're going to do is I'll go down for some food and we'll eat here in the apartment and I'll call Charlie Wong and tell him I'm not feeling good and won't be able to work tonight. Then you'll go to bed and get some . . ."

"No," Michael said.

"Dr. Ling said you have to rest."

"Dr. Ling isn't wanted for murder. What I want to do is go see this Charlie Nichols person . . ."

"No. You can call him on the phone if you like, but I won't let . . ."

"I don't *want* to call him on the phone. Every time I talk to somebody on the phone, the police show up in the next ten minutes. I am wanted for *murder,* Connie! Can't you . . . ?"

"You're yelling at me," she said.

"Yes. Because you're behaving like a . . ."

"We're having our first argument," she said, grinning.

"Let's go see Charlie Nichols," he said.

*   *   *

She did not want to ask Charlie Wong for the use of a limousine because she had already called to tell him she was sick. She did not want to go to a car rental place because she suspected the police would have contacted all such places and asked them to be on the look-out for the wanted desperado Michael Barnes. So she went to Shi Kai, who ran the restaurant downstairs.

Mr. Shi had a car he only drove during the summer months. The rest of the time, it sat idle in a garage he rented on Canal. That was because the car was a 1954 Oldsmobile convertible with a mechanism that had broken while the top was in the down position. Mr. Shi handed the keys over to Connie and told her not to freeze to death. Michael was beginning to understand that Connie had a great many friends in New York City's Chinese community, all of whom seemed willing to perform all sorts of favors for her. This may have been only because she was Chinese, but he suspected it was because she was extraordinarily beautiful as well.

He loved the way she wore her beauty.

His former wife, Jenny, was beautiful, too, if you considered long blonde hair and green eyes and a spectacular figure beautiful, which apparently not only Michael had considered beautiful but all of Harvard's football team while he was in Vietnam, and most recently the branch manager and God knew who else at Suncoast Federal. But Jenny *flaunted* her beauty, wearing it like a Miss America who was certain her smile would bring her fame, fortune, and a good seat at Van Wezel Hall, which was Sarasota's big contribution to Florida culture, such as it was. It had sickened Michael every time Jenny gently placed her hand on someone's arm and leaned in close to flash that incandescent smile of hers, and the person—male *or* female—melted into a gushing pool of gratitude and awe. Jenny knew without question that wherever she and Michael went, she was the most beautiful woman in the room. This was true. An indisputable fact. You could no more doubt that than you could doubt the certainty of the sun rising in the morning or the tides going in and out. Jenny was gorgeous. That she knew this and used this was not a particularly admirable trait.

Connie seemed not to know that she was extravagantly beautiful.

She wore her beauty like Reeboks.

Or galoshes.

It never occurred to her that Mr. Shi would feel honored when she asked to borrow his convertible with a top that could not be put up. She went to him as a supplicant, politely asking for the use of the car, generously offering to pay for the use of the car, eyes respectfully lowered when talking to this person who was older than she was, and Mr. Shi—recognizing the beauty and the grace and the modesty of this young woman who came to him as a dutiful daughter might have—handed her the keys and accepted her gratitude with a tut-tut-tut, and then cautioned her paternally against freezing to death.

Connie smiled so radiantly, it almost broke Michael's heart.

He guessed he was beginning to love her a whole lot.

* * *

"One of the nice things about a convertible," Connie said, "is you can see all the buildings."

Michael was thinking that in this city you could drive a convertible with the top down in the dead of winter and nobody paid any attention to you. That was one of the nice things about this city, the way everyone respected everyone else's privacy. Indifference, it was called.

He was beginning to learn the downtown area.

For example, he now knew that if you wanted to get out of Chinatown, you didn't have to go very far until you were in Little Italy. And if you wanted to get out of Little Italy . . .

"This is all the Fifth Precinct," Connie said.

"Thank you," he said.

. . . you either drove east toward the East River or west toward the Hudson River. On the other hand, if you wanted to get to Charlie Nichols's apartment in Knickerbocker Village, you first drove east on Canal, and then you made a left on Bowery and drove past the Confucius Plaza apartments and P.S. 124 all the way to Catherine, where you made another left that took you past P.S. 1 on your right and then a Catholic church and school on your left—there were certainly a great many educational opportunities in this fine city—and then you made another left onto Monroe, which was a one-way street, and you looked for a parking space.

You could fit all of downtown Sarasota in Knickerbocker Village. That was another thing about this city. You could drive all over the downtown area, which was really just an infinitesimal part of New York, and you'd see more buildings and more restaurants and more movie theaters and more people than you would driving through the entire state of Florida. Michael found this amazing. He suddenly wondered if Connie planned to stay in New York for the rest of her life. He hoped not.

They were surrounded now by tall brick buildings.

They walked on paths shoveled clear of snow.

The evening was cold and brisk. Connie was wearing jeans and leg warmers and boots and the short black coat she'd had on last night when she'd followed him out of the fortune-cookie factory. Michael was wearing a brown leather bomber jacket he'd bought from a friend of Connie's named Louis Klein who ran an Army & Navy store on Delancey Street, which he opened for Connie even though this was Christmas and he was leaving for Puerto Rico in the morning. He had also sold to Michael—with money borrowed from Connie—a pair of Levi jeans, a blue wool sweater reduced from sixty-four dollars to twenty-three ninety-five, and a pair of white woolen socks "to keep your feet warm," he said paternally. It was amazing how Connie brought out the paternal instinct in all these fifty-, sixty-year-old men. When Klein clucked his tongue and asked Connie how her boyfriend had hurt his arm, Connie told him simply and honestly that he'd been shot. Klein said, "This city, I'm not surprised," and threw in an extra pair of woolen socks free.

She clung to his right arm now as they wandered through the development, following signs that told them which building was which. Somehow there was no sense of urgency here in this cloistered enclave. It was close to five o'clock now. There was a hush on the city. The street lamps, already lighted, cast a warm glow on the snow banked along the paths. Window rectangles glowed with the warmth of rooms beyond, Christmas tree lights blinking red and blue and green and white. Strings of lights outlined windows and balconies. One window was decorated with a huge white star. It was still Christmas.

They found Nichols's building, located his name in the lobby directory downstairs, and took the elevator up to the sixth floor. The corridor smelled of Christmas. Birds and beef that had been roasted, pies that had been baked. There was laughter behind one of the closed doors. Music behind another. They walked to the door of Nichols's apartment and Michael pressed the bell button set into the jamb. He listened. Nothing. He looked at Connie. She shrugged. He rang the bell again. No answer.

"He's out," he said.

"Knock," she said.

He knocked.

No answer.

He knocked again.

He shook his head.

"Damn it," he said.

"What do we do now?"

"I'd like to get in there," he said.

"Do you know how to do something like that?" she asked.

"Something like what?"

"Opening a door with a credit card?"

"No. Anyway, they *stole* my credit cards."

He was beginning to get angry all over again. Just thinking about what had happened to him since seven o'clock last night made him angry.

Not knowing *why* these things were happening to him made him angry. Not knowing *who* was doing these things to him made him angry. And now Nichols not being here made him even angrier.

"Do *you* have a credit card?" he asked.

"Yes, but you just said . . ."

"I can learn."

She dug in her shoulder bag, found her wallet, and took from it an American Express card. He looked at the card, looked at the place in the jamb where the door fit snugly into it, grabbed the knob in his hand, slid the card between door and jamb, twisted the knob—and the door opened.

He looked at the door.

He looked at the credit card.

"Boy," Connie said, "you're *some* fast learner."

He eased the door open the rest of the way. There were lights on in the living room. A lighted Christmas wreath in the living room window as well. He motioned Connie in, closed the door behind them. There was a deadbolt lock on the door. In the open position. Which meant he hadn't worked any magic with the credit card, the door had been unlocked already. He turned the thumb bolt now. The tumblers fell with a small oiled click that sounded like a rifle shot in the silent apartment.

"This is breaking and entry, you know," Connie said.

They stood just inside the entrance door.

There were two lamps on end tables in the living room, casting warm pools of illumination on a sofa and a pair of easy chairs. The wreath in the window glowed red and green. There was not a sound anywhere in the apartment.

"Let's see if we can find a desk someplace," Michael whispered.

"Why a desk?"

"See what's in it."

They moved out past the kitchen, and discovered off the hallway just beyond it a room that was furnished as a study. Big window on the wall across from the door. Bookcases on the wall to the right, an easy chair and a reading lamp in front of them. A desk and a chair on the opposite wall. Michael went to the desk and snapped on the desk lamp. The wall above the desk was decorated with framed pictures, most of them in black and white, all of them showing the same man in various costumes and in various poses. But in whichever costume and whatever pose, he was definitely the man who'd stolen Michael's car, and presumably the man whose apartment this was: Charles R. Nichols. It looked as if Nichols had once played Sherlock Holmes, if the deerstalker hat and pipe meant anything. Julius Caesar, too, judging from the toga and the laurel wreath. And either Napoleon or Hercule Poirot, it was difficult to tell from the photo. There were also photographs of him playing what appeared to be the leading man to various leading women. Holding the ladies' hands, gazing into their eyes, grinning in a goofy juvenile manner. It was always embarrassing to see photographs of an essentially unattractive man who thought he was handsome and who posed like a lady-killer. Michael thought of himself as merely okay in a world populated by spectacularly handsome men. He sometimes wished he had the kind of nerve it took to pose for pictures like the ones here on Charlie's wall.

"We're looking for anything about Crandall," he

said. "Or Parrish or Cahill."

"Okay," Connie said.

She pulled out the bottom desk drawer and sat on the floor beside it, legs crossed Indian style. Michael sat in the chair and began looking through the drawer over the kneehole.

"Have you got enough light?" he asked.

"Yes," she said.

It occurred to him that he liked the way they worked together.

They were getting good at working together.

Last night in Crandall's office had been the very first time they'd ransacked anyplace together. Now, working as a team, they . . .

"The check," Michael said.

"What check?"

"The one Crandall wrote on Monday. For nine thousand dollars."

"What about it?"

"He went to the bank at two-thirty. If that's when he cashed it . . ."

"Uh-huh."

" . . . then maybe he gave the cash to Charlie . . ."

"Uh-huh."

" . . . when he came to the office at *three*-thirty. That's all on Crandall's calendar, Connie. The bank, and Charlie coming to the office."

"Okay, so what are we looking for?" she asked. "Nine thousand dollars in cash?"

"Well, I guess so."

"And if we find it? What will that mean?"

"I don't know," Michael said, and sighed heavily.

They did not find nine thousand dollars in cash in any of the drawers in Charlie's desk.

They found instead a tarnished penny in a tray

containing rubber bands, paper clips, a roll of Scotch tape, and a pair of scissors. That was all the cash they found.

They did, however, find an address book and an appointment calendar.

And for Monday, the twenty-third of December, Charlie had listed his three-thirty meeting at Crandall's office.

And for Tuesday, the twenty-fourth of December . . .

Last night . . .

The night this whole damn thing had started . . .

Charlie had written onto his calendar:

Call Mama

"Mama again," Michael said.

"Let's check his address book."

There was a listing for Arthur Crandall in Charlie's address book.

For both his office and his home.

So *that* connection, at least, was clearly established.

There was no listing for either a Parrish or a Cahill.

"Is his mother listed?" Connie asked.

"Why his mother?" he asked.

"Mama," Connie said, and shrugged.

"Why would Crandall have called *Charlie's* mother 'Mama'?"

"I don't know. Maybe she's a big, fat woman. People call big, fat women 'Mama' even if they're somebody else's mother."

"I don't even call my *own* mother 'Mama,'" Michael said.

"Sophie Tucker was big and fat and she was the last of the Red Hot Mamas," Connie said.

"Who's Sophie Tucker?" Michael asked.

"I don't know. I drove somebody to see a play about her."

Michael looked under Nichols.

He found a listing for a Sarah Nichols in New Jersey.

"Try her," Connie said.

He debated this.

"Wish her a merry Christmas, ask her if she's talked to her son lately."

Michael still hesitated.

"Go ahead," Connie said.

He was thinking that the last time he'd talked to a strange woman on the telephone—Albetha Crandall, last night—the police had come up the fire escape the very next minute. Maybe talking to strange women on the telephone had a jinx attached. In Vietnam, you did all sorts of things to avoid jinxes. Jinxes could get you killed. You wrote all sorts of magic slogans on your helmet, you hung little amulets and charms from your flak jacket, anything to ward off a jinx, anything to stay alive. He did not want any more cops coming up the fire escape. He did not want to get shot by anyone else in this city, good guy or bad guy. But if the Mama in both Crandall's *and* Charlie's appointment calendars *was* in fact Charlie's mother, then maybe she could tell him something about what was going on here. If he played his cards right. If he crossed his fingers and mumbled a bit of voodoo jive to keep away the jinx. In Vietnam, Andrew had taught him some voodoo jive. Andrew was from New Orleans, where they sometimes did that kind of shit.

He dialed the number.

"Hello?"

A woman's voice.

"Sarah Nichols?" he said.

"Yes?"

"Merry Christmas," Michael said.

"Who's this, please?" Sarah said.

"A friend of Charlie's."

"Is anything wrong?" she asked at once.

"No, no. I've been trying to locate him, I wonder if you've talked to him lately."

"Not since this morning," she said. "He was supposed to come here for an early dinner, I told him I was having some friends in, but he never showed. Well, you know how Charlie is."

"Oh, yeah, Charlie," Michael said, and chuckled. "What time this morning?"

"Oh, around eleven, it must have been. The minute Charlie hears I want him to meet some girl, he runs for the hills."

"That's Charlie, all right," Michael said. "And you haven't talked to him since, huh?"

"No. Would you like to leave your name? In case he *does* pop up? Though it's really quite late, I doubt if even my brother would walk in at nine-thirty."

"Your brother, uh-huh," Michael said. "You don't think he might be with Benny, do you?"

"Who's Benny?"

"I don't know. I thought you might know."

"No, I'm sorry, I don't."

"Do you think your mother might know Benny? Do you have a mother?"

"Everyone has a mother."

"I mean, she isn't dead or anything, is she?"

"Not that I know of."

"What do you call her?"

"I call her . . . who did you say this was?"

"Do you call her Mama?"

"Sometimes."

"Is she spry? Does she get around?"

"Yes, she's very spry. Excuse me, but . . ."

"Would you know if someone named Arthur Crandall took her to meet someone named Benny last night?"

"I have no idea. Can you tell me who this is, please?"

"Michael."

"Michael who?" she asked.

"Bond," he said. "No relation. Please tell Charlie I called."

"I will," she said. "Good night, Mr. Bond."

"Good night," Michael said.

He put the receiver back on the cradle.

He was beginning to like that name.

Maybe he'd take it on as a middle name.

It was certainly a hell of a lot better than Jellicle.

"His sister," he said.

"I gathered," Connie said.

"Let's see if there's anything in the bedroom," he said.

Charlie Nichols was in the bedroom.

On the bed.

All bloody.

11

Michael had seen a lot of dead bodies in his short lifetime, but none quite so messily dispatched as this one. Whoever had shot and killed Charlie seemed to have had a difficult time *finding* him. There were bullet holes in the headboard, bullet holes in the wall behind the bed, and several bullet holes in Charlie himself. If there were awards for sloppy murders, whoever had shot Charlie should start preparing an acceptance speech.

Connie looked as if she was about to throw up.

"You okay?" Michael asked.

She nodded.

He looked at the body again, went to the bed, and was leaning over the corpse when Connie yelled, "No!"

"What's the matter?" he said.

"Don't touch him," she said.

"Why not? Is that a Chinese superstition?"

"No, it's not a Chinese superstition."

"Then what is it?"

"It's disgusting."

"I just want to see if he's carrying a wallet," Michael said, and tried the right-hand side pocket in his pants, and found what appeared to be several white rock crystals in a little plastic vial.

"Must collect these, huh?" he said, showing the vial to Connie.

Connie looked at him.

"Rocks, I mean," Michael said.

"Crack, you mean," Connie said.

"What?"

"That's crack."

"It is?" Michael said, and looked at the vial more closely. "I thought crystallography was perhaps his hobby."

"Smoking cocaine is perhaps his hobby."

"I'll tell you something," Michael said, "if this turns out to be another goddamn *dope* plot . . ."

"A single vial of cocaine doesn't necessarily . . ."

"I've had dope plots up to here, I mean it. You can't go to a movie nowadays, you can't turn on television . . ."

"There is no reason to believe that this is linked to a *dope* plot."

"Then what's this?" he asked, and showed her the vial again.

"That's crack."

"And is crack dope?"

"Crack is dope."

"And is this man dead?"

"He appears to be dead."

"There you are," Michael said, and rolled him over.

"Irrgh," Connie said, and covered her eyes with her hands.

Michael was patting down the right hip pocket. "Here it is," he said, and reached into the pocket and yanked out a wallet.

Connie still had her hands over her eyes.

"You can look now," he said, and opened the wallet.

The first thing he saw was a driver's license with a picture of the man on the bed. The name on the license was Charles Robert Nichols.

"Well, it's him," Michael said.

"Good, give him back his wallet."

"Let's see what else is in it."

There were three credit cards in the wallet.

And an Actors Equity card.

And a Screen Actors Guild card.

And an AFTRA card.

And three postage stamps in twenty-five-cent denominations, no longer any good for first-class mail.

And this year's calendar, small and plastic and soon to expire.

And a TWA Frequent Flight Bonus Program card.

And a slip of paper with what looked like a handwritten telephone number on it.

"Here we go," he said.

"Good idea," Connie said. "Let's."

"What's the matter with you?"

"I don't like being here with that person on the bed."

"Is this a New York exchange?" he asked, and showed her the telephone number.

"Yes."

"Let's try it."

"No. Let's leave."

"Connie . . ."

"Michael, that person on the bed is dead."

"I know."

"You're *already* wanted for *one* murder . . ."

"I know."

"You've already been *shot* . . ."

"I know."

"So let's get out of here, okay? Before . . ."

"Let's try this number first."

"Michael, every time you try a number . . ."

"Maybe this time we'll get lucky," he said, and winked.

Connie did not wink back.

Instead, she followed him sullenly down the hallway and into the study again. He sat at the desk with the wall of black-and-white photographs in front of him, and he dialed the telephone number scrawled in a spidery handwriting on the slip of paper, and he waited, waited, waited . . .

"Hello?"

A woman's voice.

"Yes, hello, I'm calling for Charlie Nichols," he said.

"Sorry, he's not here," the woman said.

"I know he isn't, I'm calling *for* him. Who's this, please?"

"Judy Jordan," she said. "Who's this?"

"Hello?" he said.

"Hello?" she said.

"Hello, Miss Jordan?"

"Yes, I'm here."

"Hello?" he said.

"I can hear you," she said.

"I'll have to call back," he said, and hung up.

"Did you get cut off?" Connie asked.

"No," he said.

He was already looking through Charlie's address book again. He flipped rapidly through E, F, H . . .

"Here it is," he said. "Jordan, Judy."

Connie looked at the address. "The Seventh Precinct," she said. "Where they found the body in your car."

"Then we'd better go see her," he said.

"Why?" Connie asked.

He looked at her.

And felt suddenly foolish.

She was right, of course.

He'd found a telephone number in a dead man's wallet, and he'd called that number, and the woman who'd answered the phone was named Judy Jordan.

So?

Why go see her?

He was tired. And beginning to feel that perhaps the best thing to do, after all, was run on over to the police station and tell them he was the man they were looking for and could he please make a call to his lawyer, Mr. David Lang in Sarasota, Florida? Connie knew where all the precincts were, they could drive over to the nearest one in Shi Kai's broken convertible. Or perhaps he should call Dave first, ask him to take the next plane up to New York, hole up in Connie's apartment until he got here, and *then* go to the police togeth—

"Judy *who*, did you say?"

This from Connie.

Who not five minutes ago had been urging him to please get the hell out of here. But who now seemed to have a note of renewed interest in her voice.

"Jordan," he said, and turned to look up at her.

Connie was looking at the wall.

Specifically, she was looking at a photograph of Charlie Nichols and a teenage girl. Charlie was a much younger man in the photograph; Michael guessed the picture had been taken at least fifteen years ago. The girl couldn't have been older than sixteen or seventeen. She was wearing a white sweater and a dark skirt and she was grinning up into Charlie's face. Charlie was holding both her hands between his own.

Written in blue ink across the girl's sweatered breasts were the words *To My Dear Daddy, With Love* and beneath that the signature *Judy Jordan*.

Michael leaned in closer to the picture.

The young girl had long, dark hair.

But aside from that, she was a dead ringer for Helen Parrish.

"Also," Connie said, "does Benny have to be a *person?*"

"What?" Michael said.

"Because there's a place called Benny's in SoHo, and maybe that's where Crandall went to meet Charlie's mother, in which case we should take Crandall's picture there in case somebody might remember him from last night, don't you think?"

Michael kissed her.

The bartender's name was Charlie O'Hare.

"There are lots of Charlies in this city, you know," he said.

"Yes, I know," Michael said.

They were sitting at the bar. The place was unusually crowded for Christmas night, but then again Michael had never been in a bar on Christmas night, and maybe they were all this crowded. It was a very Irish bar. No frills. A utilitarian saloon designed for drinkers. Sawdust on the floor. No cut-glass mirrors, no green-shaded lamps like in the place last night where they'd set Michael up for theft and accusation. A nice friendly neighborhood saloon with a handful of people sitting in the booths or at the tables or here at the bar, all of them wearing caps and looking like nice friendly IRA terrorists.

"Here's his picture," Michael said, and showed him the eleven-year-old clipping from the Nice newspaper. He had taken it out of its frame. The back of the clipping was a story about a Frenchman who'd leaped into the Mediterranean to save a German tourist who should have known better than to be swimming in the sea in May. Crandall smiled out from his photograph.

"He's even fatter now," Michael said.

"No, I don't know him," O'Hare said. "Is this French here?"

"Yes."

"What's it say here under the picture?"

"Arthur Crandall before the showing of his film *War and Solitude* yesterday afternoon."

"So what is he, an actor?"

"No, he's a director."

"Sheesh," O'Hare said. "And this is a new movie?"

"No, it's an old one."

"Then how come they showed it yesterday afternoon?"

"They showed it eleven years ago."

"I musta missed it."

"Do you recognize him?"

"No."

"Take a look at the picture again. He would've been here last night at eight o'clock."

"I don't remember seeing him."

"Were you working last night?"

"Yeah, but I don't remember seeing this guy."

"He would've been meeting somebody's mother."

"Well, we get a lot of mothers in here, but I don't remember this guy sitting with anybody's mother," O'Hare said.

"Were you working the bar alone?"

"All alone."

"So he couldn't have been sitting at the bar."

"Not without my noticing him." O'Hare looked at the newspaper clipping again. "This is a French movie?" he asked.

"No, it's American."

"Then why is this written in French?"

"Because that's where they showed it."

"I can understand why they never showed it here. That sounds really shitty, don't it, *War and Solitude*? Would you go see a movie called *War and Solitude*?"

"They did show it here."

"Here? In New York?"

"I think so."

"I never heard of it. *War and Solitude.* I never heard of it. It sounds shitty."

"A lot of people agreed with you," Michael said.

"Don't she speak English?" O'Hare asked, jerking his head toward Connie.

"I speak English," she said.

"'Cause I thought maybe you spoke only Chinese, sitting there like a dummy."

"I don't have anything to say," Connie said.

"You're a very pretty lady," O'Hare said.

"Thank you," Connie said.

"She's very pretty," O'Hare said to Michael.

"Thank you," Michael said. "Who would've been working the booths last night? And the tables."

"Molly."

Michael looked around. He didn't see any waitresses in the place.

"Is she here now?"

"She was here a minute ago," O'Hare said.

He craned his neck, looking.

The door to the ladies' room opened. A woman who looked like Detective O'Brien, except that she was fully clothed, came out and walked directly toward where someone signaled to her from one of the booths. She had flaming red hair like O'Brien's and she was short and stout like O'Brien, and she waddled toward the bar now with a sort of cop swagger that made Michael think maybe she *was* O'Brien in another disguise.

"Two Red Eyes," she said. "Water chasers."

O'Hare took from the shelf behind him a bottle of what looked like house whiskey, the label unfamiliar to Michael. He poured liberally into two glasses, filled two taller glasses with water, and put everything onto Molly's tray.

"When you got a minute," he said, "this gentleman would like a few words with you."

Molly looked Michael up and down.

"Sure," she said, and swaggered over to the booth.

"Molly used to wrestle in Jersey," O'Hare said.

"Really?"

"They called her the Red Menace."

"I see."

"Because of the red hair."

"Yes."

"Which is real, by the way," O'Hare said, and winked.

Molly came back to the bar.

"So?" she said. "What now?"

Michael showed her the newspaper clipping.

"Ever see this man in here?" he asked.

"You a cop?" Molly asked.

"No," Michael said.

"You sure?"

"Positive."

" 'Cause I was thinking of calling the cops."

"No, I don't think we need . . ."

"Last night, I mean. When I heard what the two of them were talking about."

"Who do you mean?"

"Mr. Crandall. And the Spanish guy with him."

"You mean you know him?"

"No, I don't *know* him. I only recognize him."

"Arthur Crandall?"

"I don't know his first name. I only know he's Mr. Crandall."

"How do you happen to know that?"

"Because of the phone call."

"What phone call?"

"The phone call that came in the phone booth over there. For Mr. Crandall."

"Who turned out to be the man in this picture, am I right?"

"Yes."

"Arthur Crandall."

"If that's his first name."

"Then that's who it was."

"What about this phone call?"

"Don't rush me. That was later. Earlier, they were sitting at that table over there," she said, and gestured vaguely, "which is when I heard them talking."

"What time was this?"

"Around eight-fifteen."

"And you're sure this is the man?" Michael asked, and showed her the clipping again.

"Yeah, that's him all right. Though he's fatter now."

"But you say he was with another *man*? Not a woman?"

"Not unless she had a thick black mustache," Molly said.

"Why'd you want to call the cops?" Connie asked.

"Who's this?" Molly said, and looked her up and down.

"Connie Kee," Michael said.

"Is she Chinese?"

"Yes."

"I thought so," Molly said. "Is it okay to talk in front of her?"

"Yes, absolutely."

"Because Chinese people are funny, you know," Molly said.

"Funny how?" Connie asked, truly interested.

"They're always yelling," Molly said.

"That's true," Connie said. "But that's because they're not sure of the language. If they yell, they think you'll understand them better."

"Well, I wish they wouldn't yell all the time."

"Me, too," Connie said.

"It makes me feel like I did something wrong."

"Japanese people never yell, did you notice that?" O'Hare said.

"Excuse me," Michael said, "but why *did* you . . . ?"

"Yes, they're very quiet and polite," Molly said.

"Why did you want to . . . ?"

"Well, they're two very different cultures," Connie said.

"Oh, certainly," Molly said. "The Korean, too. And also the Vietna . . ."

"Excuse me," Michael said, "but why did you want to call the police?"

"What?"

"Last night."

"Oh. Well, because of what they were *talking* about, why do you think?"

"What were they talking about?"

"A *body*," Molly said, lowering her voice. "A dead *body*."

"Who?" Michael asked.

"The two of them in the booth. Mr. Crandall and the Spanish guy with the mustache."

"I mean, the body. Who was it?"

"They didn't say."

"Well, what did you hear them . . . ?"

"The Spanish guy was saying he already had the corpse. That's when I almost called the police."

"But you didn't."

"No. Because I figured the man had to be an embalmer."

"Uh-huh."

"Or one of those people who does autopsies at the hospital."

"Uh-huh."

"But then Mr. Crandall said if Charlie could de . . ."

"Charlie!" Michael shouted and almost leaped off the stool.

"Jesus, you scared the *shit* out of me," Molly said, backing away.

"Did you say *Charlie*?"

"What the hell's wrong with you?"

"What *about* Charlie?"

"I think this guy's crazy," Molly said to O'Hare.

"Nah, he's okay," O'Hare said, indicating with a shrug that in his lifetime as a bartender he had served many, many nutcases picking at the coverlet.

"Tell me about Charlie," Michael said.

Molly sighed and rolled her eyes.

"He said if Charlie could deliver what they needed . . ."

"Crandall said?"

"Yes. Said if Charlie could deliver what they needed, then they could plant the stiff before midnight."

"Plant the stiff."

"He meant the corpse."

"Uh-huh."

"He meant they could bury the corpse before midnight."

"That's what *you* think," Connie said knowingly.

"Which is when I almost called the cops again," Molly said. "Because even if the man *was* an undertaker, why would he be burying anybody at midnight? On Christmas Eve no less."

"*Before* midnight," O'Hare corrected.

"Right," Molly said, "on Christmas *Eve*. But then the Spanish guy told Mr. Crandall there wasn't any hurry, the body would keep, it was on ice, so I guessed he was a legitimate undertaker, after all."

"Did you happen to catch his name?"

"No."

"What this was," O'Hare said, "this Spanish undertaker was waiting for Charlie to bring the dead man's suit and underwear or whatever, his *stuff*, you know, so they could dress him all up before they buried him."

"That's what *you* think," Connie said again.

"Which is another thing I don't like about Chinese people," Molly said.

"What's that?" Connie asked, truly interested again.

"They think they're so fucking smart," Molly said.

"Yes, that's true," Connie said.

"That's 'cause they *are* so fucking smart," O'Hare said.

"That's true, too," Connie said.

"Excuse me," Michael said, "but did either of them say what Charlie was supposed to deliver?"

"Your I.D., of course," Connie said.

"So when they planted the corpse with *Crandall's* I.D. on it . . ."

"They could *also* drop . . ."

"Do you know what these two are talking about?" Molly asked O'Hare.

"Sure," O'Hare said.

"What?"

"The stiff's dog tags."

"What dog tags?"

"To put in his mouth. The stiff's."

"I think *you're* crazy, too," Molly said, shaking her head.

"What else did they say?" Michael asked.

"Mr. Crandall said he wanted to get moving on it, and he wished Charlie would hurry up and do what he had to do."

"Did he mention Charlie's last name?" Michael asked.

"No."

"He didn't say Charlie Nichols?"

"I just told you he didn't mention his last name, so why are you asking me Charlie this or Charlie that? What's the *matter* with this guy?" she asked O'Hare.

"He's okay," O'Hare said, indicating with a shrug that in his many, many years as a bartender he had encountered many a fruitcake who had escaped from this or that mental institution.

"It goes right back to Charlie again," Michael said to Connie. "And the pair working with him. The phony cop and . . ."

"*All* cops are phonies, you want to know," O'Hare said.

"Tell me about the phone call," Michael said.

"The phone in the booth rang, I went to answer it, and a woman on the other end . . ."

"A *woman!*" Michael shouted.

"Listen, if you're gonna keep yelling like that . . ."

"I'm sorry. Did she give you her name?"

"No."

"Helen Parrish," Michael said to Connie.

"I just told you she didn't me give her name," Molly said.

"Or Judy Jordan," Connie said.

"Who's Judy Jordan?" Molly asked.

"Tell me exactly what she said," Michael said.

"She asked to talk to Mr. Crandall. So I yelled out was there a Mr. Crandall here, and the guy in your picture gets up and goes to the phone booth."

"Then what?"

"Then the Spanish guy ordered another beer."

"And then what?"

"Then Mr. Crandall comes back to the table all smiles and tells the Spanish guy everything's okay, they got it."

"Got *what*?" Michael asked.

"Your license and your credit cards," Connie said.

"What time was this?" Michael asked.

"Around eight-thirty," Molly said.

"Right after Crandall stole my car," Michael said.

"She probably told him that, too. That they also had your car."

"So now the Spanish guy could plant the corpse in my car . . ."

"With Crandall's I.D. on it . . ."

"And my stuff alongside the body . . ."

"And set the whole thing in motion."

"What whole thing?" O'Hare asked.

"This is giving me a headache," Molly said, and walked off.

The real headache began at eight o'clock that night, as they were approaching Connie's building.

That was when the shots came.

Michael had developed a sixth sense in Vietnam, you didn't survive unless you did. You learned to know when something was coming your way, you heard that tiny oiled click somewhere out there in the jungle, and you knew someone had squeezed a trigger and a round was right then speeding out of a rifle barrel, or a dozen rounds, you didn't wait to find out, you threw yourself flat on the ground.

They said in Vietnam that the only grunts who survived were the ones who got good at humping mud. Michael had survived.

There was no mud to hump on Pell Street that Wednesday night, there was only a lot of virgin white snow heaped against the curbs on either side of the street. The plows had been through, and the banks they'd left were three, four feet high. In the bright moonlight, Connie and Michael came walking up the middle of the street, which was clearer than the sidewalks, and were about to climb over the bank in front of her building when Michael heard the click.

The same oiled click he'd come to know and love in dear old Vietnam, a click only a trained bird dog might have heard, so soft and so tiny was it, but he knew at once what that click meant.

In Vietnam, he'd have thought only of his own skin.

Hear the click, hump the mud.

Here, there was Connie.

He threw himself at her sideways, knocking her off her feet and *down,* man, out of the path of that bullet or bullets that would be coming their way in about one-one hundredth of a—

There!

A sharp crack on the air.

And another one.

First the click, and then the crack.

If you hadn't heard the click, you never heard the crack, because by then you were stone-cold dead in the market.

For a tall, slender girl, Connie went down like a sack of iron rivets. Whammo, on her back in the snow, legs flying. "Hey!" she yelled, getting angry.

Another crack, and then another, little spurts of snow erupting on the ridge of snow above their heads, better *snow* spurts than *blood* spurts, Charlie.

"Keep down!" he yelled.

She was struggling to get up, cursing in Chinese.

He kept her pinned.

Listened.

Nothing.

But wait . . . wait . . . wait . . .

"Are you crazy?" she said.

"Yes," he said.

Wait . . . wait . . .

He knew the shooter was still up there. Sensed it with every fiber in his being.

"Stay here," he said. "And stay down. There's someone up there trying to kill us."

"What?"

"On the roof. Don't even lift your head. I'll be right back."

"Michael," she said. Softly.

"Yes?" he said.

"I love you, Michael, but you *are* crazy."

It was the first time she'd said that.

The loving him part.

He smiled.

"I love you, too," he said.

The street ran like a wide trench between the banks of moonlit snow on either side of it. Connie lay huddled close to the bank on the northern side of the street, hidden from the roof. Up there was where the shooter was. Michael began wiggling his way up the street, on his belly, using his elbows, dragging his legs. Working his way toward the corner of Pell and Mott, where he planned to make a right turn, out of the shooter's line of fire. Then he would get up to those rooftops up there, and see what there was to see.

It was such a beautiful night.

Long Foot Howell, the only Indian guy in the platoon—an *American* Indian whose great-great grandfather had ridden the Plains with Sitting Bull—always used to say, "It's a good day for dying."

His people lived on a reservation out West someplace. Arizona, maybe, Michael couldn't remember.

Long Foot told him that his people used to say that before they rode into battle.

It's a good day for dying.

Meaning God alone knew what.

Maybe that if you were going to die, you might as well do it on a nice day instead of a shitty one.

Or maybe it referred to the enemy. A good day for killing the *enemy*. A good day for the *enemy* to die.

Or maybe it was a reverse sort of charm. The Indian's way of wishing himself good luck. If he said it was a good day for dying, then maybe he wouldn't get killed. Maybe whichever god or gods the Indian prayed to would hear what he'd said and spare him. If that was it, the charm hadn't worked too well for Long Foot.

On a very good day in Vietnam, with the sun shining bright on his shiny black hair, Long Foot took a full mortar hit and went to join his ancestors in a hundred little pieces.

This was a beautiful night.

But not for dying.

Not here and not now.

However much whoever was on the roof might have wished it.

Michael had reached the corner now, the two narrow streets intersecting the way he imagined country roads did in England, where he'd never been. The hedgerows here, however, were made of snow, high enough to keep Michael hidden from the sniper on the roof, who was still up there silent and waiting.

On his hands and knees, Michael came around the corner.

The building immediately on his right had the inevitable Chinese restaurant on the ground floor, a blue door to the right of it. The door had a sign on it reading TAIWAN NOODLE FACTORY. Michael figured the door to a business would be locked shut on Christmas Day. He could not afford fiddling with a locked door after he climbed over the snowbank and onto the sidewalk where he would be seen if the sniper was roaming around up there.

He crawled to a spot paralleling the next building in line.

Lifted his head quickly.

Saw a door painted green.

Ducked his head.

Waited.

Lifted it again. Saw numerals over the door, nothing else, no sign, no anything. An apartment building. Meaning steps going up to the roof. He hoped.

Ducked again.

Waited.

He crawled several buildings down the street, staying close to the snowbank, and then he took a deep breath, counted to three, and scrambled over the side of the bank as if it were a suspect hill in Vietnam except that over there he'd have had a hand grenade in his fist. He landed on his feet and on the run, sprinting for the green door, which he now saw was slightly ajar, flattening himself against the side of the building to the right of the door. He shot a quick, almost unconscious glance upward toward the roof, saw nothing in the moonlight, and shoved the door fully open.

The entrance vestibule was dark and cold.

He closed the door behind him.

Or, at least, tried to close it. There was something wrong with the hinge, the door would not fully seat itself in the jamb. He gave it up for a lost cause, went to the closed inner door just past the doorbells and mailboxes, and tried the knob. The door was locked. He backed away from it at once, raised his knee, and kicked out flatfooted at a point just above the knob.

"Ow!" he yelled. "You son of a *bitch*!"

The door hadn't budged an inch.

Still swearing, he moved over to where the doorbells were set under the mailboxes. At random, he selected the doorbell for apartment 2A, rang the doorbell, waited, waited, waited and got nothing. The sole of his foot was sending out flashing signals of pain. He wondered if it was possible to break the sole of your foot. He rang another doorbell. A voice came instantly from a speaker on the wall. The voice said something in Chinese. Michael said, "Police, open the door, please." An answering buzz sounded at once. Pleased with himself, Michael opened the door and was starting toward the steps when another door opened at the end of the little cul de sac to the right of the staircase. A short, very fat Chinese man wearing a tank-top undershirt, black trousers, and black slippers stepped out into the hallway, squinted toward where Michael was standing, and yelled, "Wassa motta?"

"Nothing," Michael said.

"You police?" the man yelled.

"Yes."

"Me supahtennin."

"Go back to sleep," Michael said. "This is routine."

"Where you badge?"

"I'm undercover," Michael said.

The man blinked.

"Wah you wann here?" he asked.

"There's a sniper on the roof," Michael said.

"I go get key," the man said, nodding.

"What key?"

"For loof," the man said, and went back into his apartment.

Michael waited. He did not want a partner. On the other hand, his foot still hurt and he didn't want to have to try kicking in another door. He suddenly wondered if in real life it was possible to kick in a door the way detectives did in the movies and on television. He knew it wasn't possible in real life to slam a car into another car and just go on your merry way. Teenagers saw a car chase in a movie, they thought, Hey terrific, I can run into el pillars and concrete mixers and I'll just bounce right off them like a rubber ball, that should be great fun. That same teenager got a drink or two in him, he decided he was a big-city detective in a car chase. He rammed his car into a bus, expecting either the bus would roll over on its back or else his car would bounce off it like in the movies and the next thing you knew a real-life steering wheel was crushing his chest or his head was going through a real-life windshield. Michael suddenly wondered if Sylvester Stallone had ever been to Vietnam.

"Okay, I gotta key," the man said, and came out into the hallway, and pulled the door to his apartment shut behind him. To Michael's dismay, the man had taken off his slippers and put on socks and high-topped boots that looked like combat boots. He had also put on a shirt and a heavy Mackinaw and a woolen stocking cap.

They climbed the steps to the fourth floor and then up another short flight of steps to a metal door. Nodding, flapping his hands, turning the key on the air, shaping his other hand into a gun, Michael's guide and new partner indicated that this was indeed the door to the roof and that he was now going to open the door to the roof, so if Michael was a real cop and there was a real sniper out there maybe he should take out a gun or something. Obligingly, Michael took out a gun. The one he had taken from Crandall, which upon inspection had turned out to be a .32 caliber Harrington & Richardson Model 4, double-action revolver.

"Ahhhhhh," the man said, and nodded. He liked the gun. He showed Michael the key again, and then inserted it into the padlock that hung from a hinge and hasp on the metal door, and as if performing a magic trick, he turned the key and opened the padlock, and grinned and nodded at Michael. Michael nodded back. The Chinese man took the padlock off the hasp, and then moved aside. If there really was a sniper out there, he wasn't going to be the first one to step out onto the roof. He almost bowed Michael out ahead of him.

"You stay here," Michael said.

"More cops," the man said, and nodded. "I call more cops."

"No!" Michael said. "No more cops. This is undercover."

The man looked at him.

"What's your name?" Michael asked.

"Peter Chen," the man said.

"Mr. Chen, thank you very much," Michael said, "the city is proud of you. But you can go back down, thank you," Michael said. "Good-bye, Mr. Chen, thank you."

"I come with you," Chen said.

Michael looked at him.

Chen smiled.

Michael sighed in resignation, opened the door, and stepped quickly out onto the roof. He paused for a moment, getting his new bearings, trying to work out where he was in relationship to Connie's building, where the sniper was. Because once he did that, the rest would be simple. The buildings here were all joined side by side, there were no airshafts to leap, it would merely be a matter of climbing the parapets that separated one rooftop from the next. So if the cross street was *here*, then Connie's street was *there*, and he'd have to go over this rooftop and then the next one to the corner—

"What you do?" Chen asked.

"I'm thinking."

"Ahhhhh."

—and then make a left turn and continue on over the rooftops till he came to the middle of the block somewhere. Long before then, on a clear moonlit night like tonight, he'd have seen the sniper. The trick was to make sure the sniper didn't see *him*.

Or his new friend, Chen, who was now behind him and staying very close as he made his way across the roof toward—

"I see nobody," Chen said.

"Give it time," Michael whispered. "And keep it down."

The snow had drifted some four feet high in places. It was almost impossible to tell where one rooftop ended and the next began. He discovered the first parapet only by banging into it. He climbed over it, Chen close behind him, and was working his way laboriously through the snow toward the corner where the buildings joined at a right angle when he saw up ahead—

He signaled with his hand, palm down and patting the air.

Chen got the meaning at once, and dropped immediately flat to the snow.

Michael raised his head.

There.

He squinted into the distance. Someone in black. Crouching behind the parapet facing the street. Rifle in his hands.

"Stay here," he whispered to Chen.

Chen nodded.

Michael began creeping forward.

He did not want to kill anyone. He had Crandall's .32 in his right hand and Frankie Zeppelin's .45 in the left-hand pocket of his bomber jacket, but he did not want to use either of those guns to kill anyone. He'd already been accused of killing *one* person, and he did not want to add to that list the *actual* murder of yet another person. It was too bad, of course, that the person lying on the roof up ahead was armed with a rifle he'd already fired at Michael. Because if that person wanted to kill him, as seemed to be the case, then he certainly wasn't going to put down his rifle and come along like a nice little boy. In which case Michael might very well have to shoot him. Perhaps kill him. The way he'd killed people in Vietnam, where it hadn't seemed to matter much. Kill or be killed. Like tonight. Maybe.

He suddenly wondered why this person wanted him dead.

Crawling across the snow—closer and closer, keeping his eyes on the man as he advanced steadily toward him, ready to fire if he had to, if he was spotted, if the man turned that rifle on him—the question assumed paramount importance in his mind.

Why does this person want to kill me?

And then another question followed on its heels, so fierce in its intensity that it stopped Michael dead in his tracks.

Who is the person they've already killed?

The corpse wasn't Crandall's, that was for sure, even though Crandall's identification had been found on it.

But there *was* a corpse, there was no mistake about that, the police of the Seventh Precinct had found a dead man in the car Michael had rented, so who was that man?

Maybe the man in black over there would have the answers to *both* questions.

Michael began moving toward him again.

He could see the man clearly in the moonlight now. Forty yards away from him now. Black watch cap. Black leather jacket. Black jeans. Black boots. Black gloves. Crouched behind the parapet facing the street, hunched over a rifle, Michael couldn't tell what kind at this distance. Telescopic sight on it.

The man suddenly got to his feet.

Michael froze.

In an instant, the man would spot him, and turn the rifle on him.

In an instant, Michael would have to shoot him.

But no, the man—

Huh?

The man was taking the telescopic sight off the rifle. He was putting the rifle and the scope into a gun case. He was snapping the case shut. He was, for Christ's sake, quitting! Giving the whole thing up as a botched job!

He rested the gun case against the parapet. Angled it against the parapet so that the wider butt end of the case was on the snow, the muzzle end up. He reached into his jacket pocket. Took out a package of cigarettes. Lighted one. Nice moonlit night, might as well enjoy a cigarette here on the rooftops overlooking downtown New York. His back to Michael. Looking out over the lights of the city. Enjoying his little smoke. So he'd bungled the job, so what? Plenty of time to get the dumb orange-grower later on.

Unless the dumb orange-grower had something to say about it.

It was not easy moving across the snow-covered roof. Silence was the only advantage the snow gave Michael. He glanced behind him once to make sure Chen was still glued in place and out of sight. He saw no sign of the fat little Chinese. At the parapet, the man in black was still enjoying his moonlight

smoke, his back to Michael, one foot on the parapet, knee bent, elbow on the knee. Not five feet
separated them now. Michael hoped the cigarette
was a king-sized one.

The man suddenly flipped the cigarette over the
edge of the roof.

And reached for the gun case.

And was starting to turn when Michael leaped
on him.

He caught the man from behind, yanking at the
collar of his jacket, trying to pull him over backward onto the snow, but he was too fast and too
slippery for Michael. He turned, saw the gun in
Michael's hand, knew that his own weapon was
already cased and essentially useless, and used
his knee instead, exactly the way Michael had used
his knee on Charlie Wong last night, going for
the money but coming up a little short, catching
Michael on the upper thigh instead of the groin,
and then looking utterly surprised when Michael
threw a punch at him instead of firing his gun.

Michael went straight for the nose, the way he'd
gone for Charlie Wong's nose yesterday, because a
hit on the nose hurt more than a hit anyplace else,
even sharks didn't like to get hit on their noses,
ask any shark. The man all in black looked like
a sixteen-year-old kid up close, but Michael had
killed fourteen-year-old Vietnamese soldiers and
this kid's age didn't mean a damn to him, the
only thing that mattered was that he'd tried to
kill Michael not twenty minutes ago. Peachfuzz
oval face, slitted blue eyes, a very delicate Michael
Jackson nose, which Michael figured wouldn't look
so delicate after he made it bleed, which was another nice thing about going for the nose. Noses bled

easily, whereas if you hit a guy on the jaw, for example, with the same power behind the punch, he wouldn't bleed at all.

The kid slipped the punch.

Ducked low and to the side and slipped it.

Michael's momentum almost caused him to fall.

He grabbed for the kid, trying to keep his balance, clutched for the kid's shoulders, and that was when the kid got him good, right in the balls this time, square on. Michael dropped the .32. Caught his breath in pain. The kid was turning, the kid was starting to run for the door of the roof. Michael reached out for him, clutched for his jacket, his head, anything, caught the black watch cap instead, felt it pulling free in his hands, and the kid was off and loping through the thick snow like an antelope.

Michael fell to his knees in pain.

Grabbed for his balls.

Moaned.

Did not even try to find the .32 where it had sunk below the snow some two feet away from him.

Did not even try to reach for the .45 in his jacket pocket.

The person running away from him across the rooftop was not Helen Parrish.

Nor was she Jessica Wales.

But she was a tall, long-legged, slender woman with blonde hair that glistened like gold in the silvery moonlight now that it was no longer contained by the black watch cap Michael still clutched in his hands close to his balls.

Maybe he didn't try shooting her because he was in such pain himself.

Or maybe he'd shot and killed too many women.

In Vietnam.
Where anyone in black pajamas was Charlie.
The roof door slammed shut behind her.
And he was alone in pain in the moonlight.

12

"**A**re you sure she was blonde?" Connie asked.

She was asking about Helen Parrish.

"Yes, she was blonde," Michael said.

"But Charlie's daughter has *dark* hair."

"She's the same person, believe me."

They were driving toward the address in Charlie Nichols's book. Judy Jordan's address. Judy Jordan who was also Helen Parrish whose dear dead daddy was Charlie Nichols. In the bar last night, Helen Parrish had told him she was thirty-two years old. Which was about right if the picture in Charlie's study had been taken fifteen years ago and if she'd been seventeen at the time.

It was very cold outside, driving alfresco this way. The dashboard clock wasn't working, which came as no surprise in a convertible with a broken top-mechanism. Michael waited to look at his watch until they stopped for a traffic light on a corner under a street lamp. It was almost ten o'clock.

He was very eager to see Miss Helen Parrish again.

The *fake* Miss Parrish, who was in reality—

Well, that wasn't necessarily true.

It was possible that Judy Jordan was now married, although in that bar last night Helen Parrish had told him she wasn't married, wasn't divorced, she was just single. Well, she'd told him a lot of things. But if she *was* married, and if Helen Parrish was indeed her real name now, which she'd have been crazy to have given him, then her maiden name *could* have been Judy Jordan, the girl with the long brown—

But no.

Charlie Nichols was her father.

Isn't that what she'd written on the photo?

To My Dear Daddy.

Then why had she signed her name Judy Jordan?

"What I'd like to know," Connie said, "is if Judy Jordan is Helen Parrish, then how come she's not Judy Nichols if Charlie Nichols is or was her father?"

"I love you," Michael said, and kissed her fiercely.

The Amalgamated Dwellings, Inc., were cooperative apartments at 504 Grand Street, but the entrance to the complex was around the corner on a street called Abraham Kazan, no relation. You went down a series of low brick steps and into an interior courtyard that might have been a castle keep in England, with arches and what looked like turrets and a snow-covered little park with shrubs and trees and a fountain frozen silent by the cold. The lettered buildings—A, B, C, and so on—were clustered around this secret enclave. Judy Jordan lived in E. The name on the mailbox downstairs was J. Jordan.

"Women who do that are dumb," Connie said. "Using an initial instead of a name. You do that, and a rapist knows right off it's a woman living alone. You can bet I don't have C. Kee on *my* mailbox."

"What *do* you have?"

"Charlie Kee."

"That's a very common name in this city," Michael said. "Charlie."

"Which is why I put it on my mailbox," Connie said, and nodded.

"Why?"

"So a rapist would think it was a common man named Charlie Kee up there."

"How about the postman?"

"Mr. Di Angelo? A rapist? Don't be ridiculous!"

"I mean, how will he know where to deliver mail addressed to Connie Kee?"

"That's *his* worry," Connie said.

Michael looked at the name on the mailbox again. J. Jordan.

"I'll go up alone," he said. "You go back to the car."

"If this blonde is as beautiful as you say she is . . ."

"She may also be dangerous."

"I'll bet."

"Connie, please go wait in the car for me, okay?"

"I'll give you ten minutes," she said. "If you're not back by then, I'm coming up after you."

"Okay. Good."

He kissed her swiftly.

"I still think I ought to go with you," she said.

But she was already walking out of the courtyard.

Michael pressed the button for Judy Jordan's apartment.

"Yes?" a woman's voice said.

He could not tell whether the voice was Helen Parrish's or not. As a matter of fact, he'd completely forgotten what Helen Parrish had sounded like.

"Miss Jordan?" he said.

"Yes?"

"Charlie Nichols sent me," he said.

"Look," she said, "this is an inconvenient time. I was just dressing to . . ."

"I'd like to talk to you, Miss Jordan, if . . ."

"Oh, well, all right, come on up," she said, and buzzed him in.

He climbed to the third floor, found her apartment just to the left of the stairwell, and was about to ring the bell set in the doorjamb when he hesitated.

If Judy Jordan did, in fact, turn out to be Helen Parrish, or vice versa, then the woman inside this apartment was the person who'd set the whole scheme in motion, the MacGuffin as she might be called in an Alfred Hitchcock film. Was he going to simply knock on the door and wait for the MacGuffin to answer it, perhaps to do him more harm than she'd already done? Michael did not think that was such a good idea. He reached into the right-hand pocket of his new bomber jacket, and took out the .32 he had appropriated from Arthur Crandall. He flipped the gun butt-side up, and rapped it against the door. Twice. Rap. Rap. And listened.

"Who is it?" a woman said. Same voice that had

come from the speaker downstairs.

"Me," he said.

"Who's me?"

"I told you. Charlie sent me."

"If it's about the money, I still haven't got it," the woman said from somewhere just inside the door now. There was a peep-hole set in the door at eye level. She was probably looking out at him. He still couldn't tell whether the voice was Helen Parrish's.

"I'd like to talk to you, if I may," he said, ducking his chin, trying to hide his face so that if this *was* Helen Parrish looking out at him, she wouldn't get such a good look.

"Just a minute," she said. "I'm still half-naked."

He wondered if this really was Helen Parrish, half-naked inside there. He thought back to the beginning of their relationship together, their gentle, easy conversation, the way they'd held hands, the way they'd looked deep into each other's eyes. He thought what a shame it was that she'd turned out to be a MacGuffin but maybe all beautiful women turned into MacGuffins sooner or later. He certainly hoped that wouldn't be the case with Connie.

He looked at his watch.

What the hell was taking her so long in there?

He rapped on the door with the gun butt again.

Three times.

Rap. Rap. Rap.

"Miss Jordan?" he called.

No answer.

"Miss . . ."

"Put your hands up, Mr. Barnes."

A man's voice.

Behind him.

"Up!" the man said. "Now!"

The thing in Michael's back felt very much like the muzzle of a gun.

Michael raised his hands over his head, the .32 in his right hand. The bandaged left arm hurt when he raised it. He almost said Ouch.

"Just let the gun fall out of your hand," the man said. "Just open your hand and drop the gun."

He opened his hand. The gun fell out of it. Dropped to the floor. Hit the floor with a solid *thwunk*.

"Thank you," the man said. "Now stand still, please."

Kneeling to pick up the gun now, Michael supposed. There was a small scraping sound as it came up off the tile floor. A hand began patting him down. All his pants pockets. Then the right-hand pocket of the jacket, and then—

"Well, well, another one," the man said.

Frankie Zeppelin's .45 came out of Michael's pocket.

"Mr. Barnes?" the man said.

And hit him on the back of the head with at least one of the guns.

He heard voices.

A man's voice. A woman's voice.

" . . . blow the whole thing," the man said.

" . . . other choice, do you?"

He opened his eyes.

A tin ceiling.

The shrink he had gone to in Boston had an office with a tin ceiling. Michael used to lie on his couch and look up at all the curlicues in his tin ceiling. He was not on a couch now. He was on a bed. An unmade bed. The bed smelled as if someone had peed in it. He wondered if it was a child's bed. The bed had a metal footboard, which he could see by lifting his head. Wrought iron painted white. He was spread-eagled on the bed with his ankles tied to the footboard and his arms up over his head and tied to the headboard, which was also wrought iron painted white.

He had never seen this room in his life.

The room looked like the sort he imagined you'd find in any cheap hotel that catered to hookers and dope dealers. He figured this had to be a drug plot. Otherwise why would a man who'd known he was Michael Barnes—or at least *Mr.* Barnes— have hit him on the head with his own gun and then tied him to a bed in what was truly a very shitty room? A drug plot for sure. Paint peeling off the walls. A pile of dirty laundry in one corner of the room. No curtain or shade on the window leading to the fire escape. And—hanging crookedly on the wall beside the window—a framed and faded print of an Indian sitting on a spotted pony. Michael was really very surprised and disappointed by this totally shitty drug-plot room because the building itself had looked so nice from the street and the hallways had been so neat and clean, which proved you couldn't always judge a book by its cover.

He lifted his head again.

A closed door. The voices beyond it.

" . . . in a garbage can someplace," the woman said.

" . . . like behind a McDonald's."

" . . . drive the cops nuts."

Three people in that other room. Two men and a woman. None of them sounded like anyone he'd ever met. All three of them were laughing now.

They thought this would be comical. Driving the cops nuts.

"Or kill him and just leave him *here*," one of the men said. "In Ju Ju's bed."

They all thought this would be even more comical. Killing him and leaving him here in Ju Ju's bed. Was Ju Ju's bed the one he was tied to? The one that stank of piss? Was Ju Ju a cutesy-poo name for Judy Jordan? Was this, in fact, Judy Jordan's bedroom? Was Judy Jordan a bed-wetter? There was hysterical laughter in the other room now. It was contagious. Michael almost laughed himself. He had to stifle his laughter.

Michael wondered who Ju Ju was.

He hated movies with casts of thousands.

"We'd better wait till Mama gets here," the woman said.

Mama again.

The *woman's* mother?

Or did *everybody* call her Mama?

Maybe Connie was right. Maybe Mama was a big, fat lady who everyone—

Connie!

She'd told him if he wasn't back in ten minutes she'd come up and get him. How much time had gone by since he'd left her down there on the ground floor? Five minutes to climb to the third floor, another three minutes while he'd waited in the hallway for the naked woman to put on her—

The doorbell rang.

Oh, Jesus, he thought. Connie!

Or maybe Mama.

Either way, that ringing doorbell could only mean more trouble.

Because if the person doing the ringing was

Connie, they would hit her on the head and then tie her up alongside him on the bed.

And then when Mama finally arrived, it would be so long to both of them. Shoot them both and leave them in Ju Ju's bed, ha ha. Or else shoot them and drop them in a garbage can behind McDonald's, which would be almost as amusing. Michael found neither choice acceptable. So he hoped against hope that it was not Connie ringing that doorbell. Because if they were going to shoot anyone at all, he much preferred it to be himself alone, leave Connie out of this entirely. The doorbell kept ringing. He began actively wishing that one of them would go answer the door and it would be big, fat Mama standing there, Hi, kids, it's me.

"Who is it?" one of the men yelled.

"Abruzzi Pizzeria," someone yelled back.

Michael listened.

Someone was coming into the apartment.

"You order a large pizza?"

A delivery boy.

"That's right."

The woman. Obviously the one who'd placed the order.

"Half anchovies, half pepperoni?"

"Right."

"Three Cokes?"

"Three Cokes, right."

"Here's the napkins, that comes to thirteen dollars and twenty-one cents."

"That sounds like a lot," one of the men said.

"How do you figure it's a lot?" the delivery boy asked.

"For a pizza and three lousy Cokes? Thirteen bucks and change?"

"Yeah, but it's a large with anchovies and pepperoni."

"Only *half* anchovies and *half* pepperoni."

"Which costs nine dollars and ninety-five cents. For the large with the anchovies and pepperoni."

"So how much are the Cokes?"

"Seventy-five cents each."

"That sounds high, too."

Cheap bastard, Michael thought.

"How do you figure that's high?" the delivery boy asked.

"For a lousy Coke? Seventy-five cents?"

"Yeah, but these are twelve-ounce Cokes."

"That's still high. That's six cents and change for an *ounce!*"

"Yeah, but that's what it *costs* an ounce," the delivery boy said.

"That's very high for an ounce of Coke."

"Yeah, but that's what it costs. Seventy-five cents for twelve ounces."

"So how do you get thirteen dollars and twenty-one cents?"

"There's an eight and a quarter percent tax. See it here on the bill? A dollar is the tax. So if you add a dollar to the nine ninety-five for the pizza and the two and a quarter for the Cokes, you get thirteen twenty-one. See it here?"

"Who added this?"

"The cashier."

"What's her name?"

"Marie. Why?"

"She's a penny off."

"What do you mean?"

"You see this here? Add it yourself. Nine ninety-five for the pizza, two twenty-five for the Cokes, and a dollar for the tax is thirteen dollars and *twenty* cents, not thirteen dollars and twenty-*one* cents."

"Gee," the delivery boy said.

"Tell Marie."

"I will."

Cheap bastard, Michael thought again.

"Here's fifty bucks," the man said. "Keep the change."

Michael heard the door opening and closing again.

The sudden aroma of cheese and garlic and tomatoes and pepperoni and anchovies wafted into the room where he was tied to the bed.

In that moment, he wanted nothing more from life than a slice of pizza.

If they told him they would kill him the moment Mama got here, his last request would be a slice of pizza.

"This is very good pizza," the woman said.

A rap sounded at the window.

He turned his head sharply.

A man wearing a black silk handkerchief over his nose and down to his chin was standing on the fire escape. He put his forefinger to where his lips would have been under the handkerchief, signaling Michael to keep quiet.

Michael looked at him.

The man was wearing a black cap to match the black handkerchief. And a black jacket bristling with little chrome studs. In keeping with his attire, the man himself was black, or at least what was nowadays *called* black even though his exposed hands were certainly not the color of his clothing. His hands were, in fact, the color of Colombian coffee.

The man hefted something onto the windowsill. A black satchel.

He opened the satchel and took out some kind of black tool.

Terrific, Michael thought. A burglar.

In the other room, they began talking about pizza.

One of the men maintained that pizza with a thin crust was the best kind. The woman said she preferred her pizza with a thick crust. The other man said extra cheese was the secret. They all agreed that extra cheese was desirable on a pizza.

Michael was dying of hunger.

The black man was working on the window with the black tool, which Michael surmised was a jimmy.

"When we finish this pizza here," one of the men said, "I think we ought to do him. Whether Mama's here or not."

Michael guessed they were talking about him.

About doing *him*.

"Anchovies I don't find too terrific on a pizza," the woman said.

"Me, neither, Alice," the other man said.

Alice.

The woman's name was Alice.

"They're too salty," she said.

"They overpower all the other ingredients," the man said, agreeing.

"Because the longer this man stays alive, the bigger the threat he is," the first man said, making a reasonable case.

"I think we should wait for Mama," Alice said.

"It was Mama sent you after him the first time," the other man said.

"I know that, Larry."

Larry. Another county heard from.

"So if Mama wanted him dead at eight o'clock tonight," he said, "why should it be any different now?"

"Because now is ten-thirty and not eight o'clock," Alice said.

"Which, by the way, you fucked up," the first man said. "On the roof there."

"No, by the way, I *didn't* fuck up, I was *ambushed,* Silvio."

So Alice was the blonde who'd been firing from the roof.

"Which it don't matter," Silvio said, "so long as we do the job right *this* time."

"That's *still* saying I did it wrong *last* time," Alice said.

"All I know is what Mama told me. Barnes was down Benny's asking questions about Arthur Crandall. So Barnes had to go. So you got sent to do him and you *didn't* do him, which is why he's tied to the bed in there now and you're telling me we should wait for Mama, which I don't know why."

"Because I say so," Alice said flatly.

"And I say we do him and leave him here in Ju Ju's bed," Silvio said, and they all burst out laughing again.

They were silent for the next few minutes or so.

Eating.

"As far as I'm concerned," Alice said, "the best combination is sausage and peppers."

"On a pizza, you mean?" Larry asked.

"No, on a piano," Alice said. "*Certainly* on a pizza. We're *talking* about pizza, aren't we?"

"I thought you were talking about a sandwich," Larry said.

"If you don't mind," Silvio said, "*I'm* talking about let's finish the goddamn *pizza* here and *do* the man, okay?"

"A grinder, I thought you meant," Larry said. "A sausage and pepper grinder."

"No, a pizza," Alice said. "Half sausage, half pepper."

Michael was hoping the burglar would hurry up and open the window. Then maybe he could talk the man into untying the ropes. Before they finished their pizza and came in here to do him. But the burglar seemed pretty new at the job. He had put the first tool back into the satchel and he'd taken out another one, but he didn't seem to be having any better luck with the new one. Meanwhile, in the other room, the pizza seemed to be dwindling. Michael was happy it had been a large one to begin with.

"Who wants this last slice?" Alice asked.

"Go ahead, take it," Larry said.

"Hey, *wait* a minute," Silvio said, "don't be so fucking generous with *my* pizza, if you don't mind."

"If you want it, take it," Alice said.

"Go ahead, Silvio, take it," Larry said.

"If Alice wants it, she can have it," Silvio said.

"No, this slice is all anchovies," Alice said.

"That's why I don't want it," Silvio said.

"I thought you *did* want it," Alice said.

"No, I only said he shouldn't be giving it away so fast in *case* I wanted it."

"Well, I don't want it," Alice said. "It's all anchovies."

"I don't want it, either," Larry said.

"Then the hell with it," Silvio said. "Throw it in the garbage, and let's go do him."

No, Michael thought. *Somebody* eat it. Please.

"Well, if nobody wants it," Alice said, "I'll take it."

"In fact, let's split it," Larry said.

"Three ways," Silvio said.

The window opened a crack. Cold air rushed into the room. And what smelled like fish. The black man all in black pushed the window up higher, letting in more cold air and the very definite stink of fish. He climbed over the sill and came into the room. Came directly to the bed. Pulled the handkerchief off his face, leaned in close to Michael's ear, and whispered, "Connie sent me."

"Untie me," Michael whispered.

In the other room, Silvio said, "It's a sin to make good food go to waste."

"This is very hard to cut," Larry said.

"Hold it with the fork," Alice said.

The black man began untying the ropes. He was no better at untying than he was at jimmying. In the other room, they were silent now. Michael figured they were concentrating on slicing the slice of pizza into three even slices, which was probably more difficult than untying a man tied to a bed. He hoped. He wished they would say something in there. The silence was somehow ominous. Maybe they had *already* sliced the slice of pizza and already eaten it. Maybe they were at this very moment loading pistols instead of slicing—

"Listen," he whispered, "don't you have a *knife* in that satchel?"

"This'll only take a minute," the black man whispered.

He had finally untied the first wrist.

That left two ankles and a wrist to go.

"Get the ankles," Michael said. "I'll try the other wrist."

"Did you hear something just then?" Larry asked.

Silence.

Oh, Jesus, Michael thought.

"No," Silvio said. "What did you hear?"

"Like somebody talking," Larry said.

"Where?"

"I don't know. Like next door."

They all listened again.

The black man had untied Michael's left ankle and was now working on the right one. Michael was plucking at the knots in the rope holding his left wrist to the headboard. He figured that in about two minutes he would be a dead man.

"I *still* don't hear anything," Silvio said.

"Are you going to finish these Cokes, or what?" Alice asked.

"I'm done," Larry said.

"Me, too," Silvio said.

"Me, too," the black man whispered.

So was Michael.

He yanked his left hand free of the rope, swung his legs over the side of the bed, and went immediately to the window. The black man was right behind him. As they went out onto the fire escape, Michael heard Silvio saying, "Let's go do him."

The black man's name was Gregory Washington.

The name of the club was the Green Garter.

Gregory told him that this was where Connie had said she would meet them. He also told Michael that the club was sometimes known as the Green *Farter* because it attracted a very old clientele. Michael looked around the place and did not see anyone who looked older than thirty. But Gregory was only nineteen.

A lot of the women standing at the bar, or sitting in the booths or at the tables, seemed to be wearing only lingerie. Garter belts and panties and seamed silk stockings and teddies and negligees and stiletto-heeled shoes that made them look a lot like either the redheaded detective named O'Brien, who'd mistaken him for a cheap hold-up artist, or the redheaded hooker named Hannah, who'd mistaken him for the man in the Carvel commercials. Michael wondered if Frankie Zeppelin had yet found someone to kill Isadore Onions. He wondered whose thigh Isadore's girlfriend had her hand on now. He wondered if all the women in New York City walked around in their underwear at Christmastime.

"You have adorable buns," Gregory said. "Has anyone ever told you that?"

Which was when Michael began to suspect that both Gregory and the Green Garter were what you might call gay, and that all these underdressed women were in actuality men.

One of them winked at him.

"Oh, look," Gregory said. "Phyllis has her eye on you."

He sounded like Eddie Murphy doing his gay bit in *Beverly Hills Cop*. In fact, he even looked a little like a younger Eddie Murphy, if there *was* such a thing as a younger Eddie Murphy. It seemed to Michael that nowadays there were no male movie stars who were his age. All the male movie stars up there on the screen were twenty years old. Making love to stark-naked women who had to be at least in their thirties. The only twenty-year-old movie stars Michael believed were the ones in war movies because in Vietnam almost everybody was twenty years old or younger. Even the lieutenants were twenty years old. The only people who weren't twenty years old were sergeants.

Phyllis winked at him again.

Phyllis was wearing a blonde wig, a red silk blouse, and a green silk skirt with high-heeled pumps to match. Most of the people in the room, Michael noticed, were dressed in either red or green in honor of the yuletide season, except for the ones who were wearing swastikas and chains and jeans and black leather jackets bristling with metal spikes and studs. They looked tougher and meaner than any man Michael had ever seen in his life, but he guessed they were gay, too, otherwise what were they doing here?

Which was probably what Phyllis, who needed a shave, was wondering about him.

"What time did Connie say she'd be here?" he asked.

"Soon as she does what she has to do," Gregory said.

"What is it she has to do?" Michael asked.

"Find out who the corpse is."

"And how does she plan to do that?"

"At the Gouverneur Hospital morgue," Gregory said. "On Henry Street. 'Cause the corpse was found in the Seventh Precinct, and that's the only hospital in the Seventh, so she figured that's where they must've took it. She knows a man there works with the stiffs."

"So that's where she is now," Michael said.

"Lucky her," Gregory said, and grinned.

"Excuse me," Michael said, "but how do *you* fit into all this?"

"Oh, very comfortably," Gregory said, and looked around the room. "I been comin' here since it opened."

"I meant, how did you happen to get the job of rescuing me?"

"Oh. Connie asked me to climb on up there."

"Why you? Are you a burglar?"

"No, I'm a dancer."

"I still don't understand how Connie knew I was in trouble."

"Well, from what she told *me,* she was waiting outside the Amalgamated when she saw this man carrying you out of the building. Unconscious. You, not the man. So she followed his car to this warehouse near the Fulton Market. The *fish* market. On Fulton Street. And that's how come you're sitting here with me now, doll."

"Connie just ran into you, is that it? And asked you to . . ."

"No, she called me on the telephone."

"And you ran on over with your satchel . . ."

"I borrowed the satchel from my brother-in-law."

"Is he a dancer, too?"

"No, *he's* a burglar. But he's white, you wouldn't *'spect* him to have no rhythm."

"So Connie called you . . ."

"Right, and asked me to meet her at this warehouse, where she was waiting outside."

"How'd she know what apartment I was in?"

"It isn't an apartment building, it's a warehouse. She watched the elevator needle. And I went up the fire escape to the fifth floor, where I found you, aren't you glad?"

"You mean to tell me Connie just picked up the telephone, and you ran on down to meet her?"

"I owe her," Gregory said, and left it at that.

"Well, I'm grateful to you."

"*How* grateful?" Gregory said, and was putting his hand on Michael's thigh when Phyllis walked over.

"Won't you introduce me, Greg?" she said.

"Michael, this is Phyllis," Gregory said, and squeezed Michael just above the knee.

"Care to dance, Michael?"

Michael figured he could do worse.

"Do you come here often?" Phyllis asked.

She was a very good dancer.

The jukebox was playing "It Happened in Monterey." Frank Sinatra was singing.

"My first time," Michael said.

"You have adorable buns," Phyllis said. "Has anyone ever told you that?"

"Yes, as a matter of fact," Michael said.

"Oh my, she's modest as well," Phyllis said.

Her beard was scratching against Michael's cheek.

"Are you married?" Phyllis asked.

"Divorced," he said.

"Oh, good," Phyllis said.

"But very serious about someone," Michael said quickly.

"Oh, drat," Phyllis said.

"May I cut in, please?" someone asked.

The someone was Connie.

"I said the Green *Garden*," she said.

13

The three of them sat in a booth.

Connie was irritated because Gregory had taken Michael to the Green Garter instead of the Green Garden, which was a health food place on Orchard Street, and a hell of a lot closer to Gouverneur Hospital than Greenwich Avenue was.

"It all gets down to a matter of precincts," she said. "The Sixth Precinct is *not* the Seventh Precinct. If I'd wanted the Green *Garter* in the *Sixth* Precinct, I wouldn't have picked the Green *Garden* in the *Seventh* Precinct."

"I'm contrite," Gregory said.

He wasn't being sarcastic, he really did sound enormously sorry for his error. Moreover, as Michael now reminded Connie, he was the one who'd charged to the rescue when—

"Well, not exactly *charged*," Gregory said modestly.

"But Michael's right," Connie said. "I'm sorry I yelled at you."

"It's the stink of the morgue," Gregory said. "Have you ever been inside a morgue?" he asked Michael.

"Never."

"About two years ago," Gregory said, "a friend of mine OD'd on heroin, and I had to go to the morgue to identify him. It truly does stink in there. It can give you a headache in there. It can also make you very anxious. All those dead people stacked up on drawers that slide out."

"Don't remind me," Connie said.

Michael was thinking that at times the stench in Vietnam had been unbearable. He could not imagine any morgue in the world stinking more than a jungle clearing littered with three-day-old bodies.

"He didn't even *look* like Crandall," Connie said.

"You saw him?" Michael asked.

"Yes. A tall, thin man. Pockmarked face. Tattoo on his arm."

"White?"

"Yes. But that's the only resemblance."

"How old was he?"

"My friend at the morgue guessed maybe forty, forty-five."

"What's his name?"

"Max Feinstein. I know him from when he was driving an ambulance for . . ."

"No, I mean the corpse."

"Oh. Julian Rainey. They finally identified him from his fingerprints. He has a record that goes back forever."

"Yes, he's a dealer," Gregory said, nodding.

"*Was* a dealer," Connie corrected. "You mean you *know* him?"

"Oh, yes, he works this entire downtown area."

"*Used* to work," Connie corrected.

A drug plot, Michael thought. I knew it.

"A red heart, am I right?" Gregory said. "The tattoo?"

"Yes," Connie said.

"On his left arm."

"The left arm, yes."

"And in the heart it says Ju Ju, am I right?"

"I don't know what it said in the heart."

"Ju Ju. That's his nickname."

"*Was* his nickname," Connie corrected.

Michael was looking at both of them.

"I think we have to go back to that warehouse," he said.

"Without me," Gregory said.

It was close to midnight when they got there.

Christmas was almost gone.

Not a light showed in the entire building.

"That's because nobody lives here," Connie explained. "This is a *real* warehouse, it's not like the buildings they're renting for lofts all over town. People actually store things here."

"What do you suppose Ju Ju was storing here?" Michael asked.

"Take a wild guess," Connie said.

Michael looked up at the front of the building. It was seven stories high, with five evenly spaced windows on each floor. From the fifth floor down, huge white letters below the windows announced the building's original intent, stating its past like a huge poster that faced the East River:

> **WAREHOUSE**
> Wholesale-Retail
> **OFFICE FURNITURE**
> Broad Street Showrooms
> **NEW YORK—MIAMI—LOS ANGELES**

The entire area smelled of fish.

"We're just a few blocks from the market," Connie said.

The metal entrance door was locked.

"It was open earlier tonight," she said. "It's on the fifth floor. I watched the needle."

They were both getting very good at using fire escapes. Michael figured that if ever they were trapped in a burning building together, they'd know how to get out of it in a minute. He supposed it was good to know such things. On the fifth floor, they found the window Gregory had earlier jimmied open. It was closed now. Michael guessed the three pizza-eaters had closed it after they'd come into the room and found only Ju Ju's bed with no one in it. He hoped the pizza-eaters were not still here. He did not think they were; not a light was burning anywhere inside. But you never could tell; in Vietnam, Charlie could see in the dark.

He eased the window open.

Listened.

Not a sound.

He climbed in over the sill, and then helped Connie into the room.

They waited, eyes adjusting to the darkness, moonlight slowly giving shapes to objects . . .

First the bed with its white wrought-iron head-board and footboard . . .

Then the bundle of clothes in the corner . . .

And then the Indian sitting his spotted pony.

Nothing else.

"I think somebody peed in this room," Connie whispered.

It was not truly a *room*, Michael now realized, but merely a space defined by a partition. The door to the other side of the partition was slightly ajar. No light beyond it. He went to the door and listened. He heard nothing. He nodded to Connie and opened the door wider. Together they moved into the space beyond the partition. And waited again while their eyes adjusted to what seemed a deeper blackness but only because of its vastness. When Michael felt certain they were alone, he groped along the wall for a switch, found one, and turned on the lights.

If he'd expected a cocaine factory, he was disappointed.

From the evidence here on this side of the partition, you would never have guessed that Ju Ju Rainey was a drug dealer. For here was a department store of the first order, stocked with television sets and cameras, record players and home computers, typewriters and silverware, fur coats and jewelry, cellular telephones—

"A fence," Connie said. "Lots of dealers accept goods in exchange for dope."

A drug plot after all, Michael thought.

There were windows on the wall facing the street. Distant traffic lights below tinted the glass alternately red and green. It was still Christmas, but just barely. The wall opposite the windows was lined with clocks. They ticked in concert like a conglomerate time bomb about to explode. Grandfather clocks ticking and tocking and swinging their pendulums, smaller clocks on shelves whispering their ticks into the vast silent room.

On a table near the metal entrance door on the right-angled wall, there was a tomato-stained and empty pizza carton and three empty Coke bottles. A green metal file cabinet was on the wall near an open door that led to the toilet. On the other side of the door, there was a huge black safe with the word MOSLER stamped on its front.

Michael went to the file cabinet and pulled open the top drawer. A glance at one of the folders told him that this was where Ju Ju Rainey kept his inventory records. A methodical receiver of stolen goods. The bottom drawer was locked.

"Do you know how to do something like that?" Connie asked.

"Like what?"

"Like pick a lock?"

"No," Michael said.

"Let's see if anybody brought in a set of tools," Connie said.

They began rummaging through the stolen goods as if they were at a tag sale. It was sort of nice. Shopping this way, you could forget that dead bodies were involved. Like that day in the jungle. With the baby. Not a thought of danger, Charlie was miles and miles away. Just strolling in the jungle. Birds twittering in the treetops. Andrew smoking a cigarette, the baby suddenly—

He turned off all thoughts of the baby.

Click.

Snapped them off.

Connie had stopped at a pipe rack from which hung at least a hundred fur coats.

The baby crying.

Click.

"This is gorgeous," Connie said.

She was looking at a long red fox coat.

Michael moved away from her, deeper into what looked like a smaller version of the *Citizen Kane* storehouse. There was a makeshift counter—sawhorses and planks—covered entirely with Walkman radios. There had to be at least a thousand Walkman radios on that counter. All sizes and all colors. Michael wondered if all those radios had come from a single industrious thief. Or had a thousand less ambitious thieves each stolen one radio? Another counter was covered entirely with books. It looked like a counter in a bookshop. Very big and important books like *Warday* and *Women's Work* and *Whirlwind* were piled high on the counter. Michael could easily understand why someone would want to steal these precious books and why Ju Ju had been willing to take them in trade for dope. He'd probably planned to resell them later to a bookseller who had a blanket on the sidewalk outside Saks Fifth Avenue.

Connie was lingering at the fur-coat rack. In fact, she was now trying *on* one of the coats, which he hoped she didn't plan to steal. The temptation to steal something from a thief was, in fact, overwhelming. The goods, after all, were not the thief's. The thief, therefore, could not rightfully or even righteously claim that anything of his had been stolen, since the stolen goods had already been stolen from someone else. Moreover, the

transaction by which the thief had come into possession of the property was in itself an illegal
one, the barter of stolen goods for controlled substances, and the thief could expect no mercy on
that count. Especially if he was dead, which Ju
Ju Rainey happened to be. On the other hand,
if it was okay to steal stolen goods from a dead
thief, then maybe it was also okay to have *caused*
that thief's death, and to have put another man's
identification on his corpse, and to have laid the
blame on a third person entirely, which third person happened to be Michael himself. It was all a
matter of morality, he guessed.

The coat Connie was trying on happened to be
a very dark and luxuriant ankle-length sable.

The coat was screaming, "Steal Me, Steal Me!"

He hoped she wouldn't.

The baby screaming.

Click.

"I would love a coat like this," Connie said.

Michael was at a counter covered with musical
instruments now. There were violins and violas
and cellos and bass fiddles and even lyres. There
were piccolos and oboes and saxophones and
clarinets and English horns and bassoons and
flutes. There was an organ. There were acous-
tic guitars and electric guitars and banjos and
mandolins and a pedal steel guitar and a syn-
thesizer and a sitar and an Appalachian dul-
cimer. There was a set of drums. And three
bagpipes. And fourteen harmonicas and a book
called *How to Play Jazz Harp*, which had wandered over from the book display across the
room. There were trumpets and Sousaphones
and tubas and French horns and cornets and bu-

gles and seventy-six trombones. Michael guessed it was profitable to steal musical instruments.

The next counter was covered with tools. More tools than he had ever seen in one place in his entire lifetime. He guessed it was profitable to steal tools, too. On the other hand, maybe it was profitable to steal *anything*. There were hammers and hatchets and mallets and mauls. There were pliers and wrenches and handsaws and drills. There were planes and rasps and chisels and files. There were circular saws and scroll saws and electric sanders and electric chain saws. Michael picked up one of the electric hand drills and a small plastic case with bits in it, and carried them to where Connie was now standing at a table covered with weapons.

"Look at all these guns," she said.

"Yes," he said.

There were revolvers and automatic pistols of every size and caliber and make. Smith & Wesson, Colt, Browning, Walther, Ruger, Harrington & Richardson, Hi-Standard, Iver Johnson, you name it, you had it. There were rifles and shotguns, too— Remington, and Winchester, and Mossberg, and Marlin, and Savage, Stevens & Fox. And there were several military weapons as well, guns Michael recognized as AK-47 assault rifles and AR-15 semiautomatics. Rambo would have felt right at home at this counter. Rambo could have picked up an entire attack arsenal at this counter.

"I think we can drill out the lock with this," Michael said.

"Is it a crime to steal stolen goods?" Connie asked.

"Yes," he said.

"Is what I thought," she said.

He walked past her to where the filing cabinet stood against the wall. He opened the little plastic case, and was searching for a bit he hoped would tear through the metal lock on the cabinet, when Connie joined him, her hands in the pockets of the short black car coat. Michael chose his bit, fitted it into the chuck collar, tightened the collar with a chuck key, found a wall outlet near the cabinet, knelt to plug in the drill, tested it to see if he had power, and then went back to the cabinet. Connie was still standing there with her hands in her pockets. He studied the lock for a moment, and got to work.

The bit snarled into the metal.

There was a high whining sound.

Baby over there, Andrew was saying.

Where?

Over there. Crying.

Curls of metal spun out from behind the bit.

The lock disintegrated.

Michael yanked open the drawer.

They were looking in at an open shoe box containing two little plastic vials of crack.

"Must've used all his dope to pay for the merchandise in here," Michael said.

"Either that, or there's *more* dope someplace else."

"Like where?"

"Like where would *you* keep a whole bunch of crack?"

Michael looked at the safe.

"Do you know how to do something like that?" Connie asked.

"No," Michael said.

"I didn't think so."

"But I have a question."

"Yes?"

"Would you lock a file drawer that had nothing but two vials of crack in it?"

Connie looked at him.

"Neither would I," he said.

He knelt beside the file cabinet, lifted the shoe box, turned it upside down, and looked at it. Nothing. He ran his hands along the bottom and back of the drawer, and then moved them forward along each side of the drawer to the front of it, and then felt along the back of the front panel and—

"Here it is," he said.

He bent over the drawer and looked into it.

Scotch-taped to the back of the panel was a slip of paper. It was fastened upside down, so that the writing on it could be read easily from above. It read:

> 4 L 28
> 3 R 73
> 2 L 35
> Slow R Open

"You're so smart," Connie said. "Do you know it's almost midnight?"

"Is it?"

"Only a minute left."

He looked at his watch.

"Yes," he said.

"And then Christmas will be gone. Forty seconds, actually."

"Yes."

"Do you remember what we did last night at this time?"

"I remember."

"I think we should do it again, don't you?" she said, and put her arms around his neck. "Make it a tradition."

Their lips met.

And even as bells had sounded when they'd kissed last night in Crandall's office, and even as bells had sounded when Michael left the Mazeltov All-Nite Deli, so did bells sound now. This time, however, the bells were not on a ringing telephone, and they weren't attached to a trip mechanism on an emergency door, they were instead the bells and gongs and chimes on the multitude of stolen clocks that lined the wall opposite the windows. This was a symphony of bells. This was bells pealing out into the vastness of the warehouse, floating out over the rows and rows of stolen items, reverberating on the dust-laden air, enveloping Connie and Michael in layers and layers of shimmering sound where they stood in embrace alongside a stolen Apple IIe computer, their lips locked, bong bong went the bells, tinkle tinkle went the chimes, bing bang bong went every clock in the place, announcing the end of Christmas Day, heralding the twenty-sixth day of December, a bright new Thursday morning in a world of abundant riches, witness all the shiny new merchandise here in the late Ju Ju Rainey's storeroom. And suddenly the bells stopped. Not all at once since the clocks weren't in absolute synchronization; but trailing off instead, a bong clanking heavily, a chime chinging tinnily, a dissonant bing here, a reluctant tink there, and then stillness.

"It's Boxing Day, you know," she said.

"I didn't know," he said.

"Yes," she said. "The day after Christmas. It's called Boxing Day."

"I see."

"I know because it's celebrated in Hong Kong, which is still a British colony."

"Why is it called Boxing Day?"

"Because they have prizefights on that day. Throughout the entire British Empire."

"I see," he said.

They were still standing very close to each other. He wondered if anyone had ever made love to Connie on a counter bearing stolen Cuisinarts.

"Listen," she said.

He remembered that she had terrific ears.

"The elevator," she said. "Someone's using the elevator."

He listened.

He could hear the elevator whining up the shaft.

The baby sitting just off the trail.

Crying.

The elevator stopped.

He heard its doors opening.

Footsteps in the corridor now.

Voices just outside the metal entrance door to Ju Ju's bargain bazaar.

When you were outnumbered, you headed for the high ground. The highest ground here was the rack holding all those expensive fur coats. He took Connie's hand, and led her silently and swiftly across the room, moving past a table bearing a sextant, an outboard engine, an anchor, a compass, and a paddle, and then past another table upon which there were . . .

A key turning in the door lock.

. . . seven baseball bats, three gloves, a catcher's mitt and mask, a lacrosse stick, and a pair of running shoes . . .

Tumblers falling with a small, oiled click.

. . . and reached the end of the rack where a seal coat with a raccoon collar was hanging.

The door opened.

"Who left these lights on?" a woman said.

Michael knew that voice.

He could not see her from where he was hunched over behind what looked like a lynx jacket, but this was Alice the Pizza Maven, who was also the lady who owned the Mannlicher-Schoenauer carbine with its Kahle scope, which she'd fired from the rooftop at them earlier today—or yesterday, as it now was officially—which gun was now snug in its case in Connie's bedroom closet, which was where Michael now wished *he* was. Because the next voice he heard belonged to Silvio, who had earlier thought it would be hilarious to kill Michael and leave him either in Ju Ju's piss-stinking bed or else in a garbage can behind McDonald's. And the voice after that was Larry's, both men now vigorously denying that either of them had left the lights on.

"In which case," Alice wanted to know, "how come the lights *are* on?"

There was a dead silence.

Michael wondered if he and Connie should have gone to hide in the bathroom.

"Check out the toilet," Alice said.

He guessed it was good they hadn't gone to hide in the bathroom.

Silence.

The sound of metal rings scraping along a shower rod as the curtain was thrown back.

More silence.

"So?" Alice asked.

"Nobody in there."

"Check out the whole floor," Alice said.

And suddenly there were more voices.

A man said, "All this stuff has to go, huh?"

"All of it," Alice said.

"The piano, too?" a second man said. "'Cause we ain't piano movers, you know."

"That's good," Silvio said, "'cause it ain't a piano."

"Then what is it, it ain't a piano?"

"It's an organ."

"Take *this* organ," the man said.

"If you don't mind," Larry said, "there's a lady present here."

"So?"

"So stop grabbing your balls and telling us what's an organ."

"I'm telling you we ain't piano movers."

"And I'm telling you it's an organ."

"And I'm telling you take *this* organ."

"Just shoot him in the balls," Alice said calmly.

"Some lady," the man said, but presumably he let go of his balls.

A third man said, "Okay, where's all this stuff has to go?"

A fourth man said, "Look at this joint, willya? What's this, a discount store?"

A fifth man said, "You want this stuff boxed?"

"What's breakable," Alice said. "And wrapped, too."

"What's that?" the third man asked. "A *piano*?"

"I already told them," the second man said.

"'Cause we don't move pianos," the third man said.

"It's an organ," Silvio said, "and don't reach for your balls."

"My father used to play drums," the fifth man said.

The first man said, "Why don't Mama move in the daytime, like a normal human being?"

Larry said, "Whyn't you go take that up with Mama, okay?"

"No, thank you," the man said.

"Then get to work," Larry said.

"Where's that combo?" Alice asked somebody.

"I got it," Silvio said.

"If he was gonna give you the combo, anyway," Larry said, "why you suppose he wet the bed?"

They all began laughing.

Even the moving men.

"'Cause if you wet the bed," Silvio said, laughing, "then a person won't shoot you."

"It's a magic charm," Alice said, laughing. "You wet the bed, the bad guys'll go away."

"First time I ever had a man wet the bed before I shot him," Silvio said, still laughing.

"Give me the combo," Alice said.

"I tell you," one of the moving men said, "this wasn't Mama, I wouldn't go near that piano."

"You could get a hernia from that piano," another one of the men said.

"It's an *organ*," Silvio said, but his voice was muffled and Michael guessed he was standing at the safe with his back turned. From where Michael crouched behind the furs with Connie, he felt like Cary Grant in *Gunga Din,* the scene where they're hiding in the temple and all the lunatics are yelling "Kali!"

"Read it to me," Alice said.

"Four left to twenty-eight," Silvio said.

"Look at this, willya?" one of the moving men said. "Roller skates, ice skates, dart boards, a pool table . . ."

"I ain't lifting that pool table, I can tell you that."

"That's heavier than the piano."

"It's an organ," Silvio said over his shoulder. "Three right to seventy-three."

"What's *this* thing?"

"A toboggan."

"What do you do with it?"

"Two left to thirty-five," Silvio said.

"I never seen so much stuff in my life."

"And this is what's left *after* Christmas, don't forget."

"Slowly to the right till it opens," Silvio said.

Silence.

Then:

"Holy shit!"

This from Larry.

More silence.

"That's got to be at least a million dollars' worth of dope," Alice said.

Yep, Michael thought. A dope plot.

"I thought Mama said Ju Ju was only small-time," Silvio said.

"Mama was wrong," Larry said.

"Or lying," Alice said, and there was another silence.

A longer one this time. A contemplative one. A pregnant one. The silence of thieves considering whether another thief had screwed them. It was an interesting silence, laden with possibilities. Michael waited. Connie squeezed his hand. She had understood the silence, too.

"Maybe Mama didn't know there'd be so much stuff in the box," Larry said.

"Maybe," Alice said.

She did not sound convinced.

Silence again.

All three of them were trying to figure it out.

"Listen, we ain't touching that pool table," one of the moving men said. "There's slate in that table, it weighs a ton."

"Fine," Alice said.

"Damn straight," the moving man said.

Silence except for the sound of newspapers being crumpled, cartons being snapped open, work shoes moving across the floor, men grunting as they lifted heavy objects.

"We got paid," Larry said.

A shrug in his voice.

"But did we get paid *enough*?"

This from Alice.

"The deal was to deliver Ju Ju," Larry said. "That's what we done."

Trying to make peace.

But he was standing with the rest of them at that safe, and he was looking in at what Alice had described as at least a million dollars' worth of dope.

"That was the *original* deal," Larry said.

"The deal changed yesterday," Alice said.

"The deal changed to doing Barnes, too."

"And cleaning out Ju Ju's store."

"Was what the deal changed to."

"But did Mama know there'd be all this stuff in Ju Ju's box?"

They were all silent again.

"The answer is no," Alice said.

Silence.

"Because I'll tell you why."

Michael was extremely interested in hearing why.

"Because if *you* were Mama," Alice said, "would *you* trust the three of *us* with a million dollars' worth of dope?"

They all began laughing.

Michael nodded in agreement.

"Sure, laugh," one of the moving men said. "It ain't you three gonna get the hernia."

"What I think," Alice said, "I think the trucks can deliver all this fine merchandise to Mama . . ."

"As agreed," Silvio said.

"But *us* three will take what's in the box here, how does that sound to you?"

"It sounds only fair to me," Silvio said.

"More than," Larry said.

"But who left on the lights?" Alice asked.

14

Michael thought it was a bad idea to be standing here behind all these dead animal skins. He should have been standing at the table with the weapons instead. Because Alice and her two chums were now fanning out over the warehouse floor, earnestly trying to determine who had left the lights on.

He guessed this was going to be a process of elimination.

This was going to be Gee, it wasn't *us* who left the lights on, and it couldn't have been the moving men, so it had to have been someone else. And maybe the someone else is still in here. Like maybe hiding behind the counter over there, upon which were displayed six Tandberg FM tuners, three Nakamichi cassette decks, and a Denon direct-drive turntable.

A woman came around that counter now.

Alice.

For sure.

The same woman who'd been firing at them from the rooftop.

The long blonde hair and slitted blue eyes, the delicate Michael Jackson nose, the pale ivory oval of her face. In her hand, a gun that looked foreign. She could have been playing a Russian assassin in a James Bond movie. It was bad enough, however, that she was an American assassin in a real-life drama starring Michael Barnes and Connie—

It occurred to him that Connie was no longer at his side.

Before he had time to wonder how or when she'd disappeared, he saw a short, thickset man coming around the sleeve of a chinchilla coat hanging at the far end of the rack. Except for his broken nose, the man looked a lot like Tony the Bear Orso or Charlie Bonano, both of whom looked like Rocky's brother-in-law. He had a gun in his hand. Michael guessed this was Silvio.

"Hey!" Silvio yelled, if that's who he was, and Michael immediately slipped between a Siberian yellow weasel coat and a Persian lamb, brushing past the furs and through the rack to emerge on the opposite side where a tall, angular, craggy-faced blondish man who looked like Sterling Hayden in *The Godfather* was coming around the end of a table upon which was displayed an open coffin with no one in it.

Michael figured he himself would soon be displayed in that coffin, which was made of fine mahogany and lined with white silk and hung with bronze handles.

If the other one was Silvio, then this one was Larry.

So there was Silvio coming through the rack of furs farther up the line now, emerging between a Mexican ocelot and a Mongolian marmot, and here was Larry spotting Michael now and also shouting "Hey!" and here, too, was Alice coming around the home entertainment center display and seeing Michael, and grinning like an African lioness contemplating a warthog dinner. Michael figured this was it. The full deck had been dealt at last and there were no more aces in it.

"Freeze!" the voice said.

It sounded like Detective O'Brien.

But it was Connie.

Standing with a gun in each hand.

Behind Alice and Larry, who had probably heard that word a great many times in their separate careers and who did not move a muscle when they heard it now. Coming through the rack swathed in furs left and right, Silvio froze, too. Connie looked like the Dragon Lady. Cool and beautiful and deadly. Ready to blow away anyone who did not take her by overnight junk to Shanghai. The guns were only .22 caliber revolvers, but in her delicate hands they looked like big mother-loving cannons.

"Help us here!" Alice shouted to the moving men, but they, too, had seen the guns in Connie's hands and the look in her eyes, and they had heard the word "Freeze!" thundering like a Chinese curse into that echoing space, and when they'd realized that they themselves were not the ones being asked to freeze, they decided this might be a good time to get the hell out of here before someone asked them to move a piano. There was a rush toward the metal entrance door, now an exit door too narrow to accommodate the sudden traffic. The moving men piled into the doorway like Keystone Kops, wedging themselves there for an impossibly tangled moment, unraveling themselves, and then hurling themselves headlong into the corridor outside.

Larry shook his head in dismay when he heard the elevator starting. Still shaking his head, he dropped his gun to the floor and looked at his watch, probably wondering if Johnny Carson was still on. Silvio raised his hands over his head. He looked like a man who did not have to be told that Chinese people stuck bamboo under your fingernails. Especially Chinese women. Or maybe it was the Japanese who did that. Either way, he wanted nothing further to do with this entire enterprise.

Only Alice seemed undecided.

Michael had his doubts as well.

Which was why he was moving so swiftly toward Connie.

Because it was one thing to have a look on your face that said handling a gun was second nature to you and you'd as soon shoot a person as treat him to an ice cream cone, but it was another thing to be *holding* a gun as if you'd never had one in your hand before. Connie was holding those pistols the way Crandall had held the .32 last night. They were both amateurs. Michael recognized this because when it came to oranges or guns, he was a pro. But so was Alice. And in thirty seconds flat, she was going to recognize that Connie didn't know a trigger from a click sight. In fact, the knowledge was seeping into her eyes that very instant, and Michael knew he had to reach Connie and grab one of those guns from her before Alice made her play.

She moved sooner than he'd expected.

Didn't say a word.

Merely fired at Connie.

And missed.

And was sighting along the gun barrel to fire again when Michael realized this was not a time for dueling in the sun, this was a time for definitive action—like throwing himself at her. He flung himself sideways, hoping to knock her off balance and realizing an instant too late that he was rushing her with his bad side, rushing her with the bandaged shoulder and arm that had been injured by one of those Car 54, Seventh Precinct cops—where were they now, when he needed them? He let out a horrible yell, similar to the "Aiiii-eeeeee!" he'd screamed at Detective O'Brien all those years ago on Christmas Eve, but this one was involuntary in that the body contact with Alice sent arrows of pain shooting from his arm clear up into his skull. There was another gunshot, and he thought, *Oh, Jesus, no!* and then Alice screamed and he thought it was because his own scream had frightened her the way it had earlier frightened O'Brien. But his hands where he grabbed for Alice were suddenly sticky and wet, and he realized all at once that Connie had actually *fired* one of those guns, Connie had actually *shot* Alice, who was stumbling backward now as Michael stumbled forward. He said something like "Watch it," or "What shit," and Alice very *definitely* said, "What shit," and then both of them collapsed to the floor in a hurt and bewildered heap.

Connie was on them in an instant.

Legs widespread.

Both guns angled down at Alice's head.

"One move," she said.

"Don't get dramatic," Alice said, and tossed her gun onto the floor.

She was bleeding from the shoulder.

"It went off," Connie explained.

"I see that," Michael said.

"Remember when I asked you if it was a crime to steal stolen goods? That's when I stole them. From the table. Because he who gathers up his nuts need never leave his hole."

"If you don't mind," Larry said, "there's a lady present here."

"Get me a doctor," Alice said.

Michael wondered if Dr. Ling would make a house call all the way over here in the First Precinct.

"Who's Mama?" he asked.

"Go fuck yourself," Alice said.

"Tch," Larry said, and rolled his eyes.

Silvio still had his hands up in the air.

"Can I put my hands down, lady?" he asked. "Or shall I go fuck myself, too?"

"You can put them down," Connie said.

"First promise me no bamboo shoots," Silvio said.

"What?" Connie said.

"And no MSG," Larry said. "It's the MSG gives you headaches."

"Keep your hands up," Michael said. "Who's Mama?"

"Quién sabe?" Silvio said.

"Are you Spanish?" Michael asked.

"No, I'm Italian. But everybody knows what *quién sabe* means."

"Sure," Larry said. "It's what Tonto calls the Lone Ranger."

"Anyway," Alice said testily, "we don't know who

Mama is, and please get me a goddamn doctor."

"Why are you trying to kill us?" Michael asked.

"*We're* trying to kill *you*?" Alice said. "This Asian person almost takes off my arm with that *weapon* in her hand, and *we're* trying to kill *you*?"

"That's certainly comical, all right," Larry said, shaking his head in wonder.

"Can I put my hands down?" Silvio asked.

"No," Michael said. "Who's Mama?"

"Call a doctor," Alice said.

"No. Who is she?"

"Call the police, too. I want to press charges against this illegal alien."

"I'm legal," Connie said.

"Sure. So's Mama."

"Go ahead, tell them," Larry said, shaking his head again.

"I didn't tell them anything."

"You told them Mama's an illegal alien."

"No, *you* just told them."

"I said Mama's illegal?"

"An illegal alien, is *exactly* what you said."

"Did I say that?" Larry asked, turning to Silvio.

"How come everybody can put their hands down but me?" Silvio asked.

"If I bleed to death here, they'll deport you," Alice said to Connie.

"Let's talk a deal," Michael said. "If you had one wish in the whole world, and you could get that wish by telling us who Mama is, what would that wish be?"

"Could I please put my hands down?" Silvio said.

"Yes," Michael said.

"You just blew your wish, dummy," Larry said.

"That wasn't my wish," Silvio said, shaking his

hands out from the wrists. "That was just a polite request."

"Just get me a doctor," Alice said.

"Is that your wish?"

"I wish my mother would go back to Palermo," Silvio said.

"I wish she'd take *my* mother with her," Larry said, and both men burst out laughing.

Alice laughed, too.

Blood was trickling from her left shoulder, but she suddenly began laughing along with her buddies. Michael was thinking it would be fun to work with these three if only they weren't killers. He tried to remember if any of it had been fun in Vietnam. Working with the killers there. He guessed maybe some of it had been fun. Before the baby.

Hell she doing out here? Andrew asked.

The baby crying.

Must've crawled out from the village, the RTO said.

"Who's Mama?" Michael said.

"You want to get us all killed?" Larry asked.

"I'll tell you what I'm going to do," Michael said. "I'm going to make the wish *for* you, okay? I'm going to wish that I don't go to that phone on the wall there, and call the police, and tell them to come up here and get you, that's what I'm going to wish."

"First Precinct," Connie said. "I have the number in my book."

"Go ahead, call them," Alice said.

"I keep all the precinct numbers handy," Connie said. "In case I get a weirdo. I know all the desk sergeants down here."

"Do you know Tony Orso?" Michael asked.

"No. Is he a desk sergeant?"

"No."

"Then I don't know him."

"Tony the Bear Orso."

"No."

"I know him," Silvio said.

"So do I," Larry said.

"Do you know Detective Daniel Cahill?" Michael asked.

"Go call all these cops, why don't you?" Alice said. "Tell them your Chink girlfriend tried to kill me."

"How would you like a punch in the mouth?" Connie asked pleasantly.

"Go ahead, hit me. That'll look good on your record, too."

"Detective Cahill?" Michael said. "Ring a bell?"

"There was a cop up Sing Sing named Cahill," Larry said.

"No, that was Cromwell," Silvio said.

"Oh, yeah," Larry said, and nodded and smiled, as though fondly remembering Sing Sing.

"How about you, Alice?" Michael asked.

"How about me, what? I'm bleeding to death here, that's how about me."

"Do you know anybody named Cahill?"

"No."

"How about Helen Parrish?"

"No."

"Charlie Nichols?"

"No."

"Did you kill Charlie Nichols?"

"How could I kill somebody I don't even know?"

"Charlie Nichols. Mama sent you to kill him, didn't she?"

"This man is deaf," Alice said to the air. "I'm telling you I don't *know* anybody by that name."

"Charlie Nichols. An actor."

"Is he related to Charlie Belafonte?"

"You mean *Harry* Belafonte," Larry said. "I know because his name is almost like mine."

"Can you sing 'Day-O'?" Silvio asked him.

"Charlie Nichols?" Michael said. "Nice little apartment in Knickerbocker Village?"

"Where's that? Westchester County?"

"The Fifth Precinct," Connie said.

"Go ahead, call the cops," Alice said.

"How about Judy Jordan?" Michael asked.

"Call her, too."

"Do you know her?"

"I don't know *any* of these people. Go call the goddamn cops. Just for spite, I'll be dead when they get here."

"Good," Connie said.

"You don't know any of them, huh?" Michael asked.

"You're deaf, am I right?" she said, and turned to Larry. "He's deaf."

"My uncle in Chicago is deaf, too," Larry said sympathetically.

"And I suppose you don't know anything about what happened to me on Christmas Eve, either," Michael said.

"The first time I laid eyes on you was through a telescopic sight. I was told to put you away because you'd been snooping around Benny's downtown, and that's all I know. Mama likes things clean and neat."

"She's a neat, clean illegal alien, huh?" Michael said.

Alice said nothing.

"Why would killing *me* make things clean and neat?" he asked.

"Go ask Mama."

"I will. Where do I find her?"

Alice shook her head.

"Where is she?"

Alice shook her head again.

"You're that scared of her, huh?"

Alice said nothing.

"Tell me where to find her."

She just kept staring at him.

"Then it's the cops, right?" he said. "You want me to call the cops, right?"

"Sure," she said. "Call them."

The last time Michael had stood in this hallway outside the door to Judy Jordan's apartment, he'd been alone. And someone, either Larry or Silvio, had come up behind him and hit him on the head with one of his own guns. Or rather, guns that had previously belonged to Frankie Zeppelin and Arthur Crandall. This time, Connie was by his side. With Connie by his side, he figured he would not get hit on the head again. The only thing that happened to him when Connie was by his side was that he got shot. Or, at best, shot *at*.

He wondered if the police had ever before walked into a warehouse full of stolen goods to discover a safe full of a million dollars' worth of crack, and three thieves swathed in furs and trussed with the electric cords from sundry household appliances. He did not think Alice—despite her dire warnings or perhaps promises—could possibly have bled to death by the time the police arrived. An axiom of the killing and maiming profession was that if a person was feeling good enough to laugh he wasn't about to die in the next ten minutes. He wished, however, that Alice had chosen to tell him who Mama was.

It was a little unsettling to know that somewhere out there in this wonderful city there was a woman who wielded enough power to order Ju Ju Rainey's murder first and next to order Michael's own, a woman who could generate such fear that three grown thieves had chosen to face the police rather than reveal who or where she was. Michael wasn't sure he ever wanted to meet Mama. He knew intuitively, however, that before this was over he would have to look her in the face and demand to know all the whys and wherefores. He tried to visualize her.

She would be fat, he knew that. As Connie had suggested, a woman named Mama *had* to be fat. Bloated and fat and as pale as a slug, a female with a breath that reeked of gunpowder and piss. She would have breasts like dugs, and she would obscenely expose them to Michael, threatening to suckle him if he did not do as she commanded. Standing before Mama, he would search her slightly crossed eyes for some sign that here was reason, here was cause, here was sanity, but there would be none. The .22 caliber pistols he was now carrying in the pockets of the bomber jacket would be of no use to him. He would be staring into the darkest part of evil, and he would be doomed. He did not want to find Mama, did not want to face what he knew was inescapable if this ever was to be resolved—but he knew that he had to. Mama was fate. If you had an appointment in Samarra, you did not drive instead to Newark, New Jersey.

But in the beginning, there'd been Judy Jordan.

Or Helen Parrish, if you preferred.

And to get to the end, you went to the beginning.

And prayed that somewhere along the way—

The village looked abandoned at first. Not a soul in sight.

Michael knocked on the door to the apartment.

"Cops listen first," Connie said.

Belatedly, he put his ear to the door and listened.

He did not hear anything.

"Nobody home," he said.

Charlie musta flew the coop, Sergeant Mendelsohnn said.

Michael knocked on the door again. And waited. No answer. He studied the locks. Four of them. One under the other. To get into this apartment, you would need a battering ram. He wondered if they should try the fire escape again. But how many fire escapes could you climb before someone yelled fire?

Careful, Andrew said.

An old man had appeared in the doorway to one of the thatched huts. Nodding. Smiling. Scared shitless. Six automatic rifles suddenly trained on him.

"We'd better go," Michael said.

Cover me, Mendelsohnn said.

Rain coming down. A light rain. Everything looking so green. So fresh. Waiting in the rain. The whisper of the rain. Mendelsohnn talking quietly to the old man. Scraps of Vietnamese, snippets of French, bits and pieces of English. Other gooks peering around doorways now. Women mostly. Some other old men. Watching solemnly. Looking scared. Big American liberators standing in the rain with their guns. All but one of them no older than twenty, scaring women and old men to death.

Says Charlie went through about three days ago, Mendelsohnn said.

All of them listening.

Took all their rice, Mendelsohnn said. Got to be miles away by now.

"Maybe you ought to knock again," Connie said.

"No," Michael said. "Let's go."

Looka the one in the blue over there, the RTO said.

Yeah, Andrew said.

Givin' us the eye.

Give her some big Indian cock, Long Foot said.

Let's move it out, Mendelsohnn said.

The rain still falling lightly.

A breeze coming up over the rice paddies.

They were coming down the steps when Michael heard the footsteps below. Coming up. Moving up toward them. Another tenant, he thought. Or maybe—but no, that would be too lucky. But why not? Judy Jordan coming home. By her own admission, she'd been naked the last time he was here, probably dressing to go out, it had been only ten o'clock. So she'd put on a robe and peeked out into the hallway to find nobody there, this city was full of mysteries, and she'd finished dressing, and had gone out on the town. But the night had vanished all at once, and this was now one o'clock in the morning on Boxing Day, and here she was, folks, home sweet home again, coming up the steps to the second floor, reaching the second-floor landing just as Michael and Connie came down from the third floor, hand on the banister, hello there, Judy, long time no—

But it wasn't Judy Jordan.

Or even Helen Parrish.

Instead, it was—

"You!" Michael shouted.

The man looked at him. His mouth fell open, his eyes opened wide in his head.

"You!" Michael shouted again.

And the man turned and started running downstairs.

Michael took off after him.

The streets were deserted. It would have been impossible to lose him, anyway, because he was wearing a yellow ski parka that served as a beacon, which Michael thought was extremely considerate of him. He was fast for a big man, but Michael was faster; he'd had practice chasing Charlie Wong all the way from the subway kiosk on Franklin to the fortune-cookie factory someplace in Chinatown on Christmas Eve, and it seemed to him he'd been running ever since. He wanted very badly to get his hands on this son of a bitch in the yellow ski parka, and so he ran faster than he'd ever run in his life, arms and legs pumping, eyeglasses steaming up a bit, but not so much so that he couldn't see the yellow parka ahead, the distance closing between them now, ten feet, eight feet, six feet, three feet, and Michael hurled himself into the air like a circus flier, leaping off into space without a net, arms outstretched, reaching not for a trapeze coming his way from the opposite direction, but instead for the shoulders of Detective Daniel Cahill. who had called him a thief after stealing his money, his driver's license, his credit cards, and his library card to boot.

His hands clamped down fiercely on either side of Cahill's neck, the weight and momentum of his body sending the man staggering forward, hands clawing the air for balance. They fell to the sidewalk together, Michael on Cahill's back, the big man trying to shake Michael off. Michael was tired of being jerked around in this fabulous city, tired of being shaken up and shaken off. He allowed himself to be shaken off now, but only for an instant. Rolling clear, he got to his feet at once, and then immediately reached down for Cahill and heaved him up off the sidewalk. His hands clutched into the zippered front of the yellow parka, he slammed Cahill against the wall of the building, and then pulled him off the wall and slammed him back again, methodically battering him against the bricks over and over again.

"Cut it out," Cahill said.

"I'll cut it out, you son of a bitch!"

"Are you crazy or something?"

"Yes!" Michael shouted.

"Ow!" Cahill shouted.

"Detective Daniel Cahill, huh?"

"Damn it, you're hurting me!"

"Let's go down the precinct, huh?"

"Ow! Damn it, that's my *head*!"

Michael pulled him off the wall.

"Speak," he said.

"You're a very violent person," Cahill said.

"Yes. What's your name?"

"Felix. And I don't have your money, if *that's* why you're behaving like a lunatic. Or anything *else* that belongs to you."

Felix. Big burly man with hard blue eyes and a Marine sergeant's haircut. On Christmas Eve, he'd sported a *Miami Vice* beard stubble, but now—at a little past one A.M. on Boxing Day—he was clean-shaven. On Christmas Eve, he'd been wearing a tweed overcoat and he'd been carrying a detective's blue-enameled gold shield, and he'd sounded very much like a tough New York cop. Tonight he was wearing a yellow ski parka over a brown turtleneck sweater, and he sounded like a frightened man protesting too loudly that he did not have Michael's—

But didn't he know that Michael's identification had been planted alongside the dead body of Ju Ju Rainey?

"Felix what?" Michael asked.

"Hooper. And I'm telling you the truth. I gave everything to Judy. And she still hasn't paid me, by the way. I mean, I think it's demeaning for a person to have to come to another person's apartment at one in the morning to ask for his money, don't you?"

"I assume you mean Judy Jordan."

"Yes, of *course,* Judy Jordan. Your friend Judy Jordan who owes me a thousand bucks."

"How do you happen to know her?"

"We've worked together in the past."

"Stealing things from people?"

"Ha-ha," Felix said.

Michael looked at him.

"I am an *actor,* sir," Felix said, proudly and a trifle indignantly. In fact, he tried to pull himself up to his full height, but this was a little difficult because Michael still had his hands twisted into the throat and collar of the parka. "I was asked to play a police detective," Felix said. "I'd never played one before I thought the role would be challenging."

"You thought stealing my . . ."

"Oh, come on, that was for a good purpose."

"A good . . ."

"In fact, you should have been delighted."

"Delighted? Do you know what Judy *did* with those things? My credit cards and my license and my . . . ?"

"Yes, she had them blown up as posters."

"She *what*?"

"For your birthday party."

"My *what*?"

"How terrible it must be," Felix said.

"What?"

"To be born on Christmas Day, do you think you could let go of my collar now?"

"Born on . . . ?"

"It's like being upstaged by Christ, isn't it?" Felix said. "I really think you're closing off an artery or something. I'm beginning to feel a bit faint."

Michael let go of the collar.

"Thank you," Felix said.

"So that's what she told you. Judy."

"Yes."

"That my birthday was on Christmas Day . . ."

"Well, her friend's birthday. She didn't tell me your name."

"And she was going to have my credit cards blown up as posters."

"Yes, and your driver's license, too. To hang on the walls. For the party."

"Which is why you went to this bar with her . . ."

"Yes. And waited for her signal."

"Her signal?"

"She said she would signal when she wanted me to move in."

"I see."

"She would hold out her hand to you, palm up."

Asking for the ring back, Michael thought.

The ring. Please, I don't want any trouble.

"And that was when you were supposed to come over and do your Detective Cahill act."

"Yes."

"Where'd you get the badge?"

"A shield. We call it a shield. I bought it in an antiques stop on Third Avenue."

"You were very convincing."

"Thank you. I thought so, too. Did you like it when I said, 'This individual is a thief?' That's the way policemen talk, you know. They will never call a person a *person,* he is always an individual."

"Yes, that was very good."

"Thank you."

"But why'd you steal my money? If Judy wanted the . . ."

"I don't know why she wanted the money. She said your money and all your identification. Which is all I took."

"Which was only everything in my wallet."

"Well, that was the job."

"Which you did for a thousand dollars."

"Yes, but I'm between engagements just now. How was the party?"

"Mr. Hooper, do you know where all that stuff ended up?"

"No. All I know is that I still haven't got my thousand dollars."

"That stuff ended up alongside a dead man."

"That's a shame," Felix said. "But I'm sure it had nothing do with my performance."

"Do you know who Mama is?"

"No. Is that a riddle?"

"Did Judy Jordan ever mention a woman named Mama?"

"No. Mama who?"

"She didn't say, did she, that it was *Mama* who wanted that stuff taken from my wallet?"

"No."

"Did she ever mention a man named Arthur Crandall?"

"Arthur Crandall? The *director*? The man who did *War and Solitude*? What are you saying?"

"Did she tell you it was Crandall who wanted my . . . ?"

"Oh my God, was I auditioning for *Crandall*?"

"No, that's not what I'm saying. I'm trying to find out if . . ."

"Crandall, oh, *God*, I'm going to faint."

"Would you know if . . . ?"

"Why didn't she *tell* me? I mean, I hardly even *prepared*! I mean, I went on cold! If I'd known I was doing it for *Crandall* . . ."

"Well, that's what I'm trying to . . ."

"I'll kill her, I swear to God! Why'd she give me that story about a birthday party? *Crandall*, I'm going to cry."

"No, don't cry, just . . ."

"I'm going to die, I'm going to kill her, I'll go kill her right this minute."

"You can't, she isn't home."

"Then where is she?"

"I don't know where she . . ."

"The *theater*!" Felix shouted.

15

The theater was on Thirteenth Street off Seventh Avenue, a ninety-nine-seat house in what had once been the rectory of a Catholic church. The church was still functional, although the theater—according to Felix—barely scraped by. All of the street lamps on either side of the block had been smashed by vandals, and the only illumination at one-forty in the morning was a floodlight bathing the facade of the church and causing it to look like a sanctuary for Quasimodo. A hand-lettered sign affixed to a stone buttress on the northwest side of the church advised that the Cornerstone Players could be found in the direction of the pointing arrow at the bottom of the sign.

"They're rehearsing a medieval play," Felix said, "an allegory of sorts."

Michael thought it odd that a group of players would be rehearsing at this hour of the morning. Then again, he did not know anything at all about allegories. Perhaps an allegory had to be rehearsed in the empty hours of the night.

"They were supposed to open just before Christmas," Felix said, "but the director's wife ran off with another woman, and they had to bring in a replacement. They'll be lucky if they make it before the end of the year. Even *with* all these crash rehearsals."

He was leading them familiarly up the lighted alleyway on the side of the church, feeling very chipper now that Michael had stopped banging him against the wall and had released his grip on the parka. On the way downtown in the open convertible, he'd told them he was really looking forward to killing Judy Jordan. Michael doubted he would actually kill her even though be sounded simultaneously serious and cheerfully optimistic about the prospect. Apparently, an audition with Arthur Crandall was an important thing. Working in an Arthur Crandall film, even if the movie didn't make any money, could help an actor's career enormously. Which was why Felix was so incensed that Judy hadn't told him the detective role was an audition. Michael assured Felix it had been nothing of the sort, but Felix thought he was just mollifying him, Judy Jordan being a good friend of his and all, who'd even thrown a surprise birthday party for him. Michael was thinking that in his own way Felix was crazier than any of the people he'd met in the past few days. But Felix was an actor; perhaps he was only *acting* crazy.

There was an arched doorway near the rear of the church, which Felix explained was the entrance to the theater, but he walked right past it and

around to the back of the church, where a metal
door was set in a smaller arch. A sign advised
that this was the stage door and asked all visitors
to announce themselves. Felix pressed a button
under a speaker. A woman's voice said, "Yes?"

"Felix Hooper," he said.

"Minute," the woman said.

There was a buzz. Felix grasped the doorknob,
twisted it, and led them into a space that looked
like a one-room schoolhouse, with students' desks
and a teacher's desk and a piano in one corner, and
an American flag in another corner. A dark-haired
woman wearing a wide, flower-patterned skirt over
a black leotard and tights came into the room, carrying a clipboard.

"Hi, Felix," she said.

"Hi. Is Judy here?"

"Onstage," she said.

Michael noticed that she was barefoot.

"I'm Anne Summers, the stage manager," she
said.

"I'm Connie Kee, the chauffeur," Connie said.

Michael did not introduce himself because he
was still wanted for murder, albeit the murder of
a dope dealer fence.

"You look familiar," Anne said.

"Everybody tells me that," Michael said.

"Okay to go in?" Felix asked.

"Sure."

"'Cause I want to kill Judy," Felix said, and
smiled.

"So does Kenny," Anne said, and turned to
Michael. "Kenny Stein, the director," she explained.

Michael figured that in the theater, everyone
had a title. He wondered if he was supposed to

recognize Kenny Stein's name. Anne was looking at him expectantly.

"Gee," Michael said.

"You'd better sit way in the back," she said to Felix. "Kenny likes a lot of space around him. Are you sure I don't know you?" she asked Michael.

"Positive," Michael said, and followed Felix across the room to a doorframe hung with a black curtain. Felix pushed the curtain aside, whispered, "Stay close behind me," and stepped through the doorframe. Connie went out after him. Anne was watching Michael. He smiled at her. She smiled back.

There was darkness beyond the curtain.

And a man's voice.

"Let's take it from Judy's entrance again."

And then a voice Michael remembered well.

"Kenny, could you please refer to me as the Queen?"

Judy Jordan speaking. The woman who'd called herself Helen Parrish on Christmas Eve. Wishing to be called the Queen on Boxing Day.

"Because if I'm going to stay in character . . ."

"Yes, yes," the man said patiently.

" . . . and you keep referring to me as *Judy* . . ."

"Which, by the way, is your name."

"Not in this *play*," Judy said. "In this *play*, I am the *Queen,* and I wish you'd refer to me as that."

"Yes, Your Majesty," the man said. "Can we take it from the Queen's entrance, please?"

"Thank you," Judy said.

Michael was following Felix and Connie up the side aisle of the small theater, turning his head every now and then for a glimpse of the lighted stage, where Judy Jordan was standing with three men. Michael stumbled, caught his balance, and then concentrated entirely on following Felix, who was now at the last row in the theater, moving into the seats there.

"What's the problem?"

The man's voice again. Kenny Stein, the director.

"Some problem, Your Majesty?"

"Did you want this from the top of the act, or from my entrance?" Judy asked.

"I said from your entrance, didn't I?"

"That's so close to the top, I thought . . ."

"From your entrance, please."

Seated now, Michael turned his full attention to the stage. The set seemed to be an ultramodern apartment in Manhattan, judging from the skyline beyond the open French doors leading onto a terrace. But the people in the set—Judy and the three men—were dressed in medieval costumes. Judy was wearing a crown and an ankle-length, scoop-necked gown. One of the men was wearing a black helmet that completely covered his head and his face. Another of the men was holding what looked like a real sword in his right hand. The third man, younger than the other two, was wearing leggings wrapped with leather thongs, and a funny hat with a feather in it; he looked like a peasant.

"They're rehearsing in the set for a play that's already in performance," Felix whispered, leaning over Connie, who was sitting between them.

"It's only two A.M.," Kenny said patiently, "just take all the time you need."

"We just want to make sure we've got the right place," the man with the sword said.

"The right place is Judy's entrance," Kenny said.

"From my line?"

"Yes, your line would be fine."

"'The White Knight? At your service, fair maiden?'"

"Yes, that is your line," Kenny said. "Can we do it now, please?"

"Thank you," the man with the sword said. "Judy, are you ready?"

"Please don't call me Judy," she said.

"Well, I'm not supposed to know you're the Queen yet. You haven't come in yet."

"Yes, please do come in," Kenny said. "Just say your line, Hal, and Judy will come in."

"The play is called *Stalemate*," Felix explained.

On the stage, the man with the sword said, "The White Knight. At your service, fair maiden."

"I'm not a maiden," Judy said. "I'm a queen."

The White Knight knelt at once. "Your Majesty," he said. "Forgive me."

Judy turned to the man who looked like a peasant. "Who are *you*?" she asked.

"I am the White Knight's squire," he said, "a mere pawn. Your Majesty."

"And this poor creature?" she asked, indicating the man in the black helmet.

"A helpless servant of the Queen, Your Majesty, tell him to put up his sword!"

"Release him," Judy said.

"He's a dangerous man, Your Majesty."

"Release him, I say."

The White Knight and his squire immediately let go of the man wearing the black helmet.

"Take off your helmet," Judy said. "I want to see your face."

"No," the man in the helmet said.

"I'm a *queen!*" Judy said. "Do as I say!"

"You're not *my* queen, lady," the man in the helmet said, and immediately turned to look out into the theater. "Kenny," he said, "I don't get this, I really don't. A minute ago, I'm calling her 'Your Majesty,' and now I'm telling her she's not my queen."

"That's because this is the first time you can really see her," Kenny said patiently.

"Why can't I see her before this?"

"Because she's standing in the dark. This is when she moves toward the fire. On 'I'm a *queen,*' she moves toward the fire. And you can see her face in the firelight, and that's when you say 'You're not *my* queen, lady.'"

"Then whose queen is she?" the man in the helmet asked.

"That's not the point, Jason. The point is . . ."

"You know, I think Judy's right, you shouldn't call us by our real names when we're supposed to be other people."

"It would be clumsy to call you 'Black Knight,'" Kenny said.

"Then call me 'Sire,'" the Black Knight said.

"Me, too," the White Knight said.

"And what would *you* like to be called, Jimmy?"

"I'm the Pawn," the young man in the peasant outfit said, looking stunned.

"Yes, that's what the playwright has chosen to call you, the Pawn, that is part of the metaphor. The chess metaphor. But shall *I* call you 'Pawn' when I address you?"

"Yes, that would be fine, Kenny," the young man said.

"Very well, then. Sire, would you please take it from your denial line?"

"Me?" the White Knight asked.

"No, the *other* sire, please."

"My *what* line?" the Black Knight asked.

"The line where you deny the Queen. If you please."

"Oh."

"Thank you," Kenny said.

Michael wondered if allegory and metaphor were one and the same thing. Whichever, it was certainly a very confusing play, at least the part of it they were rehearsing. At one point, he thought he was beginning to catch on to the idea that the Black Knight represented black men everywhere, but then the play swerved off in another direction and he figured he was wrong. Puzzled, he began to lose interest, until—

"I can still remember the day Arthur died," the Black Knight said.

"Oh, yes, of course," the Queen said, "the whole *world* remembers."

"I'd been in the woods with a friend of mine," the Black Knight said. "It was a bright, clear November day, the forest was alive with sound, we walked on crackling leaves, and breathed needles into our lungs. And when we came out of the forest, there was a beggar woman sitting by the side of the road, wringing her hands and weeping, and we said to her, 'Why do you weep, old woman?' and she answered, 'Arthur is dead.' And we didn't believe her. Arthur could not be dead. But as we walked further along the road, we came upon more and more people, all of them saying, 'Arthur is dead,' until at last there was a multitude of people, all of them weeping and saying the same words, 'Arthur is dead, Arthur is dead,' and then we believed it.

And the sun went out, and a wind rose up, and there was no longer the sound of life in this land of ours, there was only the sound of muffled drums."

He's talking about John F. Kennedy, Michael thought.

The Queen shuddered and said, "You're a very morbid person."

"He was a good king," the Black Knight said.

"Yes, but we've all got to go sometime, you know."

"Things would be different if he were still alive," the Black Knight said. "He had a vision, that man, you could see it flashing in his eyes, you just knew he had a *dream* clenched tight in those hands of his. And when a man can dream that strong, it makes you want to join him, it makes you want to move right in and, say, 'Yes, Daddy, take me where you're going, I'm *with* you, Daddy, let's yell it out together.' There was no bullshit about that man. I loved him."

Now he's talking about Martin Luther King, Jr., Michael thought.

"You talk too much," the Queen said, "and not about the right things. Also, I don't like profanity. And if you want to know something, I'm beginning to find you enormously boring and a trifle sinister."

This is *Alice in Wonderland,* Michael thought.

"Besides, I don't trust masked men," the Queen said. "Nobody does."

Everything in this city is *Alice in Wonderland,* Michael thought.

"This isn't a mask!" the Black Knight shouted.

"Then what is it?"

"My *head* is inside this black cage," the Black Knight shouted. "My *brain* is in here, I *think* in here, I *feel* in here, it is not a goddamn *mask!*"

"You're frightening me," the Queen said. "Look, the fire's going out."

"The fire went out the day Arthur died," the Black Knight whispered.

"Very good," Kenny said, "very nice indeed. Let's take a ten-minute break, and then I want to do the dragon scene, the H-bomb scene."

"Oh, God, is *that* it?" the White Knight said.

"Sire?"

"Is the dragon supposed to be the *H*-bomb?"

"Yes, Sire, that is the metaphor," Kenny said.

"I'm glad to know that. Because, actually, I was wondering why I was so afraid of a little dragon. I'm supposed to be an experienced knight, but I'm afraid of a little dragon. It didn't make sense to me. Now that you tell me it's the H-bomb . . ."

"That's the metaphor, yes."

"Well, that's an enormous relief, I can tell you. Did you know it was the H-bomb, Jason?"

"Oh, sure," the Black Knight said, and both men walked off the stage. The Pawn, looking somewhat bewildered, followed them. "Ten minutes, please," Kenny called after them, and left the theater through the curtained doorway that led to the one-room schoolhouse.

Judy Jordan sat alone on the stage.

Sat on a wooden plank stretched across several stacked cinder blocks.

Head bent, studying her script.

Looking blonde and beautiful and serene and quite regal.

"I want her first," Felix said, and stood up.

"No," Michael said.

He said it quite softly.

Almost whispered it, in fact.

There was no reason for Felix to have obeyed him.

But he sat down at once.

Michael walked up the aisle to the front of the theater. He climbed the steps onto the stage. Judy was absorbed in the script, probably trying to dope out all its inherent metaphors and allegories. He walked directly to her.

"I'm looking for a good criminal lawyer," he said.

Her head jerked up.

"Because I've been accused of murder," he said.

She started to rise.

He put his hands on her shoulders and slammed her back down onto the makeshift plank and cinder-block seat, which was undoubtedly a metaphor for a medieval bench.

"Remember me?" he said.

"Yes," she said. "Hello."

She was playing a woman in a movie about the French Resistance. She was really a Nazi spy and he was the wounded American soldier who had fallen in love with her and been betrayed by her. It was now his painful duty to turn her over to the authorities. He had come to take her away. She still loved him. She was looking up at him wistfully, her blue eyes wide.

"How have you been?" she asked.

"Comme ci comme ça," he said, in the French he had learned in Vietnam. *"Et tu?"*

"Not very good," she said. "I saw it on television."

"Oh. And what did you see, Miss Parrish?"

"My name is Judy Jordan," she said.

"I know."

"I'm sorry," she said. "That's not what I thought would happen."

"What did you think would happen?"

"Charlie said he was playing a joke on a friend of his."

"By Charlie . . ."

"Charlie Nichols."

"You call your father by his first name, do you?"

"My father?"

"Yes, Charlie. You call your father 'Charlie?'"

"No, I call my father 'Frank.'"

Michael looked at her.

"Isn't it true that you call Charlie 'Daddy'?" he asked.

"No, I call Charlie *'Charlie.'*"

"Look, Miss Jordan, I happen to *know* that Charlie Nichols is your goddamn *father.* So please don't . . ."

"No, Frank Giordano is my goddamn father, which is where I got the name Jordan, from Giordano, and I really don't know *what* you're talking about!"

"I am talking about a photograph of you and Charlie Nichols . . ."

"Oh."

"Yes, oh, inscribed 'To My Dear Daddy, With Love,' and signed Judy Jordan, who is *you,* Miss Jordan, Miss Parrish, Miss Giordano, who*ever* the hell you are!"

Nodding, Judy said what sounded exactly like, "I remember Mama."

"Good," Michael said at once. "Who is she?"

"Who?" Judy said. *"I Remember Mama* is a *play.* I was Christine in a revival. Charlie was Papa."

"What?"

"Yes. In the play. My father."

"In a play?"

"Yes. *I Remember Mama.* And at the end of the run, I signed a photograph . . ."

"To My Dear Daddy . . ."

"Yes, With Love."

"Referring to . . ."

"Yes, the characters in the play. Also, it was an inside joke, in that Charlie and I were sleeping together at the time."

"I see."

"Yes. Charlie was my first lover."

"I see."

"Yes. I was seventeen. I was a virgin at the time."

"So he wasn't your father."

"No, that would have been incest. Also, my own father would have shot him dead if he'd found out."

Michael wondered if her own father had now belatedly if messily shot Charlie dead. He also wondered if Judy even *knew* that Charlie was dead. He decided not to mention it. From seeing a lot of cop movies, he knew that this was an old cop trick. You did not mention that someone was dead. You waited for the suspect to trap himself by mentioning that the last time he'd seen So-and-So alive was Thursday, and then you yelled, "Ah-ha, how did you know he was *dead*?"

"I am really sorry," Judy said. "When I saw on television that they'd accused you of murdering Arthur Crandall . . ."

"Oh, you saw that, did you?"

"Oh, yes. I was *shocked*!"

"But I *didn't* murder Crandall, you know."

"Well, of *course* you didn't."

"In fact, I didn't murder *anyone.*"

"Well, I'm not too sure about *that.*"

"You can take my word for it. And please don't change the subject. The reason the police *think* I killed Rainey . . ."

"Who?"

" . . . is that you and Felix Hooper stole my goddamn identification and . . ."

"Yes, but that was for a joke."

"What joke? What do you mean?"

"The joke Charlie was going to play on his friend."

"What friend?"

"He didn't say."

"What *did* he say?"

"He said he needed someone's identification to play a joke on a friend of his. He said it wouldn't really be stealing . . ."

"Oh, it *wouldn't,* huh?"

"In that he would return the stuff to its rightful owner the moment he was through with it."

"And just how did he plan to do that?"

"He said he would mail it all back."

"And you believed him, huh?"

"Not entirely. But a thousand dollars is a lot of money."

"What do you mean?"

"Charlie paid each of us a thousand for the job."

"You and Felix."

"Yes."

Which accounted for two thousand dollars of the check Crandall had cashed on Friday. But where had the other seven thousand gone?

"I was the one who picked Felix for the part," Judy said. "He was very good, didn't you think?"

"Yes, excellent," Michael said.

"Yes, he's a very good actor. I still owe him the thousand, but Charlie hasn't paid me yet."

Nor is he likely to, Michael thought.

"So as I understand this," he said, "you were supposed to steal my identification . . ."

"Well, borrow it, yes. And your money, too."

"Why the money? If all you needed was my . . ."

"In case you went to the police. So it wouldn't look as if we'd been after your I.D. Actually, it was the best improv Felix and I ever did together."

"The best what?"

"Improvisation. Picking up a stranger in a bar, and then . . ."

"You mean I was chosen at *random*?"

"Well, not entirely. Charlie gave me the nod."

"What nod?"

"To go ahead."

"Go ahead?"

"Yes. He was sitting at the bar, listening to everything we said . . ."

"Yes, I know that."

"And he gave me the okay, just this little nod, you know—do you remember when I looked down the bar?"

"No."

"Well, I did. To get his okay. The nod."

"To get his permission, you mean, to *steal* my goddamn . . ."

"Well, it was only for a joke, you know."

"A *murder* was committed!"

"Well, I'm sorry about that, but Felix and I had nothing to do with it."

"Where does Crandall fit in?" he asked.

"I have no idea, but he's a very good director and I'm glad it wasn't him you killed."

"I didn't kill *anyone,* goddamn it!"

"I don't like profanity," she said at once. "And if you want to know something, I'm beginning to find you enormously boring and a trifle sinister. If the police made a mistake, you should go to *them* and correct it, instead of breaking the concentration of someone who's trying to master a very complex role."

"That was very good," he said sincerely. "You sounded absolutely royal."

"Do you really think so?" she asked.

"Positively majestic. Better than Bette Davis in *Elizabeth and Essex* . . ."

"Honestly?"

"Even better than Hepburn in *The Lion in Winter.*"

"Oh dear," she said.

"But would you happen to know a bar called Benny's?"

"No. I'm not being *too* forceful, am I? Maybe I should temper the steel with a touch of lace."

"No, I think you've got exactly the proper balance, really. On Christmas Eve, Crandall went to Benny's to meet a man sent there by someone named Mama. Would you happen to know who Mama is?"

"Well, of course."

"You do?"

"Mady Christians, am I right?"

"Who?" he said.

"That was in the original 1944 production, of course. When *we* did it fifteen years ago, a woman named . . ."

"Yes, but *this* Mama is an illegal alien. Would you know anyone . . . ?"

"Oh," she said. *"That* Mama."

He held his breath.

"Charlie's crack dealer," she said. "I've never met her, but he talks about her all the time."

"Do you know where she lives?" Michael asked.

Only her last name was on the mailbox.

Rodriguez.

The match Michael was holding went out.

The hallway was very dark again.

"Somebody peed in here," Connie said.

Michael was thinking it would be very dangerous to ring Mama's bell and then go up there to see her. He wondered if they should go up the fire escape again. Apartment 2C. Was what it said under the name Rodriguez on the mailbox.

Michael rang the bell for apartment 3B.

There was no answering buzz.

He tried 4D.

No answer.

"Is this an abandoned building?" he asked Connie.

"Not that I noticed," she said. "Why don't you just kick the door in?"

He did not want to hurt the sole of his foot again by trying to kick in yet another door. And he didn't want to throw his shoulder against the door, either, because his arm still hurt from getting shot and then hurling himself at Alice. He wondered if there were any medics here in this almost abandoned building.

What's the matter, honey? Andrew asked.

Cute little baby girl, eight months old, not a day older. Crying her eyes out. Sitting the way the Orientals did. Squatting really. Legs folded under her, feet turned back. Bawling. Birds twittering in the jungle. The village not six hundred yards behind them. Friendlies. Charlie had left three days go, the old man had told Mendelsohnn. Took all the rice, moved out. Had to be miles and miles away by now. The baby crying.

Come to Papa, sweetie.

Andrew reached for her.

Michael kicked out at the doorjamb, just above the lock. The door sprang open, surprising him, catching him off balance. He stumbled forward, following the opening door into a small ground-floor rectangle directly in front of a flight of steps. Connie was immediately behind him.

"2C," he said.

She nodded.

They began climbing the steps.

Four apartments on the second floor. 2A, B, C, and D. They stopped outside the door to 2C. He put his ear to the wood, listened the way Connie had told him cops did. He couldn't hear a thing. He took the .22 out of the right-hand pocket of the bomber jacket. He wondered if he would need both pistols. Suppose Mama Rodriguez was sleeping inside there with a .357 Magnum under her pillow? In Vietnam, you slept—*when* you slept, *if* you slept—with your rifle in your hands. But sometimes . . .

Andrew's rifle was slung.

His arms extended to the baby.

Come on, darlin'.

The baby blinking at him.

It had stopped raining.

A fan of sunlight touched the baby like a religious miracle.

"I don't hear anything in there," Michael said.

Birds twittering in the jungle. The leaves still wet. Water dripping onto the jungle floor. The baby had stopped crying. Fat tear-stained cheeks. Looking at Andrew wide-eyed as his hands closed on either side of her body, fingers widespread, lifting her, lifting her—

Michael was suddenly covered with sweat.

Terrified again.

Terrified the way he'd been that day in Vietnam when Andrew picked up the baby.

Afraid of what might be beyond that door. Afraid to enter the apartment beyond that door. Because beyond that door was the unknown. Mama. A woman named Mama who had ordered him murdered. Fat Mama Rodriguez inside there. Waiting and deadly. Like the baby.

Here we go, darlin', Andrew said.

The baby in Andrew's widespread hands, coming up off the jungle mat, the birds going suddenly still as—

Michael did not want to know what was behind this closed door.

Behind this door was something unspeakably horrible, something that went beyond fright to reach into the darkest corners of the unconscious, the baby going off in a hundred flying fragments, her arms and legs spinning away on the air, eyeballs bursting, bone fragments, tissue, blood spattering onto Andrew as the bomb exploded. A moment too late, Long Foot yelled, "She's *wired*!" and a surprised look crossed Andrew's face as the metal shards ripped through his body and blood spurted out of his chest. A piece of the dead baby was still in Andrew's hands. The hands holding what had been the baby's rib cage. But the hands were no longer attached to Andrew's arms. The hands were on the trail some twelve feet away from him. And the stumps where his wrists ended were spurting blood. And a hundred smoking wounds in his jacket were spurting blood. "Oh, dear God," Michael said, and dropped to his knees beside Andrew, and the RTO said, "Barnes, they're . . ." and the jungle erupted with noise and confusion. They were flanked by Charlie left and right. Charlie had wired the baby, had stolen a baby from the village and wired it, and left it just off the trail for the dumb Americans to find, Come on, darlin', here we go, and the baby exploding was the signal to spring the trap, Andrew hoisting her off the jungle mat and tripping the wire.

And in that instant, the true horror of the war struck home. The true senseless horror of it, they had wired a baby. And recognizing the horror, they had wired a *baby*, Michael was suddenly terrified. Running through the jungle with Andrew in his arms, and the Cong assuring him in their sing-song pidgin English that they did not want to hurt him, and the baby's gristle and blood on Andrew's face, and Andrew's own blood bubbling up onto his lips, oh dear God his *hands* were gone, they had wired a *baby*, Michael knew only blind panic. Suddenly there was no logic and no sense there was only a wired baby exploding between the hands of a good dear friend and the friend was dying the friend's blood was pumping out of his body in weaker spurts the friend was oh God dear God dear Andrew *please*, and he began crying. In terror and in sorrow. A sorrow he had never before known. A sorrow for Andrew and himself and for every American here in this place where he did not wish to be or choose to be and a sorrow, too, for a people that would use a baby that way because no cause on earth was worth doing something as terrible as that but behind him Charlie kept saying it was okay Yank no need to worry Yank nobody's gonna hurt you Yank.

Andrew was already dead for half an hour when Michael found the medical chopper.

He would not let them take the body out of his arms.

He kept holding the handless body close, rocking it.

"Come on, man," the black medic said. "Get a grip."

Michael turned to him and snarled at him.

Like a dog.

Lips skinned back over his teeth.

Growling deep in his throat.

The medic backed off.

A colonel came over to him later.

"Let's go, soldier," he said, "we've got work to do."

"Fuck you, sir," Michael said.

And growled at him, too.

Click.

A sound to his right. He whirled, terrified.

The door to apartment 2B was opening. A girl the color of cinnamon toast was standing in the doorway. She was wearing only a half-slip. Nothing else. Naked from the waist up. She stared blankly into the hall.

"You lookin' for Mama?" she asked.

"Yes," Connie said.

"Try the club," the girl said.

Michael felt a tremendous rush of relief.

Mama was at the club.

She was not behind this closed door.

She would not have to be faced just yet.

He put the pistol back into his pocket.

"What club?" he asked.

He did not want to know.

He hoped the girl would not tell him.

Stoned out of her mind, she would not be able to remember the name of the club. No older than sixteen, stoned beyond remembrance. He had seen that same glazed look in Vietnam. Young Americans going into battle stoned. To face the faceless enemy and the nameless horror in the jungle. For Michael, here and now, inexplicably here in this hallway in downtown Manhattan, the horror was an unseen, unknown woman named Mama, and he did not wish to face that horror again. Because this time it would destroy him. This time, the horror would explode in *his* hands, and he would run weeping all the way to Boston, his stumps spurting blood, only to learn that *his* Mama had given away even his best blue jacket. No cause, he thought. No cause on earth.

"Oz," the girl said.

"All the way downtown," Connie said. "Over near the river."

No cause, Michael kept thinking.

"Are you all right?" she asked him.

"Yes," he said, "I'm fine."

16

Oz was a disco on a peninsula that hugged the exit to the Battery Tunnel. Located on Greenwich Street, as opposed to Greenwich *Avenue* farther uptown, it seemed undecided as to whether it wished to be closer to Edgar or to Morris, which were streets and not people. In any event, the club was so far downtown that in the blink of an eye the West Side could suddenly and surprisingly become the East Side. Or rather, and more accurately, the West Side could become the *South* Side, for it was here at the lowest tip of the island that West Street looped around Battery Park to become South Street.

"It's all very confusing," Connie explained, "but not as confusing as the borough of Brooklyn."

They had parked the open convertible in an all-night garage on Broadway, and had walked two blocks south and one block west to the disco, passing several young girls shivering in the cold in short fake-fur jackets, high-heeled shoes, and lacy lingerie. Michael wondered if any of these girls had earlier been at the Christmas party where he'd met Frankie Zeppelin. He did not think he recognized Detective O'Brien among them.

At three o'clock in the morning on Boxing Day, there were at least a hundred people standing on the yellow brick sidewalk outside Oz. Not a single one of them appeared to be over the age of twenty, and most of them were dressed like characters from *The Wizard of Oz*. Standing on line in the shivering cold were a dozen or more Tin Men, half again that number of Scarecrows, six Cowardly Lions, eight Wicked Witches of the East, a handful of Glindas, three or four Wizards, a great many people wearing monkey masks on their faces and wings on their backs, some shorter folk chattering in high voices and pretending to be Munchkins, and a multitude of Dorothys wearing short skirts, red shoes, and braids. Michael felt a bit out of place in his jeans and bomber jacket.

The sidewalk outside the disco was not merely *painted* a yellow brick, it actually *was* yellow brick. The building itself had once been a parking garage, shaped like a flatiron to conform to the peninsula-like dimensions of the plot. Its old brick facade was now covered with thick plastic panels cut and fitted and lighted from within to resemble the many facets of a sparkling green emerald rising from the sidewalk. The name of the club was spelled out in brighter green neon wrapped around the front and sides of the building, just below the roof. There were no visible entrance doors. There was only the yellow brick leading to this huge green, multifaceted crystal growing out of the sidewalk.

The girls and boys standing on line outside were talking noisily among themselves, trying to look supremely confident about their chances of getting into the place. The man in charge of granting admission was about six and a half feet tall, and Michael guessed he weighed at least three hundred pounds. He had bushy black eyebrows, curly black hair, wide shoulders, a narrow waist, and hands like hamhocks. Despite the cold, he was wearing only a black jacket over a white turtleneck shirt, black loafers, white socks, and gray trousers that were too short. Michael heard one of the kids on the line referring to him as Curly.

There was a sudden buzz of excitement when what earlier had appeared to be part of the building's seamless facade now parted to reveal two green panels that served as entrance doors. An intense green light spilled out onto the sidewalk. There was the blare of heavy metal rock. Two youngsters walked out—the girl dressed as a somewhat precocious Dorothy in a pleated skirt that showed white panties and half her ass, the boy wearing a gray suit and a funnel on his head. Both were wearing grins that indicated they'd been allowed to meet the Wizard and all their wishes had been granted.

On the line, all faces turned expectantly toward Curly, who was now parading the sidewalk like a judge at a dog show. He chose two people at random, pressed a button that snapped the doors open again, and, with a surly nod, admitted the couple. The girl was dressed as a Munchkin with a frizzed blonde hairdo. The boy was wearing blue jeans and a long cavalry officer's overcoat. Apparently, then, admission to the club was not premised

on fidelity to the film. The doors swung shut again.
The sound of music was replaced by the keening of
the wind blowing in fiercely off the Hudson. Nobody
on the line complained, not even the kids standing
at the head of it. This was simply the way it was.
Curly decided who would go in, Curly decided who
would stand out here in the cold. Nor was there any
way of knowing upon which criteria he premised
his choice. Either you waited for his approving nod
or you went home with your dreams. That was it,
and this was Oz, take it or leave it.

Michael walked over to where Curly was disdain-
fully glaring out over the crowd.

"Mama's expecting me," he said.

Curly looked him over.

"Expecting *who*?" he said.

"Silvio," Michael said.

"Silvio who?"

"Just say Silvio."

"Mama ain't here yet."

"I'll wait. Inside."

Curly hesitated.

"Push your button," Michael said.

Curly shrugged. But he pushed the button.

The panels sprang open. Connie and Michael
stepped together into the interior of the jewel, and
were immediately inundated by a mortar explo-
sion of battering sound and emerald-green light.
The place was thronged with Tin Men, Cowardly
Lions, Flying Monkeys, Dorothys, Wicked Witches,
Munchkins, Wizards, Glindas, Scarecrows, and
even ordinary folk. Green smoke swirled on the
air. Bodies twisted on the small dance floor. On
the bandstand, five blond men wearing black
leather trousers, pink tank-top shirts, and long

gold chains played guitar and electric-keyboard backup to a young black woman standing at the microphone and belting out a song that seemed to consist only of the words "Do me, baby, do me good" repeated over and over again. She had a big, brassy gospel singer's voice. She was wearing brown high-heeled boots and what appeared to be draped animal skins. The thudding of the bass guitars sounded like enemy troops shelling the perimeter. The room reverberated with noise, skidded with dazzling light. Out of the deafening din of the music and the refracted green glare of the lights and the dense hanging fog of smoke, a young man in a red jacket materialized.

"Sir?" he asked. "Did John admit you?"

He looked extremely puzzled. Had the system somehow broken down?

"Mama's expecting me," Michael said.

"Who's Mama?" the young man asked.

Michael winked.

"John knows," he said.

"It's just that I haven't got a table," the young man said.

He seemed on the edge of tears.

"We'll wait at the bar," Michael said.

"But how will I *know* her?" he asked.

"Don't worry about it," Michael said, and winked again.

He took Connie's elbow and led her toward a bar hung with rotating green floodlights that restlessly swept the room like the eyes of Martians, striking the tables around the dance floor, exploding upon them like summer watermelons and then moving on swiftly as if there'd been a prison break, Michael's motion-picture associations recklessly mixing similes and metaphors, the probing green searchlights in a London air raid, the sky-washing green klieg lights outside Graumann's Chinese, green tracer shells on a disputed green killing field—but in reality the shells had been yellow and red and the world of Oz was green and loud and somewhat frightening in its insistence on colorization. They sat on high-backed stools alongside a young man dressed as a Cowardly Lion whose mane, awash in the overhead light, looked as green as wilted asparagus.

He turned to Michael and said, "You're in the wrong movie."

Ever since Christmas Eve, Michael had been thinking exactly the same thing.

"What are you, *Twelve O'Clock High*?" the lion asked.

"A Guy Named Joe," Michael said.

"She's *The World of Suzie Wong,* am I right?"

"Shanghai Gesture," Connie said.

"What'll it be?" the bartender asked.

"Lost Weekend," the lion said, and nudged Michael with his elbow.

Michael figured that in this splendidly green place a person should order either crème de menthe or chartreuse.

"Do you know how to make a hot rum toddy?" Connie asked.

"Come on, lady," the bartender said.

"A Beefeater martini then," she said, "on the rocks, two olives. Green."

"Tonic with a lime," Michael said. "Green."

"Hard or soft, the minimum's the same," the bartender said.

"That's okay," Michael said.

"And besides, the tonic costs three bucks."

"Fine," Michael said.

"Hello, darling," a voice behind him said. "You're out of costume."

He turned.

Glinda the Good Witch of the North was standing there in a diaphanous blue gown, wings on her shoulders, waving a wand. Wings on *his* shoulders, actually, since Glinda was in reality Phyllis from the Green Garter, with whom Michael had danced earlier tonight, oh what a small world Oz was turning out to be, not to mention the city of New York itself. Phyllis was with a Scarecrow who under all that straw turned out to be Gregory who had rescued Michael from the bad guys and then admired his buns, curiouser and curiouser it was getting to be.

"A Pink Lady, please," Glinda, or Phyllis, or both, said to the bartender.

"And a Whisper, please," Gregory said.

The room was stultifyingly hot. Michael took off the bomber jacket and draped it over the high back of the bar stool. The music was still deafening, but the beat was slower now, designed for dirty dancing, the bass guitar chords jangling insistently into the room like the bone-jarring sound of bedsprings in a cheap hotel, the black girl's gospel-singer voice soaring to the roof where the air was thin and clear, high above the poisonous green smoke, setting the rafters atremble the way it had back home in Mississippi, where Michael imagined she used to sing with the Sunday choir.

"Dance with me," Connie said.

There was—for him in the next several moments, and perhaps for Connie as well—the certain knowledge that they were the two most beautiful people in the joint, perhaps in the entire city, glowing with an inner light that shattered the emerald-green myth and illuminated them as sharply as if a follow-spot were leading them out to the dance floor. In the movies, this would have been Ginger and Fred, he in elegant tails rather than Levi's and a sweater, she in a long pale gown rather than jeans and leg warmers and a long-sleeved blouse. And in the movies, they would glide out onto a crowded dance floor—just as the dance floor here was crowded with people pressed against each other, sweating against each other, pumping against each other, dry-humping to the thud of the guitars and the angelic voice—and the crowd would part as Fred stepped out and Ginger followed, those first graceful steps indicating to the mere dancers on the floor that here were italicized *dancers,* here were goddamn capitalized DANCERS to be reckoned with! And the floor would clear at once, and they would be alone at last, a heavenly mist rising from beneath their feet, and they would dance divinely on clouds, oh so easy, oh so beautifully airy and light and incredibly easy, the way Michael and Connie were dancing now.

The black singer from Mississippi was caressing the dirty lyrics of the song as if the devil had entered her little church and corrupted not only the minister but the entire congregation. The song's double meaning was as subtle as a rubber body bag, designed to be understood by the dullest adolescent. With a forked tongue, the song spoke of "breaking and entry" and "shaking and trembling" and "taking so gently," the rhymes so slanted they were bent, the stumbling lyrics pounded home in a tune as simple as the village idiot. But transformed by Ginger and Fred, this crudest of melodies with its thinly disguised pornographic patter became a Cole Porter accompaniment to a dance of unimaginable sensitivity and skill.

Oh how they floated on that sea-green dance floor, oh how they drifted airborne on wafted winds of invention, oh how they wove intricate terpsichorial patterns around and among the stunned bystanders who watched them in envy and awe, open-mouthed and wide-eyed, here a black teenager wearing a modified Afro and a Scarecrow's stuffed suit, here a stunning brunette in a green micro-mini and braids and red stiletto-heeled shoes, here a lanky, loose-limbed fellow who strongly resembled a young Ray Bolger, and here a beautiful, long-legged woman with short blonde hair and wide brown eyes that opened even wider as he and Connie glided—holy Jesus!

It was Jessica Wales.

Dressed as the Wicked Witch, wearing a skintight black gown, and sparkly red high-heeled shoes, and pale white makeup and blood-red lipstick, and dancing with—

Arthur Crandall.

Who looked portly and pompous and pleased as punch, which was probably the way most fat men looked when they had slender gorgeous blondes in their arms.

"Long time no see," Michael said.

The self-satisfied smile vanished. Perhaps Crandall had expected Michael to be in handcuffs by now, in a holding cell at one or another of the city's lovely police stations. Or perhaps he'd expected him to be in a garbage can behind one of the city's many beautiful little McDonald's locations, which was where Alice might have left him, given her wont. But wherever he'd expected him to be, it was certainly not here in a smoke-filled disco called Oz at twenty minutes past three on Boxing Day.

He went immediately pale.

But not because he thought Michael was a murderer.

Oh, no.

That would have been good enough reason to have gone pale, oh yes, a wanton killer here inside this nice noisy club, a cold-blooded murderer here inside this jewel of a joint, good enough cause for Crandall's eyes to have grown round with fear. But whereas Michael had bought Crandall's little act in the St. Luke's Place apartment on Christmas morning—*"Careful! He's a killer!"*—he now knew far too much to accept it all over again. Green lights blinking on his round, sweaty face, Crandall was realizing that somehow Michael had tracked Mama here. Which meant that he had also tracked Mama to Crandall himself.

"May I cut in, please?" a voice said, and suddenly Michael was in the arms of a short, thin, mean-looking man with a thick black mustache, wearing a shiny silk gray suit that was supposed to make him look like the Tin Man.

"This is a knife," he said, and Michael suddenly detected the faint Spanish accent, and realized at once that this was the man Mama had sent to meet Crandall on Christmas Eve. The knife was in the man's left hand. The point of the knife was against Michael's ribs. The man's right arm was around Michael's back, pulling him in tight against the knife. The man danced them away from Connie, who stood looking puzzled as a swirl of Dorothys and Cowardly Lions and Wicked Witches flowed everywhere around her in the dense green fog. Michael suddenly remembered that his bomber jacket was draped over the back of the bar stool. All the way over there, the pistols were of no use to him. The man smiled under his mustache.

"I'm Mario Mateo Rodriguez," he said.

"You dance divinely," Michael said.

"Thank you."

"But I wonder if . . ."

"Mama for short," the man said.

Michael looked at him.

"Mama," the man said. "For Mario Mateo."

"You're a *man*?" Michael said.

"Nobody's perfect," Mama said.

Michael winced. Not because Mama had just quoted the best closing line of any movie Michael had ever seen in his life, but only because he accompanied the line with a quick little jab of the knife. Michael was suddenly covered with sweat. He did not know whether Mama planned to kill him right here on the dance floor under all these swirling green lights or whether he planned to dance him out of here at knife point, onto the yellow brick road, and over to the Hudson River, where once stabbed he could be disposed of quite easily, but either way was a losing proposition. Crandall and his Wicked Bimbo of the East had vanished into the green fog. So had Connie. There was only Michael now, and Mama, and the knife, and the pounding music and the swirling green lights and the enveloping smoke, and all of it added up to being in death's embrace for no damn reason, no damn cause.

"May I?" the voice asked.

The voice belonged to Phyllis in his blue Glinda gown and his diaphanous wings. He held his magic wand in his left hand, and his right hand was gently urging Mama back and away from Michael. He was attempting to cut in, the dear boy, which Michael considered infinitely preferable to getting cut up.

There was a sweaty, uncertain, awkward moment.

Mama naturally resisting any intrusion at such an intense juncture.

Phyllis naturally intent on dancing the light fantastic.

Michael naturally wishing to stay alive.

The scream shattered the hesitant moment. High and shrill and strident, it cut through the din as sharply as the word that defined it.

"Knife!"

Someone had seen the knife.

"He has a knife!"

Mama froze.

Suddenly the center of attention, unprepared for such concentrated focus, he smiled in what seemed abject apology, made a courtly Old World bow, his arm sweeping across his waist, and then immediately straightened up and turned to run. Phyllis was directly in his path. Mama hit him with his shoulder, knocking him over backward, his wings crushing as he hit the floor, his head banging against the waxed parquet, his legs flying up to reveal gartered blue stockings under his Glinda skirt. Mama pushed his way through a gaggle of chittering midgets dressed as Tin Men instead of Munchkins, all of them squealing indignantly as he shoved them aside. More people had seen the knife now. Someone shouted at Mama as he pushed his way off the dance floor, knocking over chairs and tables on his way to the exit doors, cursing in Spanish when he banged his knee against a busboy's cart, angrily slashing at the air with his knife. Michael was right behind him.

He wondered why he was doing this.

Chasing death this way.

He knew only that to find his way again, he had to follow Mama, follow him out of the green smoke and through the green exit doors that swung out onto the sidewalk, follow him into the cold night air past Curly and the waiting hopefuls, onto the yellow brick sidewalk on Greenwich Street, follow that to where it ended as abruptly as a shattered dream, pound along after Mama on a plain gray sidewalk now, past Rector and a girl in her underwear standing under a red-and-green neon sign that read GEORGE'S LUNCH, and then Carlisle where an armless man stood under an elegant white canopy lettered in black with the words HARRY'S AT THE AMERICAN EXCHANGE, and then Albany on the left, the street, not the city, and Thames on the right, the street, not the river, and another canopy stretching to the sidewalk, tan and brown this time, PAPOO'S ITALIAN CUISINE & BAR, and then O'HARA'S PUB on the corner of Cedar and Greenwich, the place names blurring with the street names until at last Greenwich dead-ended at Liberty and the World Trade Center loomed high into the night on the left. Michael was breathing hard, sweating in what was no longer fear but what had become certainty instead: he would follow Mama to his death. That was what this was all about. Michael dying.

There.

Up ahead there.

A black Cadillac limousine.

A China Doll car, he thought.

Connie, he thought.

But no, it was only Arthur Crandall stepping out of the car with a gun in his hand. And suddenly the limo resembled a hearse.

"Join us," Crandall said.

Michael figured he *still* didn't know how to use a gun. But as he moved toward him, Mama suddenly appeared again out of the night, and the knife was still in his hand, and besides, Michael could now see that Connie was inside the car.

Mama grinned.

"Yes?" he said.

Michael nodded.

The limo was quite cozy.

Mama and Michael on jump seats facing Connie on the left, Crandall in the middle, and Jessica on the right. Crandall still had the gun in his hand. Mama had the knife pressed into Michael's side between the third and fourth rib on the left. About where his heart was, he guessed. Jessica looked somewhat bewildered. He wondered if she knew what was going on here. Did she still think he'd murdered someone? How big a story had Crandall sold her? Her eyes kept snapping from the gun in Crandall's hand to the knife in Mama's.

"This is Mama Rodriguez," Crandall said.

"Yes, we've had the pleasure," Michael said, and then realized that Crandall was introducing Mama to Jessica. Which meant she'd never met him before tonight. Again, he wondered how much she knew about what was going on. He also wondered how much he *himself* knew about what was going on.

"How do you do?" Jessica said.

She seemed even more bewildered now that she knew this man's name was Mama. A man with a thick black mustache? Mama? Her eyes now snapped from the knife in his hand to the mustache under his nose. Michael was more worried about the knife than he was about the mustache.

"You *did* say Mama?" Jessica said.

"For Mario Mateo," Mama said, and smiled at her like one of the bandidos in *Treasure of the Sierra Madre.*

"I see," she said.

She did not look as if she saw anything at all. She looked as confused as Goldie Hawn in a hot air balloon over the city of Pittsburgh, Pennsylvania. Mama's fingers were dancing all over the handle of the knife, as if he simply could not wait to use it. This was a good movie back here in the backseat of the limousine. Beautiful Chinese girl looking gorgeous and alert. Beautiful blonde girl looking like a dumb bimbo, which she probably was, Albetha had been right. Fat motion-picture director with a Phi Beta Kappa key across his belly and a gun that looked like a Luger in his hand. Little Mexican bandido holding an open switchblade knife in *his* hand, coveting either Humphrey Bogart's high-topped shoes or the blonde's sparkly red ones. And sitting on one of the jump seats, the hayseed from Sarasota, Florida, the death-defying orange-grower who after the Tet Offensive in the year 1968, when he was but a mere eighteen years old—

"Let me tell you what I think happened," he said.

"No, let me tell you what's *going* to happen," Crandall said. "Jessica and I are going to get out of this car on St. Luke's Place, and then Mama is going to take you and your lovely little friend . . ."

"I'm five-nine," Connie said.

" . . . out to Long Island someplace . . ."

"And I don't want to go to Long Island," she said.

"The ocean breezes are very nice at this time of the year," Mama said. "You'll enjoy Jones Beach."

"Why are you sending them to Long Island?" Jessica asked, puzzled. "Why don't we take them to the police instead? This man's a murderer!"

"Don't worry," Crandall said.

"What does that mean, don't worry? This person *killed* a person!"

"There are police on Long Island," Crandall said. "Don't worry."

"Why did you do that, Mr. Barnes?" she asked, turning to him. "I'm an actress, as you know . . ."

"Yes."

"So I keep wondering about your motivation. Are you a crazy person? Is that it?"

"Ask your director," Michael said. "Ask him why he went to Charlie Nichols and asked him to hire two other actors . . ."

"Are you casting another movie?" Jessica asked.

"No, this wasn't a movie," Michael said. "This was Christmas Eve in a bar on—why'd Nichols give me your card?" he asked, turning suddenly to Crandall, who sat smiling and shaking his head as if Michael were certifiable.

Jessica, however, was not smiling.

Jessica was trying to understand what the hell was happening here.

Maybe she wasn't such a dumb bimbo after all.

"You *expected* me to go to the police, didn't you?" Michael said.

"He already knows the whole fucking thing," Mama said suddenly.

Jessica looked at him.

Michael did, in fact, think he already knew the whole fucking thing.

But this wasn't a movie. This wasn't the scene where the bad guys said, All right, Charlie, since we're going to kill you in the next five minutes, anyway, it won't do any harm telling you all about the terrible things we did. Nor was this the scene where the hero was playing for time waiting for the police to kick in the door, during which suspenseful moments he could explain to the bad guys exactly why they had committed all those gruesome murders. This was real life, such as it was, here in the backseat of this limousine, and the way Michael figured it, Mama was ready to make his move.

Dumb blonde bimbo notwithstanding, Mama was ready. Even if it meant throwing away the blonde with the bathwater. The blonde meant nothing to Mama. Mama wanted home free. Mama had gone into this to kill two birds with one stone. Get paid for ridding himself of a competitor and take over his business besides. Now he had both stones in his back pocket and a switchblade knife in his hand and the only thing standing between him and prosperity was a dumb fuck from Sarasota, Florida. And his Chink girlfriend. So naturally, they both had to go. That was the way Rodriguez thought. That was the way to become successful in America. And if the blonde accidentally happened to become a witness to something she shouldn't have seen, why then the blonde would have to go, too, and Mama would later give her red shoes to his *own* mama. The way Michael figured it, Mama was a businessman. And business was business. And 'twas the season to be jolly.

On the other hand, Crandall was now in over his head. Michael guessed that Mama was supposed to have done his job and then disappear into the woodwork again. Supply Crandall with a body, that was all. Charlie Nichols must have told him that he knew someone who could pick up a body for them. His crack dealer. A man named Mario Mateo Rodriguez, familiarly called Mama. No questions asked. Six thousand big ones and he'd deliver a corpse. Crandall was the sort of man who wouldn't want to know where the corpse was coming from. This was commerce. He needed a dead body. Period. He did not want to know about murder. He preferred believing that Mama would find a dead derelict in a Bowery hallway. Or in a garbage can behind McDonald's. No great loss to the city. Here's the money Charlie promised you, six thousand bucks out of the nine I safely drew from the bank, no questions asked, the other three already gone to Charlie and his fellow thespians for their contribution to the scheme. It was nice not knowing you, Mama, good-bye and good luck.

"Mr. Crandall?"

The chauffeur's voice, coming over the loudspeaker.

Crandall threw a switch.

"Yes?"

"We're approaching Houston, sir. Will you and the lady still be getting out on St. Luke's?"

"Yes, please," Crandall said.

In Vietnam, Michael had simply quit. He had told that colonel to go fuck himself, sir, and he had meant it. He had quit. Because after the way Andrew died, there was no sense pursuing this dumb fucking war any further. This war was all about people doing unspeakably horrible things to themselves and to other people. If he had been the one who'd picked up that baby, if he had been the one who'd reached for that little girl a second before Andrew did, then *his* hands would have been blown off, *his* chest would have blossomed with blood, Andrew would have carried *him* through the jungle, and *he* would have been the one who was loaded onto that chopper in a body bag, dead. The obscenity had been as much in the randomness of death as in the singularly callous act that had preceded it, the wiring of a baby, yet *another* random victim. The whole fucking thing was a lottery, and Michael had wanted nothing more to do with it.

He wanted nothing more to do with *this*, either.

But on Christmas Eve, for no reason and no cause, he had been chosen at random to take part in yet another obscenity.

The promotion of a goddamn *movie*.

So he went for Mama's knife.

17

A lot of people got hurt in that limousine. Including the driver. Who'd been nowhere near that slashing knife. A couple of people got hurt *outside* the limousine, too. What happened was that he had her up against this brick wall in this sort of little alleyway between two buildings on Houston Street and he had his hand up under her skirt and they were both breathing very hard and all of a sudden there was a screeching sound and lights flashing and he thought at first that perhaps he'd had an orgasm since he was only thirteen years old or perhaps *she'd* had one since she was only twelve or perhaps *both* of them'd had one together because that was when the earth was supposed to move. But instead it was only a big mother of a black Cadillac jumping the curb and coming up onto the sidewalk and almost into the mouth of the alley, forcing him to fall down on top of her with his hand still up under her skirt, causing him to break his wrist and causing her to lose her virginity, for which dire injuries their separate attorneys said they could collect big money for damages.

This was what Tony the Bear Orso told Michael in his room at St. Vincent's Hospital. It was still Boxing Day. Eight o'clock in the morning. From the window of his room, Michael could see a rooftop Christmas tree, its branches tossing wildly in the fierce wind.

"It was a terrible accident, sir," Orso said. "The driver told me everybody was screaming and kicking in the backseat and yelling in Spanish and Chinese and grabbing for guns and knives and kicking at the window separating them from where he was sitting, so naturally he lost control, just like you and me would've."

"Naturally," Michael said.

"When a person is wielding a sharp instrument," Orso said, "the backseat of a limousine can become a very small place."

The instrument had indeed been sharp.

In the Operating Room, when Michael came out of the anesthesia, the doctor told him he'd been slashed and stabbed eighteen times. He said it was a miracle that Michael was still alive, since one of the slash wounds was dangerously close to the jugular and another had almost severed his windpipe.

"Is Connie all right?" Michael asked him.

The doctor did not know who Connie was. He thought Michael was hallucinating, and asked the nurse to give him a sedative.

"Is Connie all right?" Michael asked Orso.

"Yes, she is a brave Chinese person," Orso said. "When she saw Mama carving you up like a Christmas turkey, she right away jumped on him. She got cut herself, too, on the hand, but she's okay."

"Where is she?"

"I don't know where she is now, sir. I talked to her in the Emergency Room."

"Does she know where I am?"

"I don't know if she knows where you are or not. The last she saw of you was when they were wheeling you upstairs to the O.R. She herself was bleeding, and they were bandaging Crandall's head, and the blonde was still yelling at him. There was a good deal of confusion, sir."

"Yes," Michael said.

"Yes. But everybody's okay now, including Mama. Who, if you'd have killed him, sir, the city would have given you a ticker-tape parade on Fifth Avenue. Which, as you may know, sir, is *up*town."

"Where is he now?"

"Mama? Down the hall, with a police officer outside his door. Not that he is going anyplace. He went through the window."

"What window?"

"That separated the back of the limo from the driver. Crashed through it headfirst when the car jumped the curb and almost hit them two kids in the alley. You should see him, sir. He looks like the Invisible Man all bandaged up."

"Good," Michael said.

"Yeah, fuck him," Orso agreed.

On the rooftop, the Christmas tree danced in the wind.

"Why were they bandaging Crandall's head?" Michael asked.

"Because the blonde hit him with one of her sparkly red shoes."

"She's good at that," Michael said.

"Yes, very good. She put two holes in his head like she was wielding a ball peen hammer instead of a high-heeled shoe."

"Did she say why?"

"Because she suddenly realized," Orso said.

"Realized what?"

"That something was fishy, but she didn't know what. All she knew was Crandall had a gun in his hand and Mama was cutting you to ribbons and blood was flying all over the car and the Chinese girl was throwing herself on Mama and yelling what sounded like orders to the kitchen, so she figured she might as well take off her shoe and hit Crandall on the head with it. She ain't very bright, you know."

Michael nodded.

"What I got here," Orso said, "which I will probably forget and leave on your bed and have to come back for later, is a transcript of the Q and A we done with Crandall after they bandaged his head and we got him up the squadroom. That little cockroach Mama wouldn't tell us nothing, he's a pro, the son of a bitch, he knows his rights. In fact, he threatened to sue us for false arrest, the little bastard. But Crandall spilled his guts. Without a lawyer present, no less. *He* thought he was being slick as baby shit, but he gave us enough to hang him. I was thinking that if I should leave this here on your bed, sir, because I'm so absentminded, and if you should happen to glance through it, I know you won't mention it to Crandall because then his lawyers'll say his rights were violated.

Every lawyer in this city is lookin' for a rights loophole. You get a guy he shot his grandmother, his grandfather, his twin sisters, his mother, his uncle, and his pet goldfish, the lawyer looks for a rights loophole. Which, by the way, sir, Charlie Bonano sends his regards."

"Where is he now?"

"Out on bail, of course. He read all about you killing Crandall in the newspaper, and he called me up to say if we caught you I should tell you never mind the ten bucks. He also said you couldn'ta done it, which I already knew."

"How'd you know?"

"Because nobody's so dumb he's gonna kill a person and then take the person's business card to the police, no offense, sir. Not even somebody from Florida. But Crandall was figuring . . . well, it's all in the transcript here, if I should absentmindedly leave it behind and if you should happen to read through it before I remember and come back for it in about ten, fifteen minutes."

"Thank you," Michael said.

"I'll ask around outside about Connie, case she's wandering the hospital lookin' for you. It's a big hospital."

"Thank you," Michael said again.

"Oops, I'll bet I'm gonna forget this fuckin' Q and A," Orso said, and tossed a blue binder onto the bed, and walked out of the room.

Michael reached for the binder.

His right wrist was bandaged. He wondered if there were stitches under the bandage. He wondered if he'd been stitched together like Frankenstein's monster. He wondered what his face looked like. He wondered if Mama had got to his face. If so, he wondered if Connie would think he looked okay. He hoped that she would.

He opened the blue binder.

There was a sheaf of photocopied typewritten pages inside it. Michael began reading. The Q & A had taken place earlier this morning, at precisely twelve minutes to six, in the office of someone named Lieutenant James Curran at the First Precinct. Present were the lieutenant, Detective/Second Grade Anthony Robert Orso, Detective/Third Grade Mary Agnes O'Brien, and an Assistant District Attorney named Leila Moscowitz. The lieutenant advised Crandall of his rights under Miranda-Escobedo, and then turned the questioning over to the A.D.A.

Q: Mr. Crandall, I'd like to clarify some of these points you've already discussed with the two detectives who responded at the scene of the accident, namely . . . uh . . . Detectives . . . uh . . .

A: (from Detective Orso) Orso. Anthony Orso.

Q: Yes, and Ms. O'Brien.

A: (from Detective O'Brien) *Mrs*. O'Brien.

Q: Mrs. O'Brien, forgive me. May we proceed in that way, Mr. Crandall? Would that be all right with you?

A: Yes, certainly.

Q: Very well then. As I understand it, when Detectives Orso and O'Brien arrived at the scene, you were in possession of a Walther P-38, nine-millimeter Parabellum automatic pistol, is that correct?

A: Not in possession of it.

Q: In your hand, though, wasn't it?

A: Well, yes. If you want to get technical.

Q: Is this the pistol you had in your hand?

A: Yes, it looks like the pistol.

Q: Is it your pistol?

A: It's a pistol I had in my hand at the time of the accident.

Q: Do you have a license for this pistol?

A: No, I do not.

Q: How did you come by this pistol, Mr. Crandall?

A: I have no idea. I was getting hit on the head with a high-heeled shoe and there was a pistol in my hand.

Q: Are you saying you don't know how it got in your hand?

A: Mr. Rodriguez must have put it there.

Q: Put the pistol in your hand.

A: Yes.

Q: By Mr. Rodriguez, do you mean Mr. Mario Mateo Rodriguez, alias Mama Rodriguez?

A: Well, I'm not sure he'd appreciate your using the word "alias."

Q: But Mama *is* his alias, isn't it?

A: A great many people choose names that they use for professional purposes, such as actors and writers and occasionally dentists. They do not call these names . . .

Q: Dentists?

A: Oh, yes.

Q: But Mr. Rodriguez isn't an actor or a writer or a dentist, he's a gangster.

A: Oh, I don't know about that.

Q: He had a criminal record in his native Colombia, and he's been arrested twice in the United States for trafficking in controlled substances.

A: I wouldn't know about that, either.

Q: Well, when you hired him, didn't you . . . ?

A: *Hired* him? Ho ho ho, let's slow down a bit, shall we? *I* hired Rodriguez?

Q: Isn't that what you told Detectives Orso and O'Brien?

A: That was when I was still dizzy. That was just a few minutes after the accident.

Q: No, that was at a quarter past four this morning. Which was forty minutes *after* the accident.

A: That may be so, but . . .

Q: And it's now ten minutes to six.

A: My how the time does fly.

Q: Mr. Crandall, I'm going to remind you that the conversation you had with Detectives Orso and O'Brien . . .

A: I might add, by the way, that I don't think it's seemly for a police officer to be questioning a person while she's sitting in provocative underwear. I'd like to say that for the record, if you please.

Q: It is noted for the record. But I was saying that the conversation . . .

A: Especially an officer who could stand to lose a few pounds.

Q: I was saying that the conversation you had with them—and you were aware of this, Mr. Crandall, you gave them your permission— the conversation was being taped. Just as *this* conversation is now being taped. Again, with your permission.

A: My, how very state-of-the-art we are.

Q: And I have the typewritten transcript taken from that tape, Mr. Crandall, I am holding it right here in my hand. And on this transcript, you told the detectives that you hired Mr. Rodriguez to requisition—that is your exact language, Mr. Crandall—to requisition a body for you. A dead body. A corpse. Isn't that what you told them?

A: Well, yes.

Q: Then you *did* hire him.

A: No, Charlie hired him. Listen, if we're going to get *this* technical here . . .

Q: Yes, we are.

A: Then maybe I *ought* to have a lawyer.

Q: If you'd like a lawyer . . .

A: Why do I need a lawyer? I can take care of myself just fine, thank you.

Q: If you want a lawyer, you're entitled to one. Just say the . . .

A: Dickens was right, we should first kill all the lawyers.

Q: It was Shakespeare. And the exact quote was "The first thing we do, let's kill all the lawyers." And I'm a lawyer, Mr. Crandall.

A: I *still* don't want one.

Q: Fine. May we continue, please?

A: Please.

Q: Did you or did you not hire Mama Rodriguez to . . . ?

A: Charlie Nichols hired him.

Q: How did that come about, can you tell me?

A: It was all Charlie's idea. We were talking about how it would be nice if the picture got some column space . . .

Q: By the picture . . . ?

A: My new picture. *Winter's Chill.*

Q: Yes?

A: Some column space to counteract what we were afraid might be adverse critical reaction when it opened—the similarity to *Gaslight*, you know, what the critics might perceive, in their abysmal ignorance, as a similarity to *Gaslight*.

Q: Yes?

A: And Charlie recalled an incident that had taken place several years back when this woman fell from a roof and she had a copy of Meyer Levin's novel *Kiss of the Spider Woman* in her . . .

Q: It was *Ira* Levin. And the novel was *Kiss Me, Deadly*.

A: (from Detective O'Brien) Excuse me, please, but I think it was *A Kiss Before Dying* and Carole Landis was in the movie.

A: (from Detective Orso) You're thinking of *Farewell, My Lovely*, by Dashiell Hammond.

A: (from Lieutenant Curran) 'It was easy.' That's the last line of the book.

A: (from Detective O'Brien) Which book is that, Loot?

A: (from Lieutenant Curran) The one where he shoots the broad in the belly.

A: (from Mr. Crandall) You'll forgive me, but neither the title *nor* the author has anything whatever to do with the point of my story.

Q: What *is* the point of your story?

A: The point is that in the novel the woman is about to get pushed off the roof, and in real life a woman actually *fell* off the roof with a copy of the novel in her hand and it made headlines all over the country. So Charlie said, "Wouldn't it be terrific if something like that happened to *Winter's Chill*?" and I said, "No such luck," and Charlie said, "Why does it have to be *luck*?" and that's how the whole thing came about.

Q: What whole thing?

A: Hiring Rodriguez. Who was Charlie's crack dealer and who Charlie thought would know where to find a dead body.

Q: And did he find out?

A: Yes.

Q: Julian Rainey's body, isn't that so?

A: I have no idea whose body it was. Mama supplied the body.

Q: And you supplied the identification to put on the body.

A: Well, that was the whole idea.

Q: Tell us what the whole idea was.

A: To make it appear that someone had murdered me. And then for me to show up alive, contradicting the fact. And to have the mystery continue through the opening of the film on the second. To generate publicity for the film, you see.

Q: But, of course, Mr. Rodriguez didn't simply *find* a corpse, did he?

A: I have no idea where he . . .

Q: He *caused* a corpse, didn't he?

A: I don't know where you got that idea.

Q: We got it from a woman named Alice Chaffee whom we found in a red fox coat tied up with the cord from a General Electric steam iron in a warehouse downtown.

A: Oh.

Q: Where there was something close to a million dollars' worth of crack in an open Mosler safe.

A: Oh.

Q: And something like five hundred thousand dollars' worth of stolen goods elsewhere on the floor.

A: I see.

Q: She told us that Mr. Rodriguez hired her to kill Julian Rainey.

A: Well, that's not what *I* hired him to do.

Q: I thought Charlie Nichols hired him.

A: Well, yes. I meant indirectly. All *I* asked him to do was *find* a dead body.

Q: Where? On the street? In the park . . . ?

A: Wherever dead bodies *are*.

Q: In the trees? In a garbage can behind Mc-Donald's?

A: I'm glad you find this so amusing, Ms. Moscowitz.

Q: Mrs. Moscowitz. And I find it quite serious. Whose idea was it to blame the murder on Michael Barnes?

A: Mine. But there was no harm in that. It was just a way to keep it going. To keep the headlines rolling. When he went to the police with his story about having been robbed—and showed them my *card*, no less—there'd be headlines all over again. And then while he was being investigated, there'd be more headlines. And when he was cleared, there'd be headlines again. And meanwhile the picture would have opened and it wouldn't matter *what* the critics said about it.

Q: So you chose Mr. Barnes as your fall guy . . .

A: Oh, it didn't have to be him. It could have been *anyone*. He simply presented himself.

Q: Popped up, so to speak.

A: Well, yes.

Q: And refused to lie down again.

A: Well.

Q: Which is why Mr. Rodriguez ordered *his* murder as well.

A: I don't know anything about that.

Q: Alice Chaffee *does*.

A: That's *her* problem. *And* Mama's, I would suppose.

Q: *Your* problem is that you ordered the *first* murder, Mr. Crandall. You're the one who set the whole thing in . . .

A: I did not order a *murder*. I ordered a *corpse*! And anyway, it was Charlie's idea. He was the one who contacted Mama. I had nothing to do with it.

Q: Alice Chaffee says Mama paid her four thousand dollars for the job. Who gave Mama that money?

A: I have no idea.

Q: Did Charlie Nichols give him that money?

A: He must have.

Q: Why? It was *your* movie, why would Charlie . . .?

A: I don't know anything about any of this. Charlie came up with a good idea. And he followed through on it. If someone got killed because of what Charlie did, I certainly am not re—

Q: All Charlie's idea, huh?

A: Yes. I had nothing to do with anyone getting killed! I was trying to save my movie. If Charlie was alive, he'd—

Q: Yes?

A: Nothing.

Q: He'd what?

A: Nothing.

Q: Is Charlie *dead*, Mr. Crandall?

A: I don't know what Charlie is.

Q: Well, as a matter of fact, he *is* dead, Mr. Crandall. But how did you know that?

A: I don't know anything at all about Charlie's condition, dead or alive.

Q: Then you don't know he was killed with a P-38 Walther nine-millimeter Parabellum automatic pistol.

A: I have nothing more to say.

Q: Ballistics will have something more to say, I'm sure.

A: It was all Charlie's idea. If Charlie's dead, that's too bad, but . . .

Q: I thought you had nothing more to say.

A: All I have to say is that it was Charlie's idea.

Q: Except for pinning the murder on Michael Barnes. *That* was *your* idea.

A: Yes.

Q: Why'd you change the script, Mr. Crandall?

A: *Why?*

Q: Please tell us.

A: Because I'm a *director*!

Q: Oh.

A: Yes.

Michael sensed her presence before he looked up.

Knew she'd be there.

Standing in the doorway.

Her right wrist was bandaged where Mama had cut her. There was a smile on her face. She stepped into the room. Into a bar of sunshine lying in a crooked rectangle on the floor. The sunlight touched her hair, touched her face.

"They have you listed as dead," she said. "But Detective Orso told me you weren't."

"I'm glad I'm not," he said.

"Me, too," she said, and came to the bed.

He would have to call his mother, let her know he was still alive. Tell her he'd met a wonderful Chinese girl he wanted to marry. Mom? Are you there, Mom? Please take your head out of the oven, Mom.

"Let me see your cute little face," Connie said, and sat on the edge of the bed, and cupped his face between her hands, and turned it this way and that, searching it. "I was so afraid he'd cut your face," she said. "But you look beautiful. Could I kiss you?"

"We'll have to ask the nurse," he said.

"No, I don't think we have to," she said.

Mom? he would say. I'm alive, Mom.

I'm alive again.